THE SOUNDTRACK OF THEIR LIVES

THE SOUNDTRACK OF THEIR LIVES

A True Dysfunctional Family Saga

DEBBIE WASTLING

Bell Publishing

Copyright © 2024 by Debbie Wastling

All rights reserved. No part of this book may be reproduced in any manner whatsoever without written permission except in the case of brief quotations embodied in critical articles and reviews.

First Printing, 2024

Contents

Prologue: I'll Be Seeing You — ix

1. Chapter 1 The Wedding Glide — 1
2. Chapter 2 Tea for Two 1925 — 6
3. Chapter 3 I Married the Bootlegger's Daughter — 18
4. Chapter 4 Hold Me — 23
5. Chapter 5 The Best Things in Life are Free 1926 — 35
6. Chapter 6 Baby Face — 44
7. Chapter 7 My Blue Heaven 1926 — 49
8. Chapter 8 March of the Women October 1928 — 55
9. Chapter 9 Old Man River — 61
10. Chapter 10 The Love Nest 1928 — 64
11. Chapter 11 Is Everybody Happy Now? October 28, 1928 — 69
12. Chapter 12 What'll I Do? — 79
13. Chapter 13 Brother Can You Spare a Dime? ... (For the Growing Family) — 86

14	Chapter 14 I Wanna Be Loved By You	99
15	Chapter 15 My Baby Just Cares for Me	108
16	Chapter 16 Needs a Little Sugar in His Bowl July 17, 1932	114
17	Chapter 17 Making Whoopee	125
18	Chapter 18 Thanks for the Memory	132
19	Chapter 19 The Glory of Love December 1936	140
20	Chapter 20 It's A Sin to Tell a Lie January	145
21	Chapter 21 Oh! We Do Like to be Beside the Seaside! July 17, 1937	148
22	Chapter 22 The Teddy Bear's Picnic	160
23	Chapter 23 Friendship	168
24	Chapter 24 Heaven Can Wait	175
25	Chapter 25 A Lovely Way to Spend an Evening	190
26	Chapter 26 Trouble In Paradise	197
27	Chapter 27 Dream January 1945	203
28	Chapter 28 Crying on the Inside	214
29	Chapter 29 Varsity Drag	221
30	Chapter 30 Choo, Choo, Cha Boogie January 5, 1946	226
31	Chapter 31 I'm a Bad, Bad Man January 1947	242
32	Chapter 32 You Always Hurt the One You Love	253
33	Chapter 33 Sweethearts on Parade	263
34	Chapter 34 Don't Sit Under the Apple Tree with Anyone Else	270

35	Chapter 35 La Vie En Rose	284
36	Chapter 36 Serenade of the Bells 1949	293

Acknowledgments   297
Music Credits   299

Prologue: I'll Be Seeing You

A young woman attired in an elegant black suit clacked in her high wedge platform shoes up and down the linoleum floor of her aunt's kitchen.

Her auntie Bunty admonished her, "Dorothy, stop all that clacking on my new kitchen floor. You'll wear it out."

She halted, but a gloved, clenched hand showed Dorothy was ready for a fight, and she said, "If my father walked in here now, I would hit him." She punched the air.

"You would not—your style is a shrewd verbal lashing. Move into the living room. The tea is ready."

Bunty picked up the tea tray holding fine bone china cups and teapot and continued, "Let's go in the living room, where you can beat the hell out of my cushions instead."

Dorothy smirked and moved into the carpeted room, where she took off her shoes and gloves, which calmed down her anger. She picked up a cushion and hugged it to eradicate her pain.

"My father, the vile Amos Bell, did not even acknowledge me at my mother's funeral. What an insult to me and my sisters."

As she poured tea leaves through a strainer, Bunty spoke softly. She chose her words carefully before answering her dramatic nineteen-year-old niece. "Dorothy, you were the one who estranged yourself at fifteen and moved away to work. Today Amos was heartbroken. I am not sure you realize how much he loved your mum."

Dorothy snorted in disgust. "He has a funny way of showing love. He never showed much love towards me or my sisters. Only the golden boy Roy Bell gained his father's attention. I think it was guilt."

"Remember your dad came out of a World War when he was your age and had to put his youthful emotions in a jar and keep them hidden, as he saw young men die daily. Your mother had the knack of opening that jar when she needed attention. Now that bright star has faded from his life, he's clamped down, and the jar is locked again."

Dorothy listened to her aunt as she sipped her tea, but shook her head and said, "Don't try to make me feel sorry for him—the bastard."

"Please do not use that tasteless expression in my home. I agree he let you down by not paying for your higher education, but he saw hundreds of young men fruitlessly die. I think that's why his heart closes down."

"He's like a stone." Dorothy undid her suit jacket and put her legs on the couch. "Why did she give up her career after she sang for King George V? Why the heck did she choose to marry a miserable train driver?"

"She was charmed by him at first. But she nearly didn't show up at their wedding. Did you know that?"

Dorothy stared at her Aunt and said, "No!"

"In the end, she carried on her role as the wife, to the end a dedicated performer." Bunty's eyes showed sadness, as she explained, "She knew at twenty-three, with a shortage of able-bodied men after the war, Amos was a catch—not injured outwardly, smart in his dress, and with a secure job."

Dorothy thought awhile about the statement. She nibbled one of the biscuits and said, "But whenever she sang at home, he would huff and puff and leave."

Bunty laughed, "Like the trains he drove. He has a stellar career on the Flying Scotsman, which has helped you all have a good life. I remember when they got married, I was younger than you. I had just started work in a Law Office in Hull. I was supposed to get my older sister to the registry office on time. George was not even my serious boyfriend then, but he was supposed to drive us. They held a double wedding—Grandad Percy was marrying his second wife, May—after your grandma Elizabeth died of the same ovarian disease as your mum."

Dorothy was intrigued by the family lore and asked, "They had two weddings on the same day?"

Bunty nodded, "Yes, but the wedding nearly didn't happen ..."

I

Chapter 1 The Wedding Glide

Today, we hope my sister Alice will get married. You would think it was my wedding: I made her dress and cake and finalised her wedding plans while she completed her singing contract in Wembley, London. Our Daddy will also marry for the second time today—a shared civil ceremony. Thank goodness they chose the registry office, not a church, or I may not have been alive to attend. I am exhausted.

My father called out, "Bunty, where are you?"

Oh no, what does Dad need now? I think he may be going deaf due to working in those noisy ships and will not hear me.

My father again shouted, "Pet, can you help me with these gold things that sit in the cuff?"

I took a large, deep breath and shouted loud enough for the street to hear.

"Cufflinks, Dad. Yes, come up here."

My dad entered the bedroom, smiled, and said, "Aye, your Mam bought them for me on our wedding day in 1895. My brother Fred had to fix them for me way back then."

I fiddled with the gold links, placing them into the stiff cuffs of his new shirt bought for the two weddings today.

"There you go. Thank you for wearing them—a little bit of mum with us."

I kissed his cheek, intoxicated with the smell of his cologne—better than his work odour of grease and sea salt. As a tear ran down my cheek, my dad kissed my forehead and hugged me.

"Now then, lass, no tears, please not today. Good thoughts."

As I wiped my tears, my sister stomped up the stairs. Despite her ability to sing opera beautifully, her footwork shook the house. Alice came in like Sarah Bernhard in her most dramatic role; sadly, she knows no other way.

"Bunty, I can't wear this dress." She pleaded with me, hands together.

"Really - so why have I spent four weeks cutting that expensive silk on a bias and stitching most of the lace by hand to make the style you had to have? What's wrong with it?"

"It's too long."

I looked at her feet, encased in her black, thick soled shoes, hence the stomping. I grabbed the hourglass-shaped heeled shoes we bought last week from our wardrobe to add two extra inches to her five-foot-two frame.

I ordered, as I let out an impatient breath, "Put on your new heels, then the dress might be the right length."

She changed shoes while I slid into my pale flowered lavender dress. As the only bridesmaid, I should not outshine my sister. Once she put on the shoes, the problem was resolved.

She hugged me. "I forgot I'd bought them, saved again by 'Bunty' Marjorie Neil-Gregory. Have I ever told you—you're a genius?"

"Not to my face, but to other people, often. Oh, last night I heard you were singing the Gershwin song 'The Man I Love.' Are you going to sing it to your husband today?"

She shook her head and grimaced as if I had suggested she might go to the ceremony naked.

I tossed my hair back, clipped in a gorgeous-smelling gardenia flower, and handed another to Alice, "You are about to become Alice Bell."

She plonked the flower into her hair and said, "Not on your Nelly, Bunty. My name will still be Madame Alice Neil-Gregory."

Before I had a chance to ask her if she had told Amos, her groom, about not changing her name, she left our shared bedroom of the past fifteen years, making a sweeping gesture, like she did for her stage exits at every concert.

Interesting: my sister does not intend to change her surname. Well, my stick-in-the-mud brother-in-law-to-be will undoubtedly have opinions about her not changing to his name. After three proposals over the last two years, in one hour from now, he will have got his girl.

 Not changing her name might cause more explosions, but Amos was a soldier for six long years; perhaps he can deal with her explosive personality. Perhaps that's what he found attractive about my sister.

I must find my do-not-forget list. This bedroom would become mine after today for the first time in my life, and I perhaps will not lose things so often. When Alice toured last year, I'd loved it—I could put my cutting table up and leave out my sewing machine. I'd even used her bed to lay out my clothes for work each day.

Ah! I hear my new boyfriend's 'Model T' car; George called the car 'Mabel.' He named his car after women, as he likes to treat the cars and women with good care. I think George might be the most easy-going man a girl could wish for. George and I were given orders by the groom to make sure Alice arrived on time. I have a sneaking suspicion is panicking at the thought of getting married. She acted for the last few days in this 'dreamy way' just like when she gets nervous at her big shows in huge venues as her uncertainty crept in—how would her voice sound and would the audience love her?

Perhaps she believed she was left on the shelf at twenty-four, so agreed to marry. Amos, I suppose, seemed like a good catch, even though he acts uptight at times. He works hard as a train driver for the L.N.E.R. But I believe he may *NOT* be the love of her life, but as a Virgo, she will commit to him if he signs on the dotted line. Alice would never admit if she made a mistake, even if she had changed her mind.

Daddy called again, "Bunt-teee—our taxi is here; we are leaving."

Hankie, handbag, flowers, and coat... still have not found my do-not-forget list!

"Go ahead, Dad. Alice and I will follow with George."

Where the hell has Alice got to?

I skipped downstairs and looked for my sister. I looked for her outside our front garden, where George was tying a white ribbon to his car.

"Alice, where are you?" No reply.

I ran upstairs checking the bathroom and two bedrooms of our father's early 19th-century terraced house, which our parents bought when they moved to Hull. I could not find my sister. I looked out the bathroom window and saw her white shoes under the old privy door.

"Alice, what the...?"

I ran downstairs, my pale lavender chiffon sleeves floating behind me, stepped into our backyard, and said, "Alice Neil-Gregory, what are you playing at?"

Alice emitted a groan, "I do not feel good."

"Are you sick?" I asked.

"Not really but…"

"You are scared to be wed."

Silence.

"You can sing in front of thousands of people, but saying I do in front of your family seems to be beyond you today? Do not let Daddy down. You are supposed to be the first couple married; you are now late."

Alice opened the toilet door, and her sister stood, white as the ceramic bowl of their toilet.

"I …"

"You can do this. You love Amos, right?" I stared at my pathetic sister, hands on hips.

Alice nodded with little conviction and fear in her eyes.

My nostrils flared. "Just like a show. Mummy told us to take a deep breath, smile, and perform. Plus, you cannot let Daddy down."

Alice nodded with more conviction as I dragged her into the house. I put her into her dropped waist blue coat, handed her the cloche bag and gloves, and pushed her out the house and into George's car.

I must get her to the registry office on time. Yikes, I hope no more disasters today, but with Alice, one never knows.

2

Chapter 2 Tea for Two 1925

Amos Bell strode up and down anxiously outside the registry office, checking his watch every thirty seconds, taking deep breaths to calm his worries. Two years earlier, he had proposed three times before Alice Neil-Gregory agreed to marry him. He was worried she would not turn up. But, dressed in his best suit, with a new shirt and a maroon tie, he squashed those negative thoughts. Alice had always turned up with a plausible explanation. His doubts arose from her turning down his proposals—twice.

First, he asked Alice to marry him by her mother's graveside (not his finest moment). The second time had been on his treasured train, 'The Flying Scotsman,' which he drove daily. Alice finally agreed to marry him—in front of a huge audience—when he proposed at Wembley Stadium. Dressed in cowboy gear and on horseback, Amos had succeeded in wooing her. Alice was performing as Queen Elizabeth I at the British Empire Exhibition, in front of thousands of people who sat on the edge of their seats. She said a majestic 'Yes' to marrying him.

Amos believed Percy Neil-Gregory would make sure his daughter would make her commitment. But something niggled at the back of Amos' mind after he waited two years to marry her. Would Alice sign on the dotted line?

Amos' worries were halted by the arrival of Percy in a taxi with his new wife-to-be. May, his new lady, yelled, "Hello, Amos, we're here. The girls are following with George."

"Good—you look smart, Percy. Hello, May."

As they shook hands, Percy pulled him aside. "I want you to remember your life with Alice may be unpredictable." He spoke in a solemn voice.

"I am aware of her personality, sir. I understand I will marry a brilliant woman who knows her own mind."

Alice's father looked relieved and said, "Perfect, good. I know she loves you and has great respect for you, but life with her dramatic nature may not be easy at times. I wanted to say this, man to man."

Alice's arrival in George's car halted the conversation. He would also officiate as best man and witness for Amos. Amos emitted a huge sigh of relief.

Alice looked pale but kissed his cheek and said to him, "At least this is cheaper than a church, and neither of us regularly attended church."

Amos had another anxious moment; maybe her father and sister wanted him to marry Alice more than she wished to be married to him. Maybe they wanted Alice off their hands.

The wedding party moved through into the inner sanctum of the austere government building and passed through to the waiting room. A large vase of chrysanthemums expelled their heavy odor, but were the only attractive point in the waiting area where severe portraits of George V and past Lord Mayors of Hull hung on the dusty walls. A pungent smell of wood polish hung in the air from the wooden floors, which shone like a skating ring. Alice almost slipped on the slick floor in her hourglass-heeled shoes. "Well, we know the cleaners are doing a good job," she chuckled.

"Hello George, hope the wife and you are well," she said to the King's portrait. "Alice had performed the part of Gloriana at the British Empire Exhibition and sang for the King and Queen a year earlier.

The Registrar appeared, a slightly balding man with a stoop, who would conduct the ceremony. He held the door for the Bell and Neil-Gregory families to gather in the stark registry room. He scrutinized each person and checked their respectability to enter.

Once settled behind the podium, the registrar's demeanour seemed more suitable for a funeral, rather than a double wedding. When he smiled, tobacco-stained teeth glowed. "Despite your *late* arrival, I am delighted to marry two couples in an unusual situation."

Alice whispered to Bunty, "He doesn't look delighted. He looks like he would rather be presiding over a funeral."

In a nasal whine, he intoned. "I am the superintendent registrar, Arnold Prescott, invested by the County of East Yorkshire to marry you. The two generations are Amos Bell to Alice Neil-Gregory and Percy Neil-Gregory to May Brown."

In a voice more suitable for the sentencing of prisoners, the stern man waved the younger couple to move towards the podium. "Please step forward. This place in which we are now met has been duly sanctioned, according to law, for the celebration of marriages. You are here today to witness the joining in the matrimony of Amos Gilbert Bell and Alice Neil-Gregory. If any person present knows of any lawful impediment to this marriage, they should declare it now."

His whine echoed around the room. "Before you are joined in matrimony, I have to remind you of the solemn and binding character of the vows you are about to make. Now I will ask each of you, in turn, to declare you know of no lawful reason why you should not be married to each other."

He paused for at least thirty seconds, which for the gathered guests seemed much longer. "Please say the following words after me. I do solemnly declare I know not of any lawful impediment why… may …"

While George Wiles, as best man, signed the witness papers, the Registrar asked, "Couple Two, please come forward." His yellow teeth glowed through his forced smile. "I will start the second ceremony. Mr. Bell, please stay up here. You are the witness for the Neil-Gregory wedding—quite unusual, isn't it?"

Alice moved back to her sister Bunty and whispered again, "That smile makes him look constipated."

Bunty put a finger to her lips, but both sisters were now trying to control their laughter. While Percy and May signed the official license with Amos, the crowd's mood became more vibrant. "You are absolutely wicked, that poor man," he frowned at his new wife.

Alice ignored his ticking off. "They must be hard up for registrars for weddings, to ask a funeral director to officiate. Did we get a discount for two weddings?"

Bunty now knew her behaviour came from Alice's fear of getting married.

Amos glared and shushed her while the second ceremony went without a hiccup. They thanked the Registrar, and Amos moved Alice firmly out of the room to have photos taken next door. George was the appointed photographer, armed with his new German 35mm Leica camera to capture their special day.

***

The couple had met in Alice's birth town of Newcastle, where she sang opera for the Lord Mayor's inauguration dinner. Amos had driven the Flying Scotsman train from Edinburgh to Newcastle and stayed at the Railway Hotel, where the concert was held. Tonight they would stay at the Hull Railway hotel for their honeymoon. Amos liked Railway Hotels, as they were all designed almost the same with consistent service, and anyway, he didn't like new places.

The Railway Hotel in Hull with its grand white pillars at the main door was a natural choice for their overnight wedding celebration. It was close to the registry office, offered excellent food, and was near the railway station for Amos to begin work the next day. His brother John and Janet, his sister-in-law, arrived by train from Leeds, sixty miles away. Due to work, they had not been able to attend the official wedding at the registry office.

"It's a piece of paper for me.," Alice declared, throwing her head silky bob around. "I could happily live in sin; it sounds so much more fun. A celebration with our family is more important. Please excuse me while I go up and change."

Amos seated their guests at their reserved table in the hotel restaurant.

Alice's changed into a less formal organza dress with cap sleeves in shadow blue. As the bride danced into the room with carefree grace, the other diners noticed and clapped.

While their wedding guests were eager for alcoholic drinks, Alice asked the bartender, "May I have a cup of tea, I do not trust myself to drink alcohol on this most important of days."

John Bell, her new brother-in-law, a barman by profession whom she'd only just met, teased her with a smile. "You'll put the bar out of business asking for tea."

"I am parched and do not drink when I sing." Alice replied, with her chin in the air.

In a strong West Yorkshire dialect, he asked, "Oh, aye—give us a song then, Alice."

She started with 'Tea for Two and Two for Tea' from the latest hit musical, 'No, No Nanette.' She and Bunty had recently seen the musical in Manchester, and both adored the Flappers' song. Then George came over to her and danced an impromptu charleston while Alice then sang, 'I Married the Bootlegger's Daughter.'

The gathered guests all laughed and applauded, except for Rachel, Alice's new mother-in-law. She sat with pursed lips and sniffed, apparently immune to the vitality of her son's new wife.

Her sister-in-law, Janet, nudged her husband in the ribs. "Well, that you put in your place, Mr. flippant John Bell. She really can sing and dance."

John howled with laughter. He was on his second pint and ready for a wild party. Amos diffused the enthusiasm of his new wife and brother with an announcement. "Please take your places for the meal—choose between locally caught cod or beef wellington."

Much discussion passed back and forth about Bunty's spectacular wedding cake. She'd not made a traditional wedding cake, as both couples had made it clear they disliked fruit cake. Her creation was made from the lightest Victoria sponge, covered in seasonal raspberries. She'd designed a cone-shaped bottom layer in the image of one of the hooped opera dresses Alice used to wear on stage. On top was a couple with a small toy ship to represent Percy's occupation as a marine fitter. The cone skirt had a toy train, with a railway track made of icing running around the hoop with 'The Flying Scotsman' in gold letters iced on the side of the cake. George had the task of shopping for the right scale of train to fit on the cake.

After the waiter filled the champagne glasses, Percy gave a toast to the young couple first. "I am blessed with two beautiful, talented daughters, who I hoped would find the right men to stand by them. I saw Amos' vigilance in caring for Alice. Her mum, Elizabeth, who met him in the last month of her life, told me she approved of

Amos. So please raise your glasses in a toast for a long, fruitful life to this young couple, Amos and Alice."

Alice began to cry, wishing her mum was still with them. Bunty grabbed her hand and handed her a hankie. The sisters hugged each other tight. The wedding guests knew nothing of their strong sisterly bond since their mother passed away, or how much they missed Elizabeth Neil-Gregory on a daily basis—she had been their rock.

George, as best man, delivered his speech next. "I met Amos Bell," he said, turning towards his friend, "on the engineering course while teaching for the L.N.E.R. in Doncaster. Us East Yorkshire lads were fish out of water in South Yorkshire. I invited him to the Crooked Hen, a pansy jazz club. Amos bore this visit in his stride, and only had eyes for the female blues singer. I think Mr. Bell may have a fatal attraction for singers. Later in Hull, we met up with Alice and her stunning sister Bunty, who has two names, right, Marjorie? I got to know them after a night at a 'Rebel Maid' performance, with the worst plot ever written for an operetta. The show had one outstanding actress in the show, Madame Neil-Gregory, who also has two names. By the way, why do you change your birth names in your family?" Some chuckles echoed around their lunch table.

"We became good friends at a seasonal picnic in December at Burton Constable Hall, where I tasted Bunty's fabulous pastries for the first time. What a day when I met these charming, well-brought-up lasses. However, sadness came over us when we got home and found Mrs. Elizabeth Neil-Gregory had passed. Amos and I have stayed good friends, and I hope it will be a lifelong friendship, just like their marriage. Please raise your glass in a toast to Amos Bell and a woman who now has a third name, Alice Bell, or is it now, Madame Alice Neil Gregory-Bell?"

"I will never be Madame Alice Bell." Alice muttered, and Bunty shushed her.

Amos then stood to give his speech. "Thank you, George, for

opening some memories, which are best forgotten. Now as to the other groom, Percy asked me not to make any speeches. Maybe he thinks I can't hold an audience like his beautiful performing daughter I just married, as some of you know I love Shakespeare."

Alice emitted a groan—Bunty kicked her under the table.

Amos continued, reading his notes. "Percy welcomed me into his family at a tough time in their lives: he was taking care of Elizabeth, his sick wife. Now he has May to take care of him, for you have both 'loved and lost your loves.' So please raise a toast to Percy and May."

"We are staying overnight at the Railway Hotel," Alice proudly stated, looking at the guests. "We should have shares in the Railway Hotels Empire, because we've have stayed at so many of them."

Rachel Bell shook her head in disgust at Alice's unexpected admission she and Amos had shared a room. Alice quickly glossed over it. "During my British Empire tour, they housed me in these fine hotels as I toured Northern cities singing last year."

John nudged Amos in the ribs. "Amos, my little brother, I never imagined you would bag a screwy firecracker like Alice."

Amos apologized to his brother. "I'm sorry we haven't seen much of each other since the war, John. Now I have free rail travel, I promise Alice and I will visit you in Leeds."

"Dear sister," Alice enthusiastically said as they dismantled the cake and boxed up the left-over cake, "you are the tops. My dress… the floral arrangements, and the yummy cake—delicious. You helped us look like the 'it' couple around Hull."

Amos kissed Bunty on the cheek. "I agree. My brother thinks I've married into high society. My sister-in-law thinks you should consider a career in fashion. She must know, as she works in the ladies' fashion department in Lewis Store."

The newly married couple waved their guests off and could hardly wait run off to their four-poster bed in their Victorian hotel room. Ironically, they had stayed in fourteen hotel rooms but never one in Hull, their hometown.

Amos ripped off his underwear as he said, "This will be the last four-poster bed for a good while, Mrs. Bell."

***

The next day, the couple met his brother John at Hull's famous fish restaurant, the Gainsborough. Alice chatted to her new relatives, John and Janet. The ladies talked fashions while the brothers caught up with their lives in peacetime.

When Amos exited to the bathroom, John whispered to Alice, "You are the biggest change ever to happen to my brother. I knew he would get wed because he cannot cook, but I thought he would choose a little mouse type who would do his bidding."

Alice raised her eyebrow. "I am small, but I am no one's mouse."

"Oh! We understand you are a force to be reckoned with, Alice," her new sister-in-law said. "We adore all your strength. You are so good for him; he dislikes change. I have been choosing his clothes since he came out of the army. I know he has set tastes and a big problem with changing his habits."

"During the war, the only way he could survive his gunner position was to carry out his duty in a set pattern. The gunning crew hauled those damn huge cannons to the front line. I am surprised he isn't deaf. The sergeant was a beast. All the crew—except those who died—wanted a placement anywhere but as the gunner front line. Their role in the war was as cannon fodder; they were taught a one-decision system—good soldiers did not waver from their duty, or death followed. Luckily, Amos was one of the smart ones who could work on electrics, installations, and communications construction, so they swiftly moved him onto transport. None of us would be here today if he hadn't been a brainy bugger."

"What are you talking about, John?" Amos had suddenly appeared back at the table.

"You, of course, I'm telling Alice what a brainy bugger you are, Amos."

Alice gazed at him and pulled him next to her. "I already know he is intelligent. He loves Shakespeare and music. Show me another train driver who can quote Shakespeare? Amos, Janet has kindly invited us to stay with them at my Christmas concert in Leeds."

Amos put his head to one side. "Oh, but I thought you would give up performing now you're married?"

"Think again, Amos—we need the money to buy our own place and new furniture. My concerts pay me one hundred pounds a night."

"Amos, you will be able to retire early." John said, slapping his brother on the back.

"Sadly, I only have a couple of those concerts a year, so Mr. Bell will continue to drive his darling Flying Scotsman for the foreseeable future."

"Fine with me," said Amos, and he pulled his wallet out to pay for the meal.

Janet stood and asked Alice, "Shall we go to the powder room?"

Alice understood her request. Janet asked once out of earshot. "John told me Amos proposed to you on a horse—is this true?"

"Sort of, he was behind his friend Jonathan, a stunt rodeo rider, decked out in cowboy hat and chaps. I played the part of Queen Elizabeth in the British Empire pageant. It was not the first time he had proposed."

Intrigued, Janet's eyes lit up. "Tell me more."

Alice sighed, hesitant to tell her new sister-in-law where Amos had proposed. "The first time was at my mother's graveside."

Janet's eyes widened. "Ouch, Rachel did not teach those Bell boys any social niceties."

"I agree. His mother thinks I am some social climber and has no idea that I earn more than her darling son."

Janet explained her understanding of the Bell family. "Well, compared to the way the Bells grew up, you sound posh. Rachel gave birth, fed the boys, and kicked them out the doors once they turned fourteen. You have talent and class, an attribute Rachel does not quite understand. I know Amos Senior taught his sons kindness, but they learned their values, street survival, and style from the Great War, not their parents. So you agreed to his proposal the second time?"

"That day I had just been handed the plum role of singing Elgar's new masterpiece, 'Gloriana.'" Alice's eyes glazed over as she remembered the moment. "I was not going to give up a lead part to marry, so I asked him to wait. But I think you know enough about your brother-in-law to understand he finishes any task he starts. So last July, he came down to London with my sister and her boyfriend for the pageant, and his friend set up the horse stunt while I was portrayed the Queen. He rode up on horseback and handed me his grandmother's ring. What else could I do in front of three thousand people but say yes?"

"But did you want to wed Amos?" Janet cautiously asked.

"Of course, " Alice said, trying to cover her hesitation. " I suppose he played me at my own game—and won."

"I realized he had found someone special," Janet said, her voice soft, "when he called me and asked to update his wardrobe with some spiffy clothes, not his usual flat caps and old man-style stuff. You've been a great influence on him, Alice. He will be a good provider for you."

Alice answered, "I make my own money, so not one of my major concerns. Please come and see me sing in Leeds at Christmas. I will get you both tickets to my concert if Amos can get away from his other woman."

"What on earth…" Janet frowned and asked.

"His darling Flying Scotswoman," Alice said. "If not working, he will be attend with me."

"I don't think John will take the night off from tending the bar for a concert if it's on a weekend, but I will be there with bells on. Argh, sorry for the pun! You can come and shop at Lewis's. I can give you my discount rates."

3

Chapter 3 I Married the Bootlegger's Daughter

The party ended, and at last George had Bunty to himself. After a day of planning and hauling boxes and cases, his Model 'T' Ford was packed to the gills. Bunty pressed the last bag onto his small backseat, then wedged herself into the front seat. As he pulled away from the hotel, she asked, "Did you enjoy the meal at the Railway Hotel, George?"

George nodded. He adored her, and as far as he was concerned, she could do no wrong as an expert baker. Over the roar of his car, he trilled, "Their pastry was bland and not patch on yours."

Bunty stared incredulously. "Don't be silly," she said, "as their master chef, that man cooks daily; he's much more experienced than me. My pastry might be tasty, but not as good as his!"

"I know what I like. I stick by my taste buds, and your Beef Wellington is pure heaven. Unfortunately, the soggy parts inside the Master Chef's pastry coloured my judgement."

"Now I can relax; after two years of courtship, 'Madame' Neil-Gregory married the infamous 'never likes to change' Mr. Amos Bell."

George agreed. "Yes, getting an answer from her took him some time, but he got his girl."

"Their stars lined up," Bunty said. "Alice accepted his proposal on New Year's Day, 1924. She's a Virgo, you know. But I hope Amos can tolerate her off-the-wall antics once they live together?"

"Don't take this the wrong way, but sometimes your sister has a drunken quality without having consumed a drop of alcohol."

She nodded. "I know—Dad calls it her over-creative imagination—mmm... she gets drunk on new music and the people around her."

George chuckled, "Oh, and that poor man at the City Registrar building. I could barely keep from laughing out loud at Alice's stream of comments on the surroundings in their place of union. Her whispers were not exactly quiet."

"I agree. Her cruel mimicking and lack of control remarking on the poor registrar's demeanour were in poor taste. That's how she carries on when she's nervous. But you must admit he had a distinct lack of personality, including a sombre delivery with his dour, creepy yellow teeth. That provided ammunition for Alice's witty comments. I thought he was going to halt the proceedings, but perhaps he found her attractive as he kept smiling at her with his yellow smile."

Bunty knew that after living in London and singing for the King, Alice had made a decision to marry, as she felt left on the shelf. She suspected her sister had doubts about her union with Amos but was scared to tell anyone.

George said, "Alice lit up the room with that creation you made for her—however, those stinky flowers in her hair nearly choked me. I thought she was about to break into a slinky Hawaiian dance."

Bunty defended her choice of flowers. "However, the fragrance of those expensive gardenias helped to dissipate the nasty wood polish smell of the registry office."

"Dear May also looked quite fetching in the blue dress you made for her. She was crying as she hugged me. 'No one has ever made a dress for me. Bunty is an angel!' she said. Of course, I agreed."

"George, whatever you do, you cannot share the May dress information with Alice. She hates her. I did not tell her I made it for May. Sadly, this lady my Dad has chosen rubs Alice the wrong way, simply by breathing. I know May cannot replace my mum, but I think she will take good care of Dad."

"I agree your dad deserves someone to take care of him after he took such good care of your mum during her illness."

Bunty kissed her boyfriend as he pulled up at her home and then started to unpack the cake boxes and other paraphernalia she'd taken to the wedding. He helped carry boxes and bags to her front door.

Bunty loaded more boxes into George's open arms. "Ah yes, he chose to marry my mum, and was totally besotted with her decisive personality. As you can tell, Alice inherited it." They put the final boxes down on her front porch.

"If I may say so," Bunty teased, "I inherited Mum's dark hair, good looks, and elegance. Even though Alice finds May dull, she has a good heart and a strong work ethic like my dad, and I hope they will have many long years together."

George took the last suitcase to her door. "Amos' brother John was taken with Alice; he called her 'a killer-diller.' He and his wife were the life and soul of the party, and so different from Amos."

Bunty opened her door and pulled the packages into the doorway, then suddenly bounced on her toes in excitement. "Oh, I must tell you at last, I found the secret of Amos' well-dressed look. His sister-in-law chooses his clothes! She sends him the classy, durable shirts and trousers from the store she works at, the top department store Lewis' in Leeds. Plus, she can take a forty-percent discount as a staff member and knows the time that menswear comes on sale. She will buy us ladies fashions too, if we pay for the extra cost of the postage. We're going to visit when Alice sings in Leeds at Christmas."

George leaned forward for a kiss and said, "Should I stay with you tonight?"

"No! May and Dad didn't want the expense of a hotel room, so they came home. Don't get any ideas, Mr. Wiles. I'm not free and easy like my sister."

George pretended to sulk, then grinned.

Bunty said, "After noting the bridal silk gown I'd made, Janet told me, 'You should open a house of couture, like Coco Chanel.' What a huge compliment! Janet thinks my dress-making designs are close to Miss Chanel's. Alice and I are a perfect design team. She draws the patterns, and I sew."

"Talent oozes out of you more than you acknowledge," George said, holding her around the waist and kissing her neck.

"Plus, Alice will be here tomorrow when Mr. Bell returns to work. She told me she would only be at his mother's house when Amos was in town. Rachel and Alice do not see eye to eye, as I am sure you can imagine. She still hasn't moved all her stuff out of our bedroom, and says she's missing me, but I know she really wants to use the piano. Her stacks of music are still here; they mean more to her than her clothes. She may be able to sing in three languages and charm the socks off anyone to get her own way, but her emotional state and decision-making she learned from those rotten films at the Music Halls, where she sang. The smutty jokes on the stage are her sense of humour, as are quotes from Picture Post-film star magazine."

George took in the fragrance of her dark, luscious hair and held her close, reluctant to leave. The neighbour's net curtains twitched at their open display of canoodling.

Bunty yawned. "Good night, George. Thanks for the ride home and all your help on this thrilling but exhausting day. On reflection, my sister did not take her wedding seriously. She has slept with Amos so many times already the wedding night cannot be meaningful for her, or maybe, just maybe, she is scared of the commitment she made today."

With a final kiss, he said, "And you are much more sensible than your sister. Bye-bye, lovely girl, go and get your beauty sleep."

She kissed him with a passionate goodbye kiss and waved as he pulled out of the street, then blew a kiss to the nosey neighbour who had watched them snogging.

4

Chapter 4 Hold Me

After the wedding party, Percy asked his daughters to meet at his home for afternoon tea. Of course, Amos was back at work on his driving shift. So Alice, Bunty, and their dad gather together just like old times. May now lived with them and had prepared a delightful spread. Bunty later pointed out, "At least she can cook, so Daddy will be looked after and I get more free time."

Percy began speaking as they finished their high tea. He was nervous. Even though he had rehearsed his wedding speech many times for the wedding with the strict task master Alice, he was not confident enough to inform his daughters about a change in his circumstances.

Percy coughed, "After taking care of your Mum for so long, I no longer want to spend my days banging hammers around on filthy boats. I have been a fitter for twenty-seven years. May has taken a job as a housekeeper in a large country home in Derbyshire. There is a position for me to work in this house, and we will have a secure place to live. We will be moving and selling up by the end of the year or sooner when this house sells."

A skeptical Alice came straight to the point, "You are going to work as servants?"

"Yes, a quieter life for us, and I think I will live longer if I get out of the grime and filth. So once this house sale has gone through, you can divide your Mum's furniture and paintings between you and sell whatever you do not want. So you will each have a little nest egg."

Bunty's eyes welled with tears. "I need a home, not a nest egg. Where shall we live? This has been my home for seventeen years."

Alice became pragmatic and sarcastic. "So we both have to find a new home. What date do you start your work, *as a servant*, May?"

Alice stressed servant as if total servitude for life. She disliked May, a lower class than their mother, though she had to admit May took good care of their Father. Alice's instincts told her May had taken the lead in this change for herself and her father. Brightly oblivious to the girl's reactions to this huge life change for all, May smiled. "I am going to go out in August to settle in, and your Dad will come over once the house sells."

Bunty, using her professional legal voice, grasped at straws as she did not want their dad to leave their home city. "Selling this house may not be easy; there are plans to industrialize this area. I typed the documents for one of our solicitors only last week. He manages the change of land usage for the City Council."

Percy diffused the tense situation. "This is a good reason for you girls to move and get into a brighter, cleaner place. Most of the time, you will be with Amos, Alice. But, Bunty, you earn enough to rent a little flat near work."

His cheerful optimism went down like a lead balloon with his daughters.

**

Later in the bedroom the sisters had shared for fifteen years, Bunty, with much angst, began venting to her sister, "May and Dad have thrown the cat among the pigeons." She repeated this phrase to all their friends and neighbours for weeks. But the sisters had to find somewhere to live. They started the task of looking for rental properties.

But the promised council demolition on the Bells' home was earmarked for two years hence. Rachel, Amos' mother, kept good on her promise to give them proceeds from her house. However, they all understood Hull City Council moved slower than a snail stuck in glue.

So Alice prodded Amos to decide which areas he wanted to live, so she could look for suitable rental places. The newspapers wrote daily about an upcoming general strike, which would cause house sales to slow down. People become cautious, not moving around like in the early twenties. Moreover, the British economy was weak—not an easy time to move or buy a house.

Alice, irritated, reasoned with him. "Amos, how can I go out looking for places to rent until you decide upon a good area for catching a train to work?"

Amos procrastinated (his favourite pastime, Alice frequently told her sister). He voiced his opinions, but knowing he might lose the argument with Alice, he said, "I think we should stay here until we have more money saved up—a much cheaper option than rent. Mum is rarely here now; out with her friends. She also babysits a few nights a week for a friend's daughter."

As expected, Alice counter-argued her slug-like husband and ploughed on with her reasons for moving. "We need to have a place alone, without your mother's furniture. You have bought this lovely double bed, but if I bring all my stuff here, there will be NO space for us to sleep."

She grabbed a map of the West Hull area. "Pencil around areas you will consider living. Then next Sunday, we will have an excursion and research properties."

Bunty reluctantly also looked for a bedsit within walking distance from work. Amos informed her the better name is 'Chambre de Bonne', a French term. So both sisters searched and helped each other on weekends. Alice looked for possible houses near railway stations, naturally. Eventually, they settled upon an old village, now recently formed into the small town of Hessle, five miles out of Hull, with a railway stop to link his travel to Doncaster and York stations. This small town suited Alice—a more upscale neighbourhood to give her access to the wealthier children's families. Hessle was expanding with local gentlemen farmers and professionals who had money to pay for music lessons for their children.

She explained her business plan to Amos. "I can charge them more for classes than the inner city Hull families. I am not sure how long I want to keep performing. I am only taking the well-paid concerts to build our house fund faster." His reaction was an annoyed shrug.

After she'd finished her London engagement singing at Wembley, she came back home to Hull. Alice earned a reasonable income teaching for her former voice teacher, Madame Sharrah. She took over for Mme. Sharrah if she took a holiday or produced one of her big shows. The students loved being coached by a professional coloratura singer. However, Alice was canny enough to build her own student base outside of Hull, if in a part of town with more wealth. The couple visited the Hessle Town Square for possible places to live. While Amos walked around the new square scoping out the town, Alice noted the businesses: a doctor's surgery, greengrocers, and other amenities they needed as a family.

The town lay beside Hessle Foreshore, where the river could be heard as it splashed against the shale, and gave this community a pleasant shingled beach to saunter along on warm days. Small ships flapped on the mud banks of the River Humber. Amos wandered around the centuries-old streets then suddenly rushed towards her, excitement glowing in his usually sombre face. "I have found a cottage for rent, reasonably priced. Come and look."

They strode to the end of the square and saw an eighteenth-century cottage, with a door directly onto the street with a 'FOR RENT' sign in the window.

Alice looked over the cottage. "This might work. The families around her have a comfortable life plus higher incomes in this small town of Hessle. Good position for bringing in local students, close to the railway for you. But if there is no indoor toilet, we are not taking it! I will call them tomorrow."

She wrote down the telephone number in her notebook. Amos repeated his weekly mantra to her, "Remember, you do not need to work. I am your husband, and I shall provide for you."

"My darling Amos, I have earned my own income since I was fourteen years old, and I do not intend to stop. My earnings will build our house fund faster while we wait for the monies from the sale of your Mum's house. For singing professionally, I need to purchase music and costumes. By teaching for a few hours a week, I can buy what I need and not be a burden on you."

He nodded begrudgingly, expecting this answer. But unfortunately, Amos also underestimated what a popular teacher Madame Alice Bell would become, and she would teach more than a few hours a week.

Amos looked through the dirty window. "Perhaps we need to look for a place for the three of us? This place looks too small—what about Bunty?"

"No. Bunty is looking for a place of her own in town."

They followed up and visited the rental the next day. The eighteenth century cottage Amos found did not totally please Alice. She disliked the poor addition of a bathroom with an old tub. They had to fill a coin meter with money to have hot water for a bath. However, she compromised with the cheaper rent and the odd method for bathing, so she could get away from his mother's home.

The sisters visited many 'bedsits' for Bunty, some lovely and expensive, some barely habitable. Then, finally, they found the right place in the city center. Bunty moved into her Chambre de Bonne in early September, above a dress store on Alfred Gelder Street, on the east side of town. There were two bedrooms and a friend from work was sharing the other larger bedroom with her sister, so the rent was divided in three. It offered a good-sized kitchen so Marjorie could bake, plus was only a five-minute walk to her lawyer's offices. She had recently taken a promotion—the lawyers wished her to train as a legal secretary.

She warned Alice, "I intend, after Dad leaves, to visit you in Hessle every weekend, Alice, so that I will live some city life and country life."

During the heat of the late summer, the sisters had to divide their mother's beautiful Victorian furniture to share between them. This was Elizabeth's dowry when she married. The art work she had painted or had passed to her from her parent's pub. Usually, the two sisters agreed upon who wanted or needed which furniture and effects, but the piano was the sticking point where they almost came to blows.

Alice moaned. "I cannot get the piano in our small cottage in Hessle. But we will not live there forever. I will need it for teaching," Alice stated, not even considering her sister, who also played, might want to acquire it.

Alice then noted her sister's 'take charge look'. "We both want access to it. I will find someone to store it; I cannot get it up the two stories of my Chambre de Bonne." Compromise was how Bunty moved her fiery sister to agree to keep the piano.

With sarcasm, Alice said, "Good luck! Most people we know do not have room for a piano." Alice, as usual, had the last word and flounced out of their bedroom.

***

One Friday George and Bunty had a night out at the cinema, which also happened to be her eighteenth birthday. She chose to watch 'The Phantom of the Opera' with Lon Chaney. During one of the scary moments, she whispered to George, "Do you think your parents would store our piano?"

"Fine by me—I will ask." His eyes twinkled as he started to kiss her ear lobe, just as the monster on the screen started to attack Christine, the heroine. Bunty screamed mid-kiss.

The next time Bunty dined at the Wiles' lovely detached home in Beverley, close by the historic thirteenth century Minster, she asked his parents if they would store the piano in their spacious outbuilding.

George's Mother, the ardent suffragist, replied, "Oh no, my dear—a piano cannot be outside. Too damp for a fine instrument— we must find space for your piano in this dining room. I want to get rid of those awful aspidistras; they shed every day. If I get rid of the plants, the stands can go too. A piano should be against an inside wall, nice and dry to help it to stay in tune. Will you play for us when you come for dinner?"

Bunty was delighted the Wiles family would house their mother's piano and smiled, "Of course, but I am not a professional like my sister. But I do love to play and would welcome the chance to play my favourites."

George found a friend with a moving van, so the Victorian piano found a temporary home in his parents' house. Alice sulked when she was heard the piano move was a fait accompli. However, she did not have time to argue that her life was in chaos with her belongings in two places, as she packed boxes for the move to the Hessle cottage.

Bunty was also beyond excited as George proposed to her on her eighteenth birthday—May 7, 1925—and Alice wanted to hear about the unexpected engagement.

"On Friday, my birthday night, George bought tickets for the posh Cecil Cinema at the opening of Garbo's new film, 'Flesh and the Devil.' As John Gilbert, the Captain, went for the 'the kiss,' which the newspapers are raving about, George put a small gift in my hand. I mouthed to him quietly, 'Thank you,' and carried on watching the engaging film. At that point in the story, I was also trying to work out how to design a collar like the one Garbo wore, made in a see-through fabric, for one of your stage costumes. Then the lights came on, I looked down and saw a little box with a label: 'Please Marry Me.' I opened it; inside was this diamond ring."

Her sister examined the gold band with a big stone, which impressed Alice, so different from her plain gold band with no stone. Bunty continued her engagement story, "I am about to try the ring on when ... guess what? I dropped it. The ring rolled down the slope of the cinema under the seats. George jumped over the seats to search for it, then the next seat, and the next. Luckily, people were leaving their seats. Then he borrowed the usher's torch and was on his knees for—I don't know—ten minutes. He found the ring; he shouts, 'Ah! Got you, you varmint!' The usher looked at us as if we had escaped from the asylum and demanded we leave immediately. So I had to kiss George in the lobby. I shall never forget this film or the proposal. Did you know Garbo and I are the same age?"

Alice laughed at George's escapade. "A proposal to remember, rather like mine. I am delighted for you; George is the perfect man for you, and dare I say, you for him. You balance his quirks. Well, one of my students told me the Garbo trick cigarette works."

Alice grabbed a stubby pencil to mime a cigarette. "Blow it out as he lights it, and bam! You get the kiss and the man."

The sisters broke into bursts of giggles. For quite a few years, each time Alice saw any couple light a cigarette for each other, Alice mimed her Garbo blow-out-the-cigarette move, and they'd burst into laughter every time.

***

Saturdays became Alice's long teaching day (it had, of course, expanded from the regular few hours to six hours each Saturday), and Bunty met her after her classes and rode the bus or train home with her if Amos was out of town. With their dad now living in Derbyshire, ninety-plus miles away, the sisters only had only each other. Due to the distance, the girls rarely visited her dad, only for their birthdays and Christmas, so the sisters were closer than ever.

Bunty told her sister everything. "I told George I wanted a long engagement. To my comment, he asked, 'Twenty or thirty years—what would be best?' After giggling at his silly comment, I told him, I simply want to live on my own for a while. Then hopefully, pass my legal exams and go out with him at weekends. He replied, 'Just let me know when.'"

Alice wished her life was easier with Amos. However, he did not seem at ease with being married to her, especially if sick, so she reached out to her Indian friend Patina, who was training to be a doctor via a letter, who wrote back to her.

Dear Alice:

I am just about to finish my finals to become a state-registered

Doctor. My exams coming up at the Royal London next week. Next time I come up north to visit friends, maybe we can meet half-way—Doncaster? I hope the herbs help you. Keep well and more news soon.

Yours, Patina

She shared her news with Amos when he was home after his four-day shift. Amos read the letter, "I am so pleased you have kept in touch with her, such a smart woman who will make a wonderful doctor."

Alice showed him the brown paper packet. "She sent me some of the herbs to improve my health."

He grinned and said, "What a coincidence! I had an hour or so to kill in York, found an Indian store, and brought you home some naan and this paste. The lady told me you could mix it with chicken. I miss our Indian food." Alice hugged him, which helped both of them connect again.

Amos does think of me sometimes, but on his long trips I wonder if he even remembers he has a wife.

The next evening, Alice baked her first Chicken Rogan Josh Masala. This food made her feel stronger and well fed. Then, while Amos caught up with his sleep, she attended an appointment at the local Doctor's surgery; back at home, she wanted to tell her news, but he listened intently to the radio. Alice requested in a loud voice, "Amos, could you turn the wireless down? I know you love your music. But I have something to tell you."

He looked at her anxiously, wondering if she had a concert which would leave him to find baby sitters, but she said, "I am pregnant."

Amos smiled broadly, then grabbed her and picked her up in the air. "Put me down; I may throw up." He put her gently down and rubbed her tummy.

"When is our son due?"

"I think it happened two months ago so that the baby might

arrive by autumn. Remember, we Neil-Gregory's have more girls than boys."

"Ah well, the Bell family has more boys than girls. So I will be overjoyed whatever it is! But my union is threatening a general strike."

"Wonderful," she said, irony dripping from her lips. "Just about the time the baby will be born. *You* cannot be part of the strike."

"Not an option, Alice; trains carry passengers to work. By impacting the general public, our solidarity helps get the public on our side; besides, our union will insist we all strike."

"Well, I will take on more concerts to make up for our loss of earnings next year. Build our nest egg for the baby. Never, ever insist on my not working. My income will make sure our children never go without anything. Let's hope it's a short strike, though I suspect it will not be if Mr. Stanley Baldwin has his way. The strike will drag on. I hate him profusely."

Amos stared at his wife and said, "Strong words indeed. Why?"

"Well, where shall I start? Baldwin is incapable of making swift decisions. While his slum clearance schemes seem a good idea should it ever happen, and this process might get us a house. His new employment insurance might help people if they get sick (though I think this is more Churchill's doing, when in his position as Chancellor of the Exchequer). But the poor miners and industry people hate him as I do for these reasons: he is indecisive, weak, and a 'yes' man, a dangerous choice for the country in the long term."

Amos teased her as he loved to listen to his wife pontificate, "Eloquently put. Have you ever considered standing for Parliament?" Understanding she read the Times regularly, while he read his Daily Telegraph, he told the men at work, "My wife has so many inspiring political concepts mulling around her brain I think she might explode."

Alice reflected, "When women get the vote, I might just get a city job. Then you would have to stay home and take care of our baby girl." Alice stood straight-faced, but Amos teased her wild statement and laughed, "How do you know it's a girl?"

"It will be what comes out, Benedick Bell."

She used her pet name from the Shakespeare play he loved, *Much Ado About Nothing*. They had often sparred like Benedick and Beatrice in their courting days. She started to clear the table and brushed crumbs onto plates to keep the place spotless, as Amos demanded a spotless house with everything in its right place.

She requested, "Please turn up the wireless while I wash the dishes. I think Viva de France is on."

Amos turned the wireless knob and teased her again. "If it's a boy, I think we will call him Benedick."

"Not on your Nelly, Amos Bell! Come and dance with me; I love this song."

They waltzed as the wireless played French songs, which brought back memories of the early twenties. Alice sang along with the vocals. This made Amos the happiest man in Hessle on this night as she whispered "J'taime."

He replied, "Me aussi."

5

Chapter 5 The Best Things in Life are Free 1926

Alice found the rental cottage too small for their expanding family and wanted her own home sooner rather than later. Amos wanted to continue to rent the Hessle Cottage to save money and not move again. Alice adamantly asked for the umpteenth time, "Have you called the council yet about the house? I think you have to push them to get the matter solved."

With little interest, he shrugged. "My Mum calls every month and gets the same answer. You are number one hundred and thirty-fifth on the list."

Alice narrowed her eyes and replied, "I wonder if we can get a copy of the list."

"Why?"

Alice, straight-faced, said, "Then we could make sure a few people on the list have fatal accidents and move us up the list." Amos looked shocked, but she laughed.

"Just saw it in a film—it works!"

Amos stared aghast at this new view of his wife. "I never want to get on the wrong side of you if you think in this macabre way."

"Just an over-creative imagination is what my Dad said."

To prevent a macabre line of reasoning, he changed the subject and asked, "How is Percy doing?"

"Comfortable to have a wife again, but he hopes to sell and move by the end of the year. I want us to buy sooner rather than later; prices always rise."

※ ※ ※

So, Alice took the matter into her own hands to move the Bell family up the council housing list, as she understood her husband would wait till doomsday to write a letter or make a visit.

The next day after Amos left for work, Alice called Bunty at her legal office and asked for the numbers of both the new Judge Stipendiary, John MacDonald, and Hull City Town Clerk, Mr. Alexander Pickard.

Bunty, in her business voice, inquired, "Why are you calling them, Alice?"

"To try and move our housing problem forward."

"I doubt they will see you without an appointment."

"Do you happen to know the legal assistants' name of either department?"

"Yes, for the judge, if he kept the same assistant when he took over—Miss Richardson, I think her name is Ruth. Remember her—she used to be with Madame Sharrah? Her parents are quite well to do—I think Madame taught her."

Alice was delighted to have an ally in the City Council. "Well, I suppose we will get on like a house on fire!"

Bunty continued, "The Town Clerk's assistant is Mr. Armstrong, middle-aged, very stuffy. I only call him if I have to; he is not easy to deal with, and he always says no to requests."

"Thanks, darling sister, you are a font of information—after rehearsal tonight I will come home to see Dad and you. Amos is gone for a few days. Are you any closer to finding a chambre to reside within?"

"I have a strong possibility—could you meet me after work and view it with me?"

"Yes, Madame, be there at five. Bye."

Alice's brain began hatching plots to get their housing problem solved. She visited the town hall offices to ask for an appointment with the Town Clerk. She entered his office and spoke in a seductive tone, "Hello, Mr. Armstrong. Is this a good time to ask you a question?"

The nasal-toned receptionist asked, "Your name?"

"I am Madame Neil-Gregory, and I am visiting on behalf of the Bell family—I recently married Amos Bell. Can you help me get an appointment with the Town Clerk, Mr. Pickard?"

"What is this matter about?"

"Are you one of the Armstrong's from Hedon, or a West Hull Armstrong?"

"West Hull."

"Did Madame Sharrah, the esteemed vocal and music teacher, give lessons to your daughter?"

In a dry bachelor monotone, he replied, "Niece. I am not married." Alice looked into his grey eyes.

"How lovely your niece sang, such a talented, sweet girl. I need an appointment today to discuss the housing clearance."

"We have a two-week waiting list for an appointment with Mr. Pickard."

"I would love it if you could squeeze me in at the end of his day for five minutes. I am only in Hull a few times a month. I taught your niece after my London shows singing for the King."

His eyes focussed on her for the first time since she entered and as if the Queen stood at his desk, swallowed several times, and squeaked, "You sang for George V?"

With superb elegance, Alice played the part he wanted her to play. "Yes, I was honoured." She placed a gloved hand on her heart. "Could you slip me in today around half-past four? I believe it might be his last appointment?"

Mr. Armstrong replied and conspired with Alice, "He likes to catch the half-past-five train, so he never leaves later than five-fifteen."

Alice purred, "I love structured men. It must be so wonderful to work in a city with all the power you have, Mr. Armstrong. Thank you for slipping me in to visit at four-thirty. I cannot wait to meet Mr. Pickard."

So Madame Neil-Gregory-Bell finagled her way to an appointment with the Town Clerk of Hull. Immediately she found out Mr. Pickard had a daughter who aspired to play the pianoforte, and Madame gave him one of her cards.

"I would love to teach her. But sadly, I have no house in West Hull yet to teach within. I am hoping you will put Mrs. Rachel Bell senior to the top of your list on the council buyout scheme. She needs money with which to retire. She will not take the offer of one of your council houses, but the buyout price at this year's going rate. Quite an easy transaction to arrange, do you not think?"

Mr. Pritchard was bowled over by Madame Bell and agreed. He rarely had beautiful young women within his dark chambers. She looked at the clock and, with elegance, held her hand out to shake and said, "Thank you for your time. We must not have you late for your train. Should I check with your charming clerk, Mr. Armstrong, in a week?"

Surprised by her comment, he never had considered his clerk 'charming', but packed his briefcase ready to leave. Alice noted no work taken home, simply his sandwich box and newspaper.

He sniffed as if needing time to think. "Well, it takes a month to go through the city system. The new Judge Stipendiary, Mr. MacDonald, will have the paperwork in his offices for maybe three months. He is working through the backlog. We have had no one in the position for over a year."

Alice moved towards the door with him, "Oh yes, I have an appointment with him also next week. I saw his picture in the Daily Mail, and he looked rather handsome—oops, I forgot I am married now. But once I have spoken to him, I will get back to you. Thank you for making this matter move forward. I understand now why it has been stuck in limbo for a year. It is wonderful to meet such a hard-working city servant."

She held out her gloved hand again. "Goodbye."

Mr. Pritchard shook her hand, which aroused him, and smiled, showing his uneven teeth. He sniffed her evocative Gardenia perfume with the aroma that had smitten Amos when he first met Alice. Consequently, Mr. Pritchard, the Town Clerk for Hull City Council, moved to the train with a skip in his step and headed home to his wife. Alice Bell had brightened his dull life.

***

A week later, Alice attended an appointment with Judge John Robert MacDonald. Ruth, his legal secretary, was a friendly, open young woman, thrilled to make an appointment for Alice Bell. She studied pianoforte with Madame Sharrah and was impressed to meet someone who had sung for the King. Ruth told Alice she admired her and squeezed her into an appointment time.

Alice liked the sound of this bright young woman and took some piano music with her as a gift for her. She noted Ruth's delight at the gift—an onlooker would have thought Alice had given her gold.

"What a lovely gift!" Ruth turned red in the face and demurely asked. "Would you sign it for me?"

Alice took her silver pencil from her bag and wrote, *To Ruth, keep a song in your heart!*

"This is a thank you for arranging this appointment with such a busy man. I remembered you are a serious musician and hope you like Strauss."

"I adore waltzes. Please take a seat. Judge MacDonald often runs a little late."

Alice moved to the waiting area and sat down dramatically. She watched from the corner of her eye while Ruth opened the music and her fingers played with her right hand on the desk. Alice smiled, as she now had an ally in this government office. A tall blonde-haired Scotsman came out, shaking another older gentleman's hand. "Thank you, Mr. Braithwaite; we will be in touch."

She took in the broad-shouldered, well-dressed judge in an expensive suit, who with an inquiring look turned towards Alice. She stood gracefully and bowed slightly to acknowledge the new Stipendiary Judge, John Robert MacDonald, who looked towards his secretary for guidance.

Ruth introduced Alice grandly, "Your next appointment, sir—Madame Neil-Gregory."

"I am delighted to meet you, sir. I am now Madame Bell."

He looked at Alice with a puzzled air. "You look familiar, Madame. How do I know you?"

As they moved into his chamber, she asked. "Do you have a musical daughter?"

"I hope so, but she is only three years old. Ruth told me you sang for George V, but I reside in Hull now."

"I was the lead singer in Elgar's tribute to Elizabeth I."

The Judge gushed as he remembered her performance. "Ah, I saw 'Gloriana'—the red wig and the vast gold dress—a memorable evening."

Alice fluttered her lashes. "I am honoured you saw the spectacle; thank you for remembering. I hope the singing was better than the dreadful red wig."

"Indeed, it was an excellent show. My wife and I lived in London at that time. After we saw that show, Lucy wanted to listen to nothing but Elgar!"

How awful for the poor man!

However, she smiled seductively at the young judge.

"I am honoured that you remember me and saw my once-in-a-lifetime opportunity to sing for our Monarch. I am here to query a delay that needs a mind of judiciary excellence like yours to solve it."

He guided Alice into his chambers and held out a leather chair for her, which she slid into like a cat who would not move from her position. But the cat was now in charge. He looked over her fine, dark blue wool ensemble with a fur collar. He stepped with a commanding air around his gigantic desk and sat politely waiting to hear what this lady needed.

He scrutinized her, which threw her off her path, so she flirted with him, "You are much better looking than the picture in the Hull Daily Mail."

He blushed, which reminded her of Amos. The judge had similar light skin colouring. But MacDonald did not rise to her bait. He continued in a business-like mode, "Thank you... Madame, but you are here for..."

Alice flowed into her prepared speech. "My family, my husband's mother, Rachel Bell, was informed one year and three months ago that she would be rehoused. She wishes to retire to the country once money comes forward and has handed over the property to Amos, my husband. She needs to retire sooner rather than later. We do not need re-housing in a city council house; we wish to buy it. The city offices have sat on this matter for a year, and I hope you can find out which office and in whose desk it is stuck?"

Judge MacDonald smiled, "You seem familiar with City Council's procedures."

Alice nodded. "I am. My grandfather assisted the Lord Mayor of Newcastle. His cousin was the City Clerk for parks and entertainment, though it was way back in the 1880s, and life was not so well structured back then. But Grandpa Sutherland, a brewer and publican, found if you find the correct person who can give you the right stamp, you could move mountains, or in his case, spaces."

She paused; the judge wrote all her comments down. Then she continued, "No one has dealt with this house matter for a year or so. Either they have died on the job, or we have been waiting for a person with your command to sign the necessary document."

Judge MacDonald laughed, then said, "How clearly you think Madame Bell. But, you may know, I have only been two months in the position. I will look into it and get back to you."

"I am on a very tight schedule with all my concerts. Could I make an appointment now with Ruth for two weeks hence and follow up on this matter?"

MacDonald looked sharply at her. "I may not have an answer in two weeks, but you may call."

Alice continued her speech with an edge. "I hope by asking for your help, many families will be impressed by your decisive actions and then plan their lives and future. I am sure some coverage in the Hull Daily Mail would help your plight. A newsworthy article of how monies have been moved from the already passed ordinance into the hands of the ordinary folk. It would be a splendid success story to present the council and yourself in a positive light."

MacDonald recognized Alice's political suggestions were spot on;

her suggestions would give him some acclaim with his new constituency. However, he also understood the demands of this well-dressed but shrewd woman in his office. Alice had used the skills taught by her mother to move bureaucratic blockages.

After the next City Council meeting, true to his word, MacDonald followed up with this ongoing matter. Those who needed to be re-housed would have a four-year wait, but for those who wanted the money, the City would release the funds by April 1926. Two and half years after Rachel Bell read the first information letter.

6

Chapter 6 Baby Face

Alice performed at local opera concerts once she arrived home from London. With a known name, she was able to impress agents who found her bookings due to singing for the King at the newly built Wembley Park. By choosing not to return to London, more income came from opera concerts as a solo artist. Staying local, she can also spend more time with Amos. She sang again in most major Northern cities with concert or grand assembly halls such as Halifax, Harrogate, and York. The audience loved her, and this income helped build their house fund.

Her doctor told her to take life easy now that she was pregnant again. His advice was disregarded as she wanted to work and grow their house fund. She was offered dinner at a prestigious music dinner at Durham University. So Bunty as her unpaid secretary called and informed the college that Madame Neil-Gregory only drank water and tea before she sang. They should not expect her to eat; Alice could not be sick during a performance.

In Durham, she met her influential Sutherland relative. She

called her Aunt Alice Joel, who she stayed at Gateshead, about the concert. Her Aunt told her, "But Alice, we are already on the guest list. Arthur Sutherland, the College Trustee is a distant relative. He is the main donor to the college and does business with your Uncle Charles."

This information surprised Alice, but she understood this evening was a high-end banquet affair. The University fed the wealthy guests in return for big cheques. In her changing room with tea and water, she nibbled some McVities biscuits, which she could hardly keep down. In her vocal performance, she shared a selection of coloratura songs and opera favourites to please the astute and wealthy guests. The political audience from her birth city of Newcastle adored her performance.

After her show, she mingled in the sumptuous Victorian Performance Hall and thanked guests for their gracious comments about her performance. A middle-aged man appeared by her side, a stout gentleman wearing the robes of a university's trustee, a gold chain glistening on his opulent belly. He introduced himself, "Hello, my name is Arthur Munro Sutherland. I am a distant cousin of your late mother Elizabeth."

Alice almost curtsied to this benefactor, "I am delighted to meet you, sir."

"Arthur, please. Good to meet you too. May I introduce my wife, Fannie? Our uncle is Benjamin John *Sutherland*, your mother's brother."

Alice nodded to his wife and graciously explained to them, "I did not know all my relatives. My Mother moved us to Yorkshire when I was six."

Arthur reminisced, "Lizzie, your Mum used to sing at our Christmas family parties—she passed on her vocal genes to you. She was a lady much better than all the other mishaps in the Sutherland family."

Alice was intrigued to hear about her mother's family. However, his wife, Fannie, replied in a lilting Scottish accent, "Oh, Madame Neil-Gregory, there are so many scandals in the Sutherland family that one of us should write a book. My husband owns the Chronicle newspaper now, but they only publish political scandals, nothing meaty."

Her husband coughed, and she moved back behind him with a vacuous smile.

Alice tightly smiled at his treatment of his wife. "I suppose this means we are cousins, somewhat removed."

"I suppose it does. Good to meet you. I enjoyed your song selection."

He turned in his fur-lined orange-red Trustee robes, and Fannie skittered after him like a blonde Labrador puppy. Alice became aware Elizabeth Neil-Gregory nee Sutherland was from a different class of people. She looked around the grandness of Durham University and the guests; her mother turned her back on this kind of life.

Suddenly, Alice began to feel nauseous and escaped to her dressing room, hoping she would have the strength to continue to sing once she had given birth.

***

Back home in Hull the next day, Alice still believed a singing career with a baby was possible. Bunty knew before Alice told her that, due to her expanding waistline, her sister was pregnant. Her dresses needed to be taken out for her concerts. Amos no longer attended her performances, as he worked weekend shifts to build up their income. Alice told Amos about the baby in late July after it was confirmed. Her heart was not in Motherhood yet, more focussed on bringing in fifty pounds or more per concert to build their savings.

Bunty mused as she took out the seams of a blue evening gown. "Your breasts are expanding, and this is only your first trimester. Should I take the darts out?"

"Whatever it takes, I cannot always wear jackets or shawls in these hot theatres and hotels, but on autumn evenings, it's usually cold or even freezing. I want to add to my earnings to show Amos I can earn more than him. I have twenty-two bookings between now and the New Year—over one thousand pounds. I must make him understand by singing at concerts; we have more cash for a down payment and even to furnish a house; he is an old fuddy-duddy."

Bunty laughed and said, "Well, what a silly statement—you know Amos was born old."

They both giggled, knowing in many ways Amos was not a modern man, more Edwardian or even Victorian in his mores. Alice, in a vulnerable mood, asked, "Do you think I will end up like him?"

"Not a chance. My darling sister, you are too wild and creative. OK, dress done—all pinned up. Take it off; I will bring it back by Monday, all spic and span. Can you choose the film? Anything you tickle your fancy?"

Alice flicked through the newspaper and read the cinema listing. "I fancy *We Women*—a comedy, and as the men are not here, it's our choice."

She scanned the Hull Daily Mail entertainment section for times of showings. "Oh, too late; it just started. What about *Lady Windermere's Fan?*"

"Yes, that would be perfect; it will be well-costumed. What time does it start?"

"Eight o'clock—grab your hat and coat—let's go."

"Hold on a minute, let me pack your dress."

"Oh, and I must visit the bathroom before we leave—babies

seem to want to push one's bladder. The bus should get us there just in time."

The ladies sat down in the Regal Cinema as the film began to run the animation shorts.

***

By the New Year of 1926, her pregnancy had started to show, so Alice had to cancel some concerts. Instead, she taught private voice students who wished to learn from Madame Neil-Gregory, so money still rolled in. Like a squirrel, she stashed away her pile of singing income. Although Alice understood she would be a full-time wife and mother, in her heart, she was a performer. Instead, she became the best vocal teacher, following in the footsteps of her teacher Madame Sharrah, a force of inspiration to help aspiring singers.

7

Chapter 7 My Blue Heaven 1926

The Bells needed a place to live, as Alice could not bear living with Amos' mother after a few months. After much-heated discussion, the couple settled on the recently renamed small town of Hessle, situated close to the railway station for Amos, within walking distance. Later, he purchased a bicycle and cycled the five minutes to the tracks. So for him, his only life change was the house he lived in with his wife of just under a year. When he came home, he expected Alice to be home waiting for him, but she taught rich people's children in their homes, so he usually came home with no supper prepared, which did not please him.

Alice was adamant. "I cannot change my students' classes if your schedule changes. I always leave a cold cut in the icebox; you know how to make a sandwich. You must have understood I was not a stay-at-home wife but a singer. This income is needed so we can buy our own house."

Amos never learned to cook, as he believed this was one of the reasons you married. She laundered Amos' clothes, and Bunty brought freshly baked bread and pastries every weekend. But the Bell family lived well, better than their parents when they were first married, and Alice told him, "All your needs are catered for."

Madame Neil-Gregory, or Madame Bell, the name she now used for teaching, followed her musical path. One of Alice's budget priorities was to add a telephone. Unfortunately, the eighteenth-century cottage had never had one installed, so it proved more expensive to start from scratch. Still, Alice shouldered the cost: her students' parents had the income to afford telephones. Plus, the device was convenient for Amos; if he took an extra shift or a train delay occurred, he could call. However, much energy came from Alice to persuade him the cost was worth the convenience of having a phone. He grumbled, "I call when I can, but no one answers when you are out teaching."

"Well, call back when you reach the next station—I am usually home by seven o'clock. You will never get hold of me on a Saturday daytime. I teach at Madame's Spring Bank studio."

Her tetchy husband replied, "I understand your schedule, but I have not found my feet here in Hessle. I miss living in Hull near the town centre and popping in for a pint at the Alex."

"Ah, you've had to change your habits," Alice sighed. "The main problem of Benedick Bell. There are three pubs within walking distance of our cottage. So on the days you know I teach, go and have a pint with pie and peas."

His reluctance showed on his face. "I might give it a try."

Once again, Alice has made her point: I need to get to know people.

The best excuse he can muster quickly falls tumbling out of his lips: "But I want more time with you."

She moved seductively over to him, "To do what exactly?"

He smiled, "To spend time with you again in railway hotels."

She pulled him up and led him to their bedroom by the hand in a low, tempting voice, "Close your eyes and delve with me to my imaginary four-poster bed. Tonight you are in the Hessle Railway Hotel, Mr. Bell, and you get some special moves here in this hotel."

Their creative night left nothing to his imagination. This rare moment created Baby Aline, who was born in May 1927. Sadly, Alice had a tough pregnancy. The baby brought on anemia. The local doctor believed Alice was highly strung due to her pregnancy and knowledgeable opinions. His formal comment was, "You should learn to bear the pain; you are having a child."

Alice called him a 'quack' to his face and did not return. Instead, Alice relied on a young midwife to help her with the birth, as she had no mother to help her. She also wrote to her old friend Patina, who was in her third year of medical training at the London School of Medicine. Packets of herbs and spices arrived for Alice at least once a month with ways to control her pain and anemia. The baby was born while Amos was away working, and Alice's strength and wit came back once the burdensome child was in the world.

Despite the fact Alice still had her Marie Stopes book on contraception, she became pregnant again six weeks after baby Aline was born. She had not even had a period as the baby Aline was taking much of her milk. Alice changed her feed to evaporated milk, which displeased the midwife. Due to her anemia, Alice had to find some milk from an outside source. Alice understood her body better than the medical people treating her.

**

Amos came home from a four-day shift. The minute he hung his work bag and hat, he could hear his wife with a cooing baby. *She didn't call me and tell me she had given birth.*

"Alice, where are you?"

She called from behind a door, "In the bathroom."

"You have given birth? Why didn't you call me on your new telephone?"

Alice came out of the bathroom with a quivering, thin voice. "I did. The L.N.E.R. office told me you had left for Edinburgh and would pass on the news."

His superior, the damned superintendent John Jenkins, didn't want to get another driver. He listened and heard a child. "It's crying."

"Babies cry." Alice, exhausted, pulled herself to the sink and washed her hands. She stared at him and sarcastically said, "Hello, Amos." She pulled the baby onto her hip and placed her in a sling. He moved toward her and hugged them both. "How are you, Momma Bell?"

Alice pushed him away. "Never call me that name again—I am Aline's Mum or Alice."

She placed the baby back in the cradle, who tried to focus on her surroundings. Amos was taken aback by Alice's belligerence. He looked into the cradle. "It's a girl. You chose a name without consulting me." He touched the baby's hand, and she grabbed at his finger.

A pained, watery gaze emitted from Alice's face. "I named Aline after my Mother's cousin."

Reading the dangerous stare from Alice, he said, "I suppose it is an unusual but fine name." He shook the cradle, and the baby moved towards the movement. "Hello, Aline. I am your Daddy."

Alice slowly made a bottle for her newborn with the breast pump. "I hate this metal contraption; it hurts like hell."

"Why are you pumping milk? Why not just give her some direct from you?"

"I need some rest, and now you are here, I can rest." She pulled off the vacuum from her breast with 'ugh' and poured the milk into the warmed baby's bottle.

Alice moved with a bottle; baby Aline immediately found the teat, followed by the sound of suckling. She handed the bottle to her husband, saying, "Here, Amos, you can feed your daughter."

He panicked, his voice high with panic, and said, "I don't know how."

Weakly, she slid onto a chair. She wrapped up the contraption with all tubes and milk residue and then wiped her hand on a cloth. Her look told him he must take care of the baby.

Trying to keep peace with his wife, he said, "I can take care of the baby, I think."

"Thank God you are home today. I cannot cope on my own, and the midwife was with me for one day only. I needed longer—another problem socialized medicine needs to fix. Aline is all yours. Make sure your hands are clean. Welcome to Fatherhood."

Alice left the room and headed to bed. He picked up his baby daughter, who once fed, fell asleep in his arms, which would always happen if her dad held her. Aline, or Biddy as she grew and developed a nickname; she bid everyone to fulfill her needs at one year old, and she would forever be Daddy's girl.

Amos learned how to feed the baby, which he soon got the hang of, but trying to please Alice he found much more difficult. Exhausted from giving birth, Alice slept for four hours, rising to make supper. She switched on the radio, which played 'My Blue Heaven'. She asked Amos, "What's the latest news about the General Strike?"

Amos carefully explained the unfortunate turn of political events: "We are the main force for moving goods and food, and we are expected to support the miners, ship workers, and everyone in unions or industries. I do not want to appear to be a scab. The power stations will function on strike day. It might get cold here. I will chop wood so you and baby don't suffer."

Alice had her pulse on the strike situation. "Those damn politicians are just playing the miners; their families will lose the money needed to feed their children. We can manage, but you must buy some candles? If they cut the electricity, we will need them. When does it start?"

Amos was frustrated with trying to balance Alice's opinions with his working life belonging to a union. "On May 4, I have asked for a two-day run so I can be home that night and be with you. They owe me compassionate leave. I will push Jenkins, who has not replied to my request. Just so you are aware, I will have to go out on the railway picket lines on my bike for a few hours. Will you both be OK alone?"

Indignant and not easily appeased, Alice said, "I suppose so! But remember, I earn more singing in one show than those poor miners who are paid *two pounds a week* to go down a dangerous mine, but I believe they are pawns for this snarly government. I hope you will not be out too long for the sake of our small family and for those who will struggle more than us."

Feeling more supported, she kissed Amos on the forehead while he cradled the baby. Arguing politics made her vibrant, as did her ability to analyze both sides of a problem. Amos astutely stayed quiet. While she made supper, they listened to the radio news, then the light program. She sang along with 'Me and My Shadow' one of the current popular songs. Amos loved hearing her—a private concert for him and their new baby. When 'My Blue Heaven' came on the radio, he was the happiest he had been for some time—they became a family on the same page—but for how long?

8

Chapter 8 March of the Women October 1928

Alice strolled through the throng of women wearing white dresses with purple sashes and worked her path to the podium. Her swollen ankles throbbed. She felt pregnancy was a fight with a devil in her body, each day a new pain in a new place. However, today she would celebrate the right for women to vote. A large group of women gathered at St James Parish Hall, usually used by the Central Hull Conservative Party, but it was also the regular meeting place for the Women's Suffrage Association. The hall's long arched windows sent bright sunshine into the vast meeting hall. The Suffragists had waited ten long years for women to be able to vote—now it had happened.

Despite a huge argument recently with Bunty, Alice had shown up for her sister, who was now the event organizer for the Hull Suffragist Movement. Bunty stood at the podium, coughed, and said, "Thank you for showing your power today by attending. I will hand over to my sister, as Mistress of Ceremonies, who some of you know is a performer, to introduce our guest speaker."

Bunty stepped back to the wall to allow the heavily pregnant Alice space to stand at the podium and gave her a look of 'You better get this right'.

"I wish to introduce our guest speaker, Margaret Wiles, who runs the East Riding branch of the Movement. Those of you who have been involved for some time know Bunty has modernized us, plus the refreshments are always top class."

Many ladies clapped and laughed.

"As you can see, soon I will give birth to another Suffragist. This bulk will not prevent me from opening the event as the mistress of ceremonies. On this majestic day, I am honoured to open today's meeting. I am delighted my daughters will have the vote." Alice patted her pregnancy bump. "My sister asked me to make the opening speech in less than three minutes. Here goes."

She placed her wristwatch on the podium. Bunty rolled her eyes, annoyed at her sister's dramatic gesture, and moved away to lay out her cakes at the buffet table. "If you do not know me, I am Mrs. Alice Bell, and my stage name is Madame Neil-Gregory. There are two women who I wish could be present with us today. My mother, Elizabeth Neil-Gregory, whom most people know did not live long enough to see women gain the vote, as she passed away in 1923. My mother trusted that Parliament would hold firm on their promise ten years ago to allow us to vote. However, I am much more cynical, but it is happening today, ladies; now any person over twenty-one can vote—male or female."

The audience applauded with cheers.

Alice got into her stride with her presentation, and though a croak in her voice was heard, she brought the audience into her story. "The other woman who sadly did not live to see the vote died in 1916. She did not live to see the National Union of Women's

Suffrage Society fight the great fight. Some of you who lived through that tumultuous time remember she was the first woman GP in this area, Dr. Mary Murdoch. I remember that day in 1907 as a small six-year-old girl holding my Mum's hand; my sister was still in her pram, not knowing suffragette history was being made. Emmeline Pankhurst and Dr. Mary Murdoch drove in an open-topped car on Hessle Road. The crowds appeared in force, with their purple sashes singing brightly in the sunshine, just like you all today. Mummy made me one too. Purple balloons shot up from the pram carrying my sister."

The audience chuckled, and others nodded, remembering how their mother dressed her baby's pram with balloons.

"So I suppose you can say Bunty and I were brought up in the movement, and I feel lucky to live at this time. I will be on my mortgage deed with my husband, Amos Bell, the third woman in our family able to own a house or business."

Some nods came from some of the stalwart members. "Plus, my great-grandmother Martha Sutherland owned a pub in Newcastle, The Barley Mow, and met the great Florence Patton. Our Mother, Elizabeth, designed the banners and posters for her campaigns. Bunty and I will carry forward what my Mother wanted. But I believe our fight is not over. Please speak to every woman in your life. If she cuts your hair, tell her to vote; perhaps she washes your laundry, tell her how important her vote is, inform shop girls anywhere; take them to the voting booths, everywhere you meet women. We must balance politics out and make sure they are a way to democratically change the balance for both women and men of this country."

Hurrahs from the audience, as Alice continued, "Our speaker today is Margaret Wiles. I was delighted to meet Margaret when Bunty started to date her son. I remember he told me back in 1923, 'You must meet my mother'. She, like our mother, is an ardent suffragist! However, today Margaret has more interesting news to report. As she comes up to the podium, please sing with me, written by that amazing opera composer Elyse Smyth, 'March of the Women.'"

A lady gave Alice a chord on the piano, and she led the women in their anthem:

Shout, shout, up with your song!
Cry with the wind, for the dawn is breaking;
March, march, swing you along,
Wide blows our banner, and hope is waking.
Song with its story, dreams with their glory
Lo! They call, and glad is their word!
Loud and louder it swells,
Thunder of freedom, the voice of the Lord!

At the end of the song, Alice conducted the audience with a flourish. "Please give a big hand to our speaker, Margaret Wiles of the National Union Women's Suffrage."

The audience clapped enthusiastically as George's mother took the podium. The audience settled down to listen to Margaret. She informed them, "Thankfully Churchill came on board with the female vote during the last minute, due to needing our numbers to win the election. I wanted to slap Stanley Baldwin. He can get neither male nor female votes, as he made a pig's ear of the General Strike." There followed thunderous applause in agreement from the audience.

At the end of Margaret's stellar speech, the audience mingled and held lively arguments as the delicious tea and cakes were served. This certainly was a celebration to remember; Bunty could finally relax. She took her now-famous mouthwatering pastries around the room.

Alice was perched on a high stool, trying to get her baby to settle into a non-kicking spot. A well-dressed, highly perfumed lady spoke to Alice, whose name tag read, 'Mrs. Lucy MacDonald.'

"Hello, Miss Neil-Gregory."

Alice corrected her by pointing to her name tag. "I am Mrs. Bell now."

"Ah yes, Madame Neil-Gregory was your stage name in London. You met my husband in his office a few years back. I am Lucy MacDonald, his wife."

Bunty, who was passing by with a plate of pastries, looked at her sister, with a questioning 'How do you know her?' expression on her face.

With a fake smile (Bunty could tell), Alice replied, "Ah! Yes, I was delighted to meet him. Although we are still waiting for our own home, Judge MacDonald helped clear the backlog of limbo housing and got those checks out to poor families. It is wonderful to meet you."

"I love Elgar and was charmed by your 'Gloriana' performance at the British Empire Exhibition at Wembley Park. I hope we can see you perform locally soon."

"Occasionally I perform, but I have one and a half babies now." She pointed to her large tummy. "So I only teach some select students, which takes up much of my time."

"I would love my daughter to take classes. Where do you teach?"

Alice negated her inquiry immediately. "I have no openings at the moment. But I suggest you call Madame Sharrah's studios on Spring Bank. She taught me everything I know. I am pleased to have met you, Mrs. MacDonald."

Alice struggled off the stool and moved away to the refreshment table. Bunty followed and whispered, "She would have been a good contact for students and concerts. So why did you not give her your telephone number? You went to all the expense of having cards made."

Alice showed disdain at Bunty's interference. "Think practically. Can you imagine trying to teach her little girl in our chaotic life in an old cottage in Hessle? Nappies and baby stuff everywhere? Even when the move to the West Hull house happens, that is not exactly judge wife territory either. I cannot be tripping everywhere to teach. Amos has a fit when I teach any student other than on Saturdays. I know this well-connected woman who would have got me many more clients, but we do not live in the right place yet."

Bunty wanted to help her sister and had been impressed by the well-to-do lady and her request suggested, "Let's look for a small studio for you in Hessle."

"Do you think I've not been looking? Nothing big enough, or in our price range." Alice said, miffed with her interfering sister. "Plus, I have not forgotten Margaret still has our piano. I cannot take more students until we move into the right place. But if I set up in a studio at home, Amos might never come home."

Bunty said, miffed, "I was only trying to help. The piano is easy to move. However, Amos is a much tougher nut to crack."

She had enough of her sister's interference in her life. Alice grabbed her belongings and left the meeting, annoyed with her sister, her unborn baby, plus her husband. But instead of a ride home, she took the omnibus, which was jammed with people. A young lad gave her his seat. Her life was not panning out the way she expected.

9

Chapter 9 Old Man River

Bunty travelled home after the big 'Vote' day with her beau George. Bunty sat in the front of the car, full of news. "George, the 'Celebrating the Vote' Party was a tremendous success. Do you know how long I have been planning this event?"

George nodded, as he had not seen her for weeks, and said, "Yes, every day after work."

"Guess what? I even had the support from the older ladies who had the real fight for women's suffrage at the beginning of the century, said Bunty. "I had lots of 'well done, my dear' and comparisons with the events my Mum used to organise. The North East organiser told your Mum, 'Margaret, your son should get married to this stellar young organiser immediately. Nominate her for the North East Committee.'"

George perked up with a sly grin. "So when are we going to set a date for our wedding, Marjorie Neil-Gregory, or do I have to ask three times to marry me as Amos did with Alice?"

"You have asked me, and I agreed. But we cannot make it this year as we are still looking for a house. Alice worries me. She has not been herself since Biddy's birth. She misses singing and performing, but she made her path with Amos, which sometimes seems rocky."

George interrupted, "Hey, that's my friend you are talking about. He's a good man."

"He is, no doubt, but he lives in the past. My sister is a woman of this age, while Amos resides with his mind at the turn of the century. He never makes decisions and though only in his early thirties, he acts like an old man. He even has a pipe. Alice gave an excellent speech at the gathering, touching on controversial topics, which the younger ladies liked. She led the 'March of the Women' song, and the ladies uplifted their unified voices to the cause: singing for the Suffragist movement—we came together. I had the shivers as if Mum was there with us."

She dabbed a tear from her eye. "Plus, I am encouraging Alice to open her vocal studio. Now they live at the 'right' end of town."

George arrived at her flat and pulled the car into a parking space. "So when will you start living your life with me and stop being on call for the Bells?"

She stared at him, puzzled. "I see you most nights."

"But if we were married, we could be together all night, no interruptions."

He raised his eyebrows, and she understood his suggestion. "Ah, you want to sleep with me?" She shook her head and ignored his sulking, then continued to describe their event. "Oh, you will love this—Alice turned down the judge's wife's request for voice classes for her little girl. I have learned from working for a solicitor's office that 'it's who you know' that usually makes or breaks your success. Unfortunately, Alice seems to have lost her desire to plan and use her gift of teaching; I hope that's not from having babies."

George accepted his advances did not work tonight. He sighed and kissed her hand. "Well, here we are at your 'chambre de nombre.'

You can sleep happily knowing your efforts worked. But I wish I could go in with you and cuddle up." He put his arm around her shoulders, sniffed her hair, and kissed her ear.

Still excited about her meeting, Bunty sat upright and continued talking. Her eyes sparkled as she added, "Plus, I can vote at the next General Election; I am thrilled that the government brought the age down to twenty-one, which vexes Alice no end; she has waited so long and I get to vote when I am twenty-one. But though women will be able to vote, we must keep fighting for equality with men and make it easier to take male-dominated jobs and earn income like men. Amos was shocked when I expressed a wish to drive a train. He stated flat out, 'We do not employ women drivers.'"

This declaration made George laugh, and he continued to move closer to his girlfriend. "Yes, that's his way of thinking. But, unfortunately, I think his lack of a college education did not improve his thought process. Though intelligent, he has not expanded his opinions since he came out of the war. But I am pleased it went well. Where's Alice?"

"Oh, she went home on the bus; probably I said something to upset her, or the baby bulk was the cause. But I think you are right about Amos. Do you think it's like shell shock? Does what he experienced stop one from digging deep inside? I was about to reply to him when Alice piped up, 'They should employ women… another issue the women's suffrage has to deal with and change.' I love my sister's quick thinking. She started humming 'Old Man River' and Amos was not amused."

George grinned and kissed her.

10

Chapter 10 The Love Nest 1928

One evening, Amos arrived home and found his sister-in-law Bunty babysitting his two daughters. Little Biddy (who was never called Aline by her family) munched her way through an apple cut into small chunks, and baby Madge was asleep in her cot. Bunty smiled and told him, "She will be in late. Alice was offered a well-paying concert as the scheduled vocalist was sick."

Amos shrugged but his expression showed annoyance. He stood at the sink, washing his hands. "When will Alice realize she is now a full-time wife and a mother?"

He slammed the soap in the water; it splashed outside the sink.

Toddler Biddy sat at the kitchen table, giggled, and said, "Oops, water." Even his daughter's giggle could not change Amos' mood.

He growled, "Where is the concert?"

"St James Parish Room's—you know it will be a snooty crowd tonight with all the toffs. The mayor is likely to show."

Biddy repeated the word 'toffs' mimicking Bunty. Amos eventually laughed. His heart began to melt as his daughter repeatedly said the word. Biddy reached out to him to pick her up from her high chair. Her Daddy lifted her out and hugged her like he might never let her go.

"Amos, children need both their parents; Alice is with them all day and night. With her extra performing work, Alice can take some of the money burdens off you as the sole earner and allow her to have some spending money to buy what she needs for your home."

Amos disputed her statement, "Biddy and Madge need their mother more than money."

Bunty stared at him, but her brown eyes narrowed. "What an interesting screwball idea! Those girls radiate smiles the minute you enter any room. They need both parents equally. I do not want to fall out with you, Amos, but *you* need to discuss why she performs. Do you not understand why Alice agrees to sing when they offer her a ton of money?"

Amos struggled to voice an answer but eventually came up with, "So we can get stuff for the house."

"Alice needs a beautiful house; we grew up with some luxuries, as my mother worked most of her life. She wants a creative home, not just a roof over her head."

Amos attempted to put down Biddy, but this toddler happily clung to his leg as if she would never let him go. He understood he needed to be home more to help with the children. Memories of Alice's parents' home returned to him—a warm, loving creative space.

Again trying to be tactful, Bunty continued, "Both your girls need you—at home." He nodded but looked tense and said, "I am such a poor husband."

Bunty tried to uplift his mood. "No, you are not; you are a

good provider, but you are not here daily to see Alice through her bad days."

Amos' face showed concern, remembering when he nursed Alice in London. "Is she suffering from it again?"

Bunty spoke with care, knowing her brother-in-law reacted in extremes, as did her sister sometimes, one trait they had in common. "Yes, sometimes. Alice sought the advice of Dr. Patina, her old friend, now a qualified doctor. Unfortunately, the 'quack' doctor in Hessle village, with his old-fashioned views, fobbed her off, telling Alice to grin and bear her pain. So we are looking for a new doctor locally who will prescribe her more than iron tablets. Both of us think there is more to her problem."

A grim smile appeared on Amos' face, while he cuddled Biddy. "Ah. I am sure the Doctor received a barrage of strong opinions from Alice. But why does she not share her ailments with me?"

With a pained expression, Bunty attempted to explain, "You usually come in after she falls asleep with the shifts you work, plus you attend your territorial meetings on your off days. I understand the babies distract you both. But you must have planning time together."

Amos hung his head in his hands. "Argh—I am a weak man, not giving her what she wants."

Bunty continued, "You need to discuss and plan together. Alice must take care of her health and realize she gets weaker after childbirth. It takes her longer after each baby to bounce back."

With a jutted jawline, Amos spat out, "But she can go out and sing..."

Bunty stated the obvious to Amos. "Of course, silly, music is her lifeline; Alice's reason for breathing. The music will never stop. You must have understood that when you married her, she survives through singing, plus her earnings allow herself to buy small luxuries."

Amos stared as if this was a new idea, then sighed deeply. "I thought she was coping. I wish a map was issued when you get married on how to navigate being a good husband."

Trying to make the mood lighter, Bunty smiled. "What a great idea; they should give them out at the marriage registry. Alice is coping in some areas but fails when her health weakens her. I want to be brutally honest with you in your 'Love Nest' Amos. You are doing fine; talk to each other more often."

He stood with Biddy in his arms and planted his feet firmly like the soldier he once was ready for action. "I will call my Mother and see if anything has moved on the house front. Shall I take this little one to bed?" Biddy giggled as he ruffled her hair.

Bunty nodded and picked up Madge to take her into the one bedroom, "Come on, let's give you a lick and promise wash, and Daddy can put you to bed. Maybe he might manage a story."

On the way to the bedroom, Biddy repeated, "Story, story…"

Poor Alice has got more than her hands full with this truculent husband, who has no clue of women's or baby's needs. While his army training might make him the best driver on wheels, Amos must consider the needs of Alice and the children. Her anemia should be his paramount concern; if she gets weak again, he will have to take time off work to care for the girls.

❋❋❋

The next day Amos left for his shift, at five o'clock in the morning and met the train at Hessle station. At this time of day, only the Station Master was on the job. Joseph Oliver, an older man with three almost grown boys, opened the station for the first train to Doncaster. Joe was helpful to customers and a great friend to Amos. Without bothering to make small talk he asked Joseph, "Tell me, with your unsocial hours, how do you manage to see much of your family – how does your wife deal with you leaving so early?"

Joseph thought for some time before answering, "We have had our ups and downs, but listening and reading a woman's signs are the best guidance I can give you. Bring her flowers or a treat whenever you are on your travels. You see the world. She only sees children all day and does housework. Plan a day out. I bet you visited many places when you courted."

Amos smiled as he remembered their travels around the country whenever Alice sang.

Joseph continued, "So take her and the bairns out for the day. Your mother lives close by. Ask her to babysit the girls and spend a few hours together."

Amos looked at his friend and asked, "This worked for you, did it?"

"Yes, we can't wait for retirement to spend time together, and if this doesn't work, get a mistress."

Shocked by his remark Amos said, "What?"

"Just kiddin' lad, here's the train. Anytime you need a chin wag, I'll be here! Have a good day at work."

Amos pondered Joseph's words on his journey to Doncaster. Joseph Oliver and Amos would stay good friends for thirty-plus years, even as Joseph went into his retirement. They would meet up often, have a pint, and 'chin wag.'

11

Chapter 11 Is Everybody Happy Now? October 28, 1928

The day arrived—the Bells had the keys to their new house. They packed on a Friday and moved in on a Saturday. Amos and George moved the large furniture (chairs, tables, and beds) with a friend who had a truck. Amos went straight to work, putting beds together in the new house.

Alice and Bunty were left in Hessle packing up the kitchen; both women took to wearing trousers for the move. Alice adapted an old pair of Amos' work bib overalls and cut them down to fit her. She told him, "Much easier to feed the baby and climb ladders to take down curtains and paintings. Yours are so chic too!"

Bunty smiled and rubbed her hands along a pair of gabardine navy blue pants. "I had to make them after seeing Coco Channel's yachting trousers in a fashion magazine."

"Mum would be so proud of us. We are working like men and dressing like them. Did George comment when he saw you wearing them?"

"Nope, I don't think he noticed, but they are so much easier to move in."

Both young women had covered their heads with gypsy-style scarves to keep their bobs out of the way. "Amos saw my hair tied back and said, 'Good idea; you won't get paint on your hair!' He's nuts if he thinks we will paint ceilings today."

George returned to Hessle to load the rest of their household belongings into the truck. Bunty travelled with George in his open-top Ford 'T', piled high with boxes and the baby's cot.

Alice arrived at her new home in West Grove first. She scrambled out of the truck with her screaming baby, with a look of relief from the driver.

A woman from next door approached her and introduced herself, "Hello, Mrs. Bell, I just met your husband. Welcome to the neighborhood! I am Mabel Norman. Want a cuppa?"

Alice shouted over Madge's piercing cry, "Oh yes, on the tea. I'm parched. Good to meet you. This screaming bundle is my daughter, Madge."

Mabel reached out for the baby's hand, smiled, and prepared to take her in her arms and said, "May I?"

Alice gladly handed her youngest over to Mabel, who smiled and cooed at her. Of course, intrigued by anyone but her mother, she stopped crying instantly. Alice relaxed at the silence from her daughter. "Ah! Why does that always happen?"

"Well, in my experience, babies are curious. I am new to her, and she's cried out from the noisy truck. I love baby girls. I only have a boy."

"Well, thank God for the silence."

The van driver unloaded boxes and nodded in agreement, having heard a screaming baby for six miles. He said, "She has a fair pair of lungs; she must be going to be a singer."

He was puzzled when Alice replied, "I hope so."

Mabel asked, "Would you like me to take her while I make you and your driver a cuppa?"

Alice was thrilled by her kindness. "Do you mind?"

"Nope, just next door." She pointed to her back door over the wooden fence. "I will leave the door open—just pop in."

Alice was not only relieved but thankful. She grabbed the baby's stuff, a case full of belongings and entered her new home—a house with her name on the mortgage! She called out to locate Amos. His head popped out over the top of the bannister.

"Got one bed up, putting up the single in case Bunty wants to sleep over tonight? We need sheets up here. Can you get out the baby's cot up here first, please? It's the same spanner for bolting them together."

Alice ran upstairs, kissing the top of his head, and said with joy, "Hello Amos, we are in our new home at last, which one day we will own." She hugged him. " I just met the neighbour."

"Ah yes, Mabel seems like a nice lady. Hey, where is Madge—asleep?"

"I wish. She screamed to hell all the way here. I think the truck driver will ask for extra pay."

"Where is she?" Amos asked.

Alice started to walk downstairs and said, "With Mabel."

"What? You let a perfect stranger take your baby?"

"She is our new neighbour and she offered to help. It's only next door." He stared at her as if she had made the worst mistake ever.

"Please go and get her back."

Alice shrugged then ran back downstairs, clattering on the uncarpeted stairway. She saw George and Bunty arrive with the cot as she went out of her front door.

"His Master's Voice has spoken. He wants the cot upstairs first. I am going next door to pick up Madge."

Alice knocked on Norman's back door. Mabel quietly opened it and said, "Shh." She pointed to a drawer lined with a soft wool blanket, right next to the stove. Madge lay fast asleep like an angel. "How did you do that?"

"She is teething, so I dabbed her dummy in a little of my husband's whisky. It sent her straight to sleep. Hope you do not mind."

"No brilliant, Mabel. Thanks."

Mabel handed Alice a mug of tea.

"Ah, perfect! I needed this, thank you." She looked out at her neighbour's back yard garden.

"Oh, you grow your vegetables. We hope to do the same."

She heard a noise and turned. A big boy of around fifteen put his fingers in his mouth and looked gently at the baby. Mabel introduced her son, "This is Philip, my son, Mrs. Bell."

"Please call me Alice. Hello, Phillip." He grunted at her and then smiled.

Mabel explained, "Phillip is mostly non-verbal but is learning to sign. He can hear you. Once he gets to know you, he will speak a little."

Alice recovered her surprise and used the little sign language, which spelt, 'I like your hat.' He looked at the cap in his hand and grinned at her.

Alice started to sing a gentle lullaby for baby, and Philip said, "Bab-bee."

"I must get back to help Amos. My sister and her fiancé are also here."

"Leave the bab-bee here to asleep. You will get more unpacked."

So for the next three hours, the Bells unpacked, set up the kitchen needs, and moved the furniture. Alice went back for baby Madge around four.

She asked Mabel, "Would you let us buy you some fish and chips in return for babysitting Madge?"

"No need, but thank you; I love babies. She was no trouble, happy to help out any time."

Stunned by Mabel's generosity of spirit and friendliness, Alice was so grateful—what a great ally to have right next door. She said, "Well, I hope I can return the favour sometime. Thank you, Mabel."

She picked up Madge from the drawer, and by the time they arrived in their new house, she cried again and wanted to feed. Amos quickly disappeared upstairs, as he did each time the baby cried. Once fed, Alice laid Madge down to rest again. Alice shouted upstairs to Amos, "Bunty is going for fish and chips. Want some?"

Amos answered, "Yes, hanging the bedroom curtains then, I will come down."

Bunty said, "OK, Alice, while we are gone, try and find the big heavy drapes box. Then George and I can hang the front room ones if you can find them in that stack of boxes. Where have you been hiding all this stuff, Alice?"

Alice called upstairs. "Amos, take a break and run the first bath in our new house. You have been slaving for two days, moving and setting up. Then you can eat with us."

Amos was relieved Alice had suggested a bath; he needed to get the grime and pain out of his body—he ached in every joint. Proud at thirty-five to have bought his own house, he had already lived two lives. One in the army, one as a suitor to Alice, and now he had family responsibility, which often weighed him down. He ran the bath and searched for a packed box labelled 'BATHROOM' to find the Lavender Epsom salts. He soaked as he thought about his journey—not on trains for once, but his life. He was ready to tackle a fish supper and more unpacking after the respite from a hot bath and the stress of moving house.

***

By eight o'clock a blazing fire was lit in their front room, and four long burgundy and gold curtains hung in the bay window to keep out the cold. They made the room look like a place of warmth and substance. Amos had been unpacking his clothes upstairs and stopped stock still as he entered the front room. "Bunty, remember that night I called for Alice, and she was working. I tasted your Eccles cakes for the first time. Your red curtains made me think you were a wealthy family, and then I saw the piano and thought, how marvellous to be able to play and have singalongs."

Bunty remembered the night he ate six of her Eccles cakes and added, "Then I gave you the address to where she was rehearsing that awful musical, 'The Rebel Maid.'"

Alice chuckled as she filled a bookcase with her Jane Austen schoolgirl books. "Ah, please do not remind me. The only time I have played an old bitch!"

Bunty said, "On stage, yes!" Her sister threw a pillow at her.

Amos looked at his wife, remembering when he fell for her. "Then we went to the Old English Gentlemen pub. You sang blues to me."

Bunty sat at the piano and started to play the hit song 'Someone to Watch over Me'—one of Alice's favourite songs. She began to sing the Gershwin song. Amos sat with the baby, who was mesmerized by her mum singing. George, Amos, and even toddler Biddy clapped at the end.

"The house is blessed by music now," George said. "Let's dance Bunty and christen the floor with some dance steps." He grabbed Bunty and asked Alice, "Maestro, can you manage 'Ain't She Sweet?'"

The couple danced and then Alice segued into 'Is Everybody Happy Now?' to show off their two-step and faster balboa steps.

Amos bounced along in time with his daughter on his knee, who gurgled along. He loved music as much as his wife and enjoyed the free concert.

"Alice, you were correct to put the piano in first. If these two will be here regularly, we might not need to put down any carpet."

A joyful first-night scene happened at 42 West Grove, Hull, where the family would expand to more children and experience many ups and downs. They would hear the soundtrack of their lives played out on their Edwardian piano and Amos' gramophone.

❅ ❅ ❅

The following Monday, Amos left on an early driving shift. Alice planned to do laundry in her new machine, the dolly washer, which was electric and plugged into a brown socket in the kitchen. She connected the washer to the water taps and tightened everything per the instructions. This new washing machine was a super saver for women. She had bought it with her little nest egg from her Mother's estate and helped shorten a full day of laundry to a few hours. The new machine needed cranking, and you slid the wet clothes through a wringer before hanging them outside on the line.

She remembered to put on her to-do list, 'Ask Amos to build an indoor clothes high hanger before the weather turns.'

Waiting for the water in the metal dolly canister to heat up, she soaked the baby's nappies to prepare the laundry ready to wash. An hour later, while putting the baby down to sleep, a loud explosion shook their home. She rushed downstairs and found the electrical wiring had burned through the new dark brown plug in the kitchen.

Not knowing how to fix the problem, Alice called Bunty at work, who called electrical engineer George. He called Alice and asked, "Explain to me what looks like which coloured wire has melted?"

"It smells awful. The brown cable at the wall has melted."

"It seems like the cable has burnt. It sounds like it has shorted out and perhaps wired incorrectly. I can come over after work and see if I can help."

"Thank you, George; you are a lifesaver. Are you working in Hull today?"

He said, "No, Selby. It might be after seven by the time I get to you."

Alice said, "I will have food ready for you."

She put her phone down and felt alone with the world on her shoulders, alone with babies and no husband. Thank goodness she knew George, and he was available by phone. Amos would not be back for two days as he was on the Flying Scotsman run to Edinburgh, so she had time to get her new investment working. George, their knowledgeable friend, diagnosed their house had been wired incorrectly. So it was not her new dolly washer but the house electrical installation.

He advised Alice, "Call the council and get someone to come and check the whole house. I think you had a drunk or blind electrician set this up. I brought a heavy-duty extension cable from the railway supplies. Plug this in while we eat and see if the machine boils up."

That was the evening Alice had to leave wet nappies in her kitchen overnight to try and dry them. Thankfully, they were hung on the line and dried by the time the council sent an electrician the next morning. He confirmed their downstairs had been wired backwards and told Alice not to plug anything in until it was fixed. He was good enough to see she had a young child and red-alerted the work order for immediate repair. (They fixed it three days later; after all, this was the Hull City Council, who were as slow as snails!)

Alice called the council and said, "As you know, we are in a brand new house, and if you send me any bills, the local newspapers will hear about it—immediately."

Amos returned Thursday while two electricians tested every

room for faults, and he promised to build her desired drying rack in the kitchen for laundry so she'd have a place to dry clothes if needed.

With a blunt reply, Alice said, "I have had a hell of a week, and sometimes I wish you were home every night. I understand you earn more on these long runs, but we are doing alright. But I need more support at home. Can you change to days and shorter runs?"

But Amos, whose penny-pinching ways were ingrained in him, did not answer and went on a new tack and asked her, "Where are we getting the money for this dolly canister thing?"

Alice had had a stressful week. She took a deep breath before answering him. "I have a small nest egg from my Mum's estate. I do not want to spend a full day a week doing laundry, and we do not have a local laundry—this seemed like a good investment. It's not costing you a penny."

"Well, it will—I pay the electric bill."

She stared at him, stony-faced, then took another deep breath and asked, "Do you want me to wash your clothes or not?"

"Of course, that's a wife's duty."

Her anger rose. He was living in another world to hers.

"Who did them before I was your wife?"

"You know who, my Mum or Maeve, the laundry lady in our street."

"Well, ask her to come and do your laundry."

"You know they moved out of town. Do not be silly, Alice."

"The one thing I am not is silly. I am a woman with half of this house, two babies, and a half-absent husband; please take Biddy and change her nappies. I will wash your clothes as we are sharing the work."

Amos had learned when Alice was on her high horse, there was no sense in arguing. He nodded and panicked inwardly—how to deal with cleaning those nappies?

12

Chapter 12 What'll I Do?

Alice and Amos' home became the talk of the West Hull neighbourhood. Her brightly painted red door, with bright yellow blooms in the garden, plus a red gate with a musical note informed everyone Alice taught music. Her daughters wore matching outfits on trips out, as Bunty bought cheap bolts of fabric in the market and made the same dresses for both girls. The Bells appeared to have more income than most, and the girls always looked well-dressed due to their mother and aunt's savviness.

But once Alice settled at their new house in West Hull, she had few friends and only Bunty for support. Her mother had died over five years ago, and neither of the two grandparents lived close to the Bell family. Amos' mother found the babies challenging to pick up with her arthritis, so rarely visited. She only had her sister, Bunty, to help with the girls while she taught her voice students.

Their next-door neighbour Mabel was a great support to Alice. Now just over forty but looking much older, she also did not have many friends due to her disabled son, but she loved children, especially girls. So she treated Alice's girls like they were her own.

"After Philip's birth, I did not want to risk having more children with disabilities," she informed Alice. So when Alice walked with the girls in the pram for fresh air or to pick up supplies at the local shops, Mabel chatted to them. In return, Alice picked up provisions for both families from the corner shop in return for some babysitting. Mabel became like an older sister to her.

Wash day was always on a Monday (unless it poured with rain), in working-class Yorkshire homes. Alice learned Mabel had the arduous task of cleaning her family laundry by hand in the bath. So she offered her the use of Bell's new electrical dolly washing machine. Mabel was beyond grateful in return, she brought the Bells fresh vegetables from her garden, which Alice cooked in the steamer, making a baby mash for the toddlers to eat more solid food.

One wash day, Alice shouted over the fence, "Mabel, I will be complete with my wash by lunchtime today with my piles of laundry. Then pop round and start with your loads."

"Thank you. I have a cabbage ready and some baby carrots shooting up—they are yours."

"Wonderful. The girls love what you grow. As soon as you see me hanging my dark clothes on the line, you can start your wash. "

Alice took extra time to drain the dirty water onto the garden to eradicate the bugs and help their recently sown seedlings grow. She borrowed Mabel's husband's sturdy wheelbarrow and filled it with soapy water, releasing the water onto the rows, where Amos turned over the soil to make it easier to hoe.

"I am here." She heard Mabel call out while she fed her girls their lunch.

"OK, I'll start heating the water. I will call you once the bell dings."

The electric dolly washer took about a half-hour to warm up.

Once the toddlers laid down for their afternoon nap, Alice watched how Mabel handled the machine. She wrung out her first load of whites through the wringer and handed them to Philip over her garden fence to hang the shirts on her washing line. The air smelt of soap suds. Mabel called out instructions on hanging the clothes: "Turn the shirt the other way around, Phillip. The tail end of the shirt pin at the top."

Suddenly, around the corner came Amos into the back garden. Alice did not expect him back until tomorrow. "Hello, wash day, I see." He kissed Alice on the cheek and looked for the children. "Where are the girls?"

"Asleep; we did not expect you today."

"No, having the rest of today off so I can take an extra three-day shift. Someone is ill; it's extra income."

He took his work boots off, sat on the small stool by the back door, and cleaned them on the boot scraper. He watched Mabel with narrow eyes, busy with her laundry. Then, without a word, he headed inside his house, his mouth hardened in a line.

Alice moved outside to bring in her laundry, now dry from the line, but she did not hurry to find out what had upset his Lordship. She brought the laundry basket of nappies and towels into the kitchen. Amos munched on a sandwich and bit into one of the recently picked carrots. Glaring at his wife, "Since when do we let the neighbours use our new washer?"

Alice slowly shook her head and said, "Amos, please wipe that hardhearted expression off your face. She repays us with fresh veg and looks after the babies if I need to pop to the store. Neighbours help each other."

He bit into the sandwich, chewed, and replied with a sneer, "It's a rocky road to choose. Some take advantage."

"Look, I purchased the dolly washer, and if someone else can be helped by loaning it out, I am fine with it. It does not affect you."

"The electric bill does."

Alice stood in a confrontational stance and retorted, "I will not wheel it over to her house each wash day. Looking after the girls is much more time spent than a measly electric bill. As you are not home every day, our neighbour's help is invaluable to me. Plus, have a look at your veggie beds. Charlie almost completed digging them. He was out there until darkness crept in last night. So do not crib to me about money or neighbours. Now you can get our plot sewn and feed our family."

They stared intensely at each other, and Amos gripped the table in anger. Then he looked away, comprehending she had the upper hand in this fruitless argument.

Alice spoke with a bitter edge, "Perhaps while you are cribbing about money, I should inform you I have treatments with an Oriental doctor for my anemia. I am paying for this treatment from my savings, but I want you to know so you do not think I am taking out of the Bell housekeeping." She spat out his name.

Amos discerned he had overstepped the mark with his estimation of the home situation. Nevertheless, he had to dig deep to show he cared and asked, "What type of treatment? Does treatment help you?"

"Acupuncture: They put needles in my feet and head to help blood flow. So, thank you for asking. The treatment does help my weakness; it gives me vigor so that I can be more energetic with the girls."

"Thanks for letting me know." He understood he must now appease Alice and diffuse the situation.

"Shall I complete the digging, or can we take the girls to the swings in the park?"

Alice relaxed a little now she had made him understand the situation. "Let's go to the park. The girls will wake up as you take your bath, and then we can go and let them run off their excess energy.

So pleased to have you home, and by the way, the fresh carrot you just enjoyed is from Mabel's garden." Alice, the actress, delivered the closing line with aplomb.

He made his way upstairs but understood her superlatively well-delivered last line. She'd essentially won the argument.

Alice sighed as she put away the pile of laundry. Still, furious at his narrow-mindedness and how she had to handle this inhibited man, she worried her love for him was fading. Plus, she now had more dirty overalls to wash, once Mabel finished her weekly wash. She heard him run a bath, but her thoughts, like ragged rats, ran amok in her mind.

After all the Normans have done for us since we moved in, Mabel and Charlie are incredible, kind neighbours. She helps me every day with the girls. I hope he apologizes at the park.

***

Later, out in the green expanses of Pickering Park, the Bells appeared like the picture-perfect family on this calm, warm afternoon. Baby Madge gurgled away in the pram, and toddler Biddy walked, holding her Daddy's hand, and behaved well, though she clung to him constantly. She pulled him to the baby swings, where he pushed her repeatedly at her insistent requests. Biddy, still teething, called out 'puth' every time Amos tired of pushing the swing. Alice watched them amused from a park bench. Her daughter was milking every moment with her Daddy.

Ha! She knows already how to manipulate her father. I wish he came home at the same time every day so the girls could spend time with him. Why does this man have to have control all the time? He followed me around the country for two years; he took care of me during my illness, and I was flattered by his actions. Once we had a marriage certificate, he behaved like he owned me. Our love is like the leaves—changing colour and fading.*

The park trees around them sprouted green buds in the late April sun. Madge sat in her pram and watched the tweeting sparrows in the high branches. Alice looked down at her feet and saw a crack had broken across the path, with multitudes of ants busy running between the weeds that had sprouted.

She laughed to herself. *Bunty would call it a sign—my life has a large crack dividing Amos and me. Maybe I am an ant!*

She viewed the empty lake. The seagulls splashed in the rainwater, captivating Biddy, who pulled her Daddy towards the birds. She loved to feed the birds crumbs, and Alice always kept a stale bread bag in the pram to excite the girls into feeding the wildlife. Madge cried out to her Daddy for a cuddle, and he took her back to Biddy, who fed the birds. While he played with the girls, Alice scrutinized Amos' behaviour.

Does he not realize marriage has many shifting parts like a train, and we must nurture them? Probably not, but the newspapers named us the bright young people who would change everything! Please apologize to me, Amos.

Amos returned with the girls and said, "It will be great to have a place to sail little boats with our son."

Amos looked towards the expanse of the empty lake. Alice's suffragist hackles lifted with this comment, that only boys would sail boats. "Our girls might like to sail a boat too. Did we discuss having more children?"

Amos flushed red and replied, "Ah, the girls can sail if they wish, but I want a son, Alice." He gazed at her the way she remembered during their courting days, his eyes almost full of tears.

Alice stood defensive, arms folded in her suffragist militant pose. "You are talking to the wrong woman here. I cannot have any more children at the moment. My body can't take it. And, just so you are aware, I want Biddy and Madge to be equal in life with their husbands—equal pay, good jobs, and to understand men do not have to get everything they want."

Come on, apologize to me. Tell me you made a mistake.

Amos shrugged. He never would argue with Alice in public but showed his annoyance by putting his youngest daughter back in her pram. He then gathered Biddy from the side of the lake area and lifted her on his shoulders. Their visit to the park was over, and they bounced along back to their home. Alice tucked Madge's bright yellow blanket into the vehicle to prevent her from climbing out, followed with the pram, and began to sing an Irving Berlin song softly.

What'll I do when you are far away, and I am blue?

What'll I do?

What'll I do when I wonder who is kissing you?

What'll I do?

Amos thought at first Alice was entertaining baby Madge, but as she sang several times, he was baffled as to the reason.

Once back home, Amos intended to rake the soil for the final beds of his garden, but his neighbour Charlie had almost finished the Bells' garden. It was his quiet way of thanking them for the loan of the washing dolly for their laundry. Amos began to comprehend the kindness of his new neighbours. He kicked himself; he'd been small-minded about Alice's needs for good neighbours.

"I am so grateful, Charlie. Thanks for doing this. I can get sowing some seeds; here's a beer."

"What'll I Do?" Alice sang while she watched the men interact and pondered why they misunderstand women and need their attention. She never received an apology from her husband; cracks appeared deep in her heart.

Chapter 13 Brother Can You Spare a Dime? ... (For the Growing Family)

The new year of 1930 in Yorkshire began with a freezing blizzard. The River Humber estuary was frozen solid, and the boats had to cut through the formed ice, so fog horns blared day and night. Snow came down daily and added to the misery for many families who'd suffered through the Depression, which began in 1929—the bad weather was the vile icing on the cake. In addition, failing banks caused the stock market to crash, the rumours of fascism spread through England, worse than potato blight, and uncertainty made life more challenging for ordinary people in the British Isles. Amos and Alice entered into their fifth year of marriage, but 'married bliss' was not a term for how either would describe their lives.

January moved as slowly as the men on the snow plough cleared the iced streets. The piled-up snow and the icy cold weather prevented Alice from taking the girls for their walks for several weeks, with no sunshine to melt the snow. But closeted at home morning to night gave her time to clean and spruce up their home.

During the cold winter months, Alice kept a fire burning all day or her girls spent family hours in the kitchen while she cooked. Mabel became a genuinely supportive friend, listening to Alice's moans and helping daily with her girls. Mabel loved knitting, so she offered to make Biddy some bootees with leather on the bottom to keep her warm but active. Biddy laid out tea parties in the front room for her bears and dolls and invited Auntie Mabel to share and play tea-parties with her, but rarely asked her mother.

It was Madge's second birthday early in January. Alice took down their first live Christmas tree and placed it in the garden for firewood. She planned a celebration to cheer everyone, but primarily for herself. "Come to our Pick-Me-Up New Year's Birthday Party" was the request on her home-made invitations. She also intended the day as a celebration for Amos, whose birthday they hardly ever celebrated as it followed so close to Christmas: a month later on January 19.

She told friends and neighbours, "A little party to cheer everyone up and celebrate my husband and daughter's birthdays."

Alice felt like a squirrel in hibernation. She needed friends to dance and speak to on an icy winter's evening and planned for high tea at the Bells.

Bunty arrived wet and cold and shook out the melting snow from her sodden fur hat. George, also soaked from the rain, followed her. He carried a soggy box full of gifts. Bunty said, "I would have arrived about midnight if I had relied on the buses. Unfortunately, they are getting stuck on the ice all over town."

Alice collected their wet coats. "This damp fur smells—is it rat or chipmunk? Hand me your wet coats, and I will hang all on the kitchen drying line."

"I think it is stoat, but at least it keeps my neck warm," said Bunty.

Bunty peeled off her wet gloves and handed Alice their dripping coats and hats. George took off his fur lined boots.

Amos came out of the front room. Bunty handed him the birthday cake—another special cake for her niece. He said, "Hello, you two. Oh, goody, birthday cake. Thank you, Bunty, for making it—smells delicious! What vile weather. But I've got your slippers warming by the roaring fire."

Bunty thrust a wet brown paper parcel into his hands. "Sorry, your present is soaked. Happy Birthday for next week, Amos; the wrapping paper might be dry by then."

Amos smiled, happy that someone had remembered it was his birthday. The couple came around most weekends to the Bells, so Alice had bought them new warm slippers to keep at her house as their Christmas gift. Biddy bounded out of the front room and threw herself at Auntie Bunty, hugged her knees, and struggled to climb up her body. George picked her up and threw her in the air, catching her while she screamed in delight, "We are getting a cake."

"Yes, we are, but it's not for you, button." Bunty patted her niece on the nose. "It's for Madge's first birthday; we cannot eat it until we sing to her."

"Come with me." Her Aunt dragged her to the warm kitchen, lifted her to table level, and showed her the delicious-looking circular cake with a ballerina on top and a ton of white sugar icing, trimmed with pink flowers for her niece's birthday. Bunty then sat Biddy at the kitchen table and placed a bib around her neck. "You can have a sausage roll but do not touch the cake until we sing." She handed a sandwich to her niece.

Bunty looked around as she wanted to get the birthday cake into the front room. "Where's the Doulton cake stand, Alice?"

"Oh! I forgot to get it out. Sorry, in the high-top cupboard."

"George!" called Bunty.

They commandeered George, the tallest man in the house, to climb up to the plethora of boxes, pottery, and packed-away items rarely used to find their highly-prized birthday cake stand. It had belonged to Elizabeth Sutherland, their mother. Bunty pointed to the required box so George could pass it down to her.

Bunty reminisced, "Mummy was given the cake stand as a wedding present."

Alice, with a puzzled expression, chimed in, "I didn't think her family spoke to her when she and Daddy got married." The sisters' mother had married beneath her station and spent her life estranged from her siblings and family.

Bunty explained, "But when they came to the wedding, Mum told me not to miss the free booze at their after party."

The cake stand was wiped, a doily was added, and the impressive birthday cake positioned in the front room. Bunty carried it through to the living room; the guests applauded and complimented Bunty's creation.

Alice declared, "The buffet is now open: sandwiches, hot sausage rolls, and jacket potatoes on the cooker. But, just so you all know, Biddy must eat at the table."

The adults piled plates high with the steaming hot food and then moved to find chairs or sit on the sofa to sit and eat. Alice brought a small tray to the front room with cups of tea and food for Amos and his mother. He stoked up the fire with pine logs and kept an eye on baby Madge, happily sleeping through her birthday party. He chatted with his mother and caught up with her simple retired life. Rachel Bell rarely saw her grandchildren; she'd visit for a few hours once a month only when Amos was home, as she was now riddled with arthritis, but she bought a gift of books for both girls.

"Thank you, Mum. Alice will love reading Bambi to them, ah … and Winnie the Pooh, that new story I read about in the paper, an excellent choice for the girls. We try to read to them every night as you did with me."

"Well, you turned out well, didn't you? How many times did we read Oliver Twist?" They overheard Alice reprimanding her daughter in the kitchen. Rachel tutted loudly, countering Alice's strict treatment of her grandchildren.

Rachel complained to Amos, "Gets you nowhere yelling at kids—send them to bed hungry works better." Amos ignored his mother by putting more logs on the fire.

Once Biddy had eaten her sandwich, she yelled at her mother, "Cake!"

Alice said severely, "No cake until we sing to Madge. She is like this all day and never takes no for an answer." The guests laughed as Alice wiped her daughter's mouth and took her down from her high chair in her best dress, pink and blue flowers with a bow to match, all of course, made by Auntie Bunty.

Bunty whispered to Mabel, "Like mother, like daughter."

Alice snapped back, "I heard your snide comment, Bunty, but let me tell you, she likes your cakes even more than her Dad does. She has a sweet tooth."

Now in a sulk, little Biddy slinked into the front room while no one was watching her. She saw her father and grandmother busy with her sister by the fire, chatting away. She sneaked to the back of the cake unnoticed, on display next to the birthday gifts. She dragged her finger across the pink frosted icing and licked her finger as if this cake was the only food she had eaten all day. This four-year-old was aware of how to get her way. Not until she sneakily snagged the ballerina from the top of the cake did her father see her actions.

He jumped up, "Oh no, Biddy, not the cake! Right, young lady, early to bed for you."

Amos picked her up and smacked her bottom. The tears flowed

and screams caught all their friends' ears, and George caught all on his camera. Amos took her upstairs, and she screamed to high heaven, kicking and making a scene. Amos said, "You cannot come back to the party. You are a bad girl." Tears continued, but Amos returned to the party without her.

Alice placed the tiny toy ballerina upon the cake and lit the pink candles.

"As my oldest daughter just made us aware, we have this lovely cake made by Bunty for baby Madge, who is now awake. But we have two birthdays this month. Amos will be 35 next Sunday. Today we found the train from our wedding cake from five years ago so it will share the cake with the ballerina. But Amos will not join the corps de ballet as his next career." The guests politely smiled at her pithy comment.

Alice exclaimed, "Happy Birthday to you both!"

Amos blew out the birthday candles while Alice played the birthday song on the piano. The crowd joined in with a joyful 'Happy Birthday' to a gurgling Madge and repeated for Amos. Biddy listened from the top of the stairs. She sulked but dare not come down. Finally, they cut the show-stopper pink cake and blew out candles for the baby. Amos had one of the last pieces of cake and said, "Give me the section my daughter had her dirty little fingers upon."

Mabel, their neighbour, licked her fork and asked, "Super cake, did you make the almond paste, Bunty? And the pink icing matches the lovely bows the girls have in their hair." Bunty nodded with her mouth full of cake.

Alice sighed. "We both try to make them look well-dressed. Bunty makes their dresses, and I buy ribbons to match. I cut their hair almost every month; they take after my mother, with tangles and thick jungle-like hair. I hate washing Biddy's hair. She screamed to high heaven as I washed her thick mane. It's Sutherland hair, all over the place and loads of it!"

Mabel smiled kindly, as she often heard the shrieks but would never tell Alice.

"They are always well turned out, Alice. You dress them in lovely colours. They are the talk of the street."

"Last night, I put a bowl on her hair to snip it with the scissors; otherwise, every time I brush her hair, Bunty squiggled away and then yelled." Their neighbours smiled, nodding. They understood as they heard Alice, the baby and Biddy yelling daily.

Alice opened the gifts for baby Madge. The hit present was Bunty's home-made gift—a white winter fur cape with a soft lining to keep baby warm, but as they wrapped her in the cape, she screamed.

Amos commented over Madge's yelling, "I wonder who she gets her volcanic volume from?" Alice smiled graciously. The guests laughed. Amos said, "Thank you all for coming tonight and making my girls look so beautiful at this cold time. Methinks Alice will ask for a white cape to match our daughters."

Bunty picked up the still damp gift, which had been drying by the fire; their guests were intrigued. "Amos, you have an early birthday gift from us, but it is so cold, I think we should get you to open it now."

He opened the soggy parcel containing a leather fur-lined hat with ear flaps—extra-large size as Amos had quite a big head.

George put in tuppence worth and said, "To keep you warm on those early morning bicycle trips." Amos grabbed his brother-in-law and friend and gave him a rare bear hug. Amos smiled broadly. He had found calm and peace in his family life and was pleased to be home for once.

The party started to liven up. Baby Madge lay in the grandmother's arms. Rachel Bell asked, turning her pinched lips into a smile. The baby became the life and soul of her party as she passed from guest to guest. Bunty stood by the fire drying off her damp dress and read the Picture Post. Suddenly, she laughed out loud. "I love this quote—listen. 'A husband today is of no practical value unless he can do the charleston without falling over.'"

Baby Madge gurgled happily to her grandmother, asked: "What the heck is the charleston?" Bunty turned up the wireless and started to dance a charleston solo to show her the steps, then grabbed George, who danced doubles charleston with her.

"A swift and loose dance," noted Rachel, whose insult to the couple washed over them. They understood her old-fashioned Puritan ways in her choice of music, which she had passed to her son Amos. She often showed disapproval of Alice's way of pandering to the girls. According to her mother-in-law, Alice's loose way of disciplining her children would make them criminals. Then Bunty cheekily turned to Amos, "Brother-in-law, want to see if Alice should be married to you? Come on, charleston, with me."

Amos shook his head, embarrassed to dance with their friends watching, "I can foxtrot with you anytime, Bunty. But your dancing will be smoother with George. Men who can charleston like him are in short supply."

"I know. Oh, I wanted to tell you all. We have set a wedding date. Two years from now."

Amos asked, "Why so far ahead?"

"I want everything to be hunky-dory, not rushed and slapdash. I have a large wedding to plan for. I want to have your lovely daughters walk down the aisle. They will be flower girls, so I must wait until Madge can walk. My wedding day will be held on September 2, 1932."

Alice hugged her sister. "I am so pleased you have found a church and set a date, Bunty. I will feed my two daughters so they can grow and throw petals with style. However, with two million unemployed and a weak and sterile government …" Amos coughed to guide Alice away from spouting her political opinion at this gathering.

Hands on her hip, she asked, "What?" She looked at Amos. "I can have my own opinion of Stanley Baldwin." She smiled at their gathered friends. "I hope people will have enough money to give you wonderful wedding gifts by then, Bunty."

Bunty dramatically raised her hands and stopped them all. "Please, everyone, I thought this was a one-year-old's birthday party and a treat for Amos, not a Labor rally. Poor Madge will grow up thinking she has to be in politics."

Rachel sneered at Alice, as she disagreed with most of Alice's radical opinions; she came from a generation where you followed your husband's political leanings. She added her tuppence worth to the discussion, "I thought you sisters would love to have your daughter be the first female prime minister in charge of all the men in this country."

Alice glared at her mother-in-law. Bunty smiled sweetly and diffused the tension by laughing. "Nothing our mum would have liked better, but I cannot see it happening in our lifetime."

Bunty picked up Madge from the lap of her Grandma. Rachel stood up, ready to leave, and Amos rushed to get her thick winter coat and hat from the hallway.

Bunty spoke to Madge in her arms. "So, my little one, make sure it happens in your lifetime! But while we are talking politics, Alice, I am inviting the Newcastle branch of aunts to my wedding, as a peace offering to the Newcastle Sutherland family, so they will come and finally bury their snobbish vendetta for our mum marrying a working-class lad. They still blame him for her death."

Alice looked at her sister, concerned. "But have you asked Daddy if he minds?"

Bunty shook her head. "Nope, not yet. But I am informing you now gentlemen: you will wear full wedding regalia, top hat, and tails, a la Fred Astaire, to impress them. George is renting for you,

Amos, and my Dad. You need to practice wearing top hats for the next two years."

Amos' face showed his lack of desire to dress up, or to wear a top hat for any event. But he did not argue with either of the Neil-Gregory sisters. He left the house and walked with his mum to the bus stop to have a chance for a smoke.

Rachel asked, "Did these snobbish relatives kill Alice's mother?"

Confused, he puffed at his cigarette. "What? – Oh no! Mum, it's their dramatic Neil-Gregory turn of phrase. Bunty meant the Newcastle family did not talk to their mother after she married Percy. They thought she married beneath her and blamed him for her cancer."

Rachel tutted, "Those girls live in a way I do not understand."

On his return home, the female guests twittered like birds in spring, chatting excitedly about the wedding. The bride-to-be had chosen her wedding date. The men were thankful when the discussion turned to music. Alice was seated on the piano stool. "Play us a song, Alice."

Evenings at the Bells always ended with singing or dancing. George and Bunty danced the foxtrot and charleston. They danced three or four nights a week; many dance halls were shooting up in the city of Hull. To warm up, Bunty insisted Amos dance with her to show off his foxtrot steps while Alice played the piano.

Amos danced slowly with Bunty and thanked her, "My lovely new leather helmet was great. You noticed mine is dropping apart."

Serving his ego, she replied, "You are the breadwinner and deserve the best. Can we start up your old gramophone?" She whispered, "Don't tell Alice, but we prefer dancing to your band records than the piano."

He grinned, wound up his gramophone, placed the needle on a 78 rpm record and played their favourite dance tunes. Alice watched them wistfully while she picked up her baby to get her ready for bed.

I do miss singing, meeting people, and dancing. We can dance at Bunty's wedding, which is two years from now. We have much to plan for my darling sister's wedding. She has known dear George for almost five years. Maybe I should have waited longer and discovered Amos' character traits. Ah, well, I cannot turn back the clock.

April 1932

One rainy morning, Amos had a stopover in York and popped into the L.N.E.R. business offices to speak to his Superintendent, Jenkin Jones. This Welshman was not popular with the crews at L.N.E.R. and had moved from across the country. There was much gossip and speculation about why. Amos had heard the rumors this new superintendent refused every request made. Amos never judged bosses until he had given them a fair berth and listened to their opinions. He knocked at his office door and heard a sing-song Welsh accent, who said, "Come in."

Entering the office, he pulled his cap off in respect. "Good morning, Mr. Jones. Did you get my request for a change in my routes?"

"Yes, I did Bell, but may I ask why? You have been on this route for almost seven years."

"My wife is pregnant again and has always has a tough time later in her pregnancy as she is highly anemic. I want to be home some nights rather than being on long-distance trips. I need to be around to help my other two children while she rests."

"This is inconvenient as you are one of our most experienced drivers." Jones stared with a disapproving look. "What date do you need this proposed 'change' to start?"

"As soon as possible, please. I understand it takes time to change some drivers' schedules. However, by giving you four months' notice, I believe this request is more than fair. The baby is due mid to late October, but my wife might be bedridden most of the summer. During May would be ideal, but definitely by June."

"I suggest you take more precautions against more pregnancies, Bell."

Amos took a deep breath, and then stated, "Sir, your remark is uncalled for. It is not your place to dictate mine and my wife's choices."

"But your request will cause much upset with our schedules. If every driver who has children asked for a schedule change, we would not be able to run the trains."

Anger bubbled inside him. Amos replied, "I am sorry, but I have never asked for any changes to my work schedule. I will resign if the L.N.E.R. cannot make these arrangements by May 1."

"You understand two million people would gladly take your job."

Amos furrowed his brows and glared at this man. "With all due respect, many of the two million could not do my job. During my eleven years with the L.N.E.R., I've never brought in a train late. All my reports are thorough and handed in on time. Please let me know if you have had time to look at the schedules or if I should look for another position."

Amos turned, fuming, and allowed the door to slam on his way out. Edith in the office smiled; she was not fond of her new boss either, and liked Amos. "Is Mr. Jones on his high horse again?"

Amos asked her, "Who sets the drivers' schedules, Edith?"

"I do. He checks them and usually says, 'Perfect, Ms. Bradley.'" She mimicked Jones's sing-song Welsh accent.

"Thank you, Edith. I thought so. See you soon."

Amos reported the outcome of his meeting with Superintendent Jones to one of his old former colleagues, who had moved up the L.N.E.R. ladder. Within a week, Eileen called the Bell household, and Amos changed his schedule to the Hull to Leeds line so he would be around to help Alice carry their third child.

14

Chapter 14 I Wanna Be Loved By You

Today Marjorie 'Bunty' Neil-Gregory will change her surname and officially become Marjorie 'Bunty' Wiles. She has known George Wiles for seven years and engaged to him for five. Even Amos, as his best man, questioned a few times if the couple would ever marry, though he had first-hand experience of a Neil-Gregory sister who never rushed into anything. It took him three proposals to have her sister Alice agree to marry him.

Although Great Britain was in a severe depression, a passer-by watching the wedding at the Church of the Transfiguration on Albert Avenue in Hull, East Yorkshire, might judge this event as a society wedding. Many wore their furs and plush Garbo slouch hats on this chilly day in September.

In attendance, Alice noted well-dressed people from the Yorkshire legal world, political women from the Suffragist Movement, and, of course, the Newcastle relatives of her mother's side of the family, the wealthy Sutherlands. Many men wore full society wedding regalia—top hats and tails.

Despite the biting wind, the groom arrived in his open-topped nineteen-twenties sports car with his best man, Amos Bell. Both were kitted out in white bib tails with top hats, which George had rented for the occasion for himself, his best man, and the father of the bride. The bride wore a long gown and arrived with her father—fashionably late. She had her dress made for her, paid for by her mother-in-law, Margaret Wiles, who had no daughters, and stated, "It is a pleasure for my son to marry a woman with compelling political principles, and I will happily treat you as I would my daughter."

Bunty, of course, designed her cream sheath silk dress, cut on the bias, the latest fashion, ankle-length, with long lace sleeves, her hair dressed with the faux sparkling diamond tiara borrowed from Alice Neil-Gregory, ran the gamut from: 'Is someone famous getting married?' and 'What a beautiful dress!' to 'Oh, look at the lovely little flower girls.' The bride's nieces carried purple flowers in baskets, handing the small bouquets to the congregation. Their mother, Alice the Matron of Honour had trained them well: smile, hand over a flower, and curtsey.

This was the first marriage of the Neil-Gregory family carried out in a high Anglican Church. When she read her sister's invitations, Alice asked, "When did you start attending church?"

At the wedding, Alice informed the relatives who arrived from Jesmond, near Newcastle, "The couple purchased a new three-bedroom house on Meadowbank Road in 1930, only a quarter of an hour walk from the church. They have been painting and decorating since they bought it."

To Bunty's friends from work, Alice pretended she knew them: "You know Bunty. She has to have a picture-perfect home. So George has been living there and dolled it up to be decorated, while she continued in her bedsit, close by your legal office."

Finally, the bride arrived in a hire car paid for by Percy, her father. Told by his daughter to hire a Daimler, he carried out her wishes. Like a blossoming white flower, she emerged elegantly from the leather backseat; she held a bouquet of purple peonies to match the flowers strewn across the church aisles by the small flower girls, of course, Alice's two young daughters.

Her friends from work and the bridesmaids eagerly waited to lift her fifteen-foot length of purple gauze train; they spread the fabric wide in a dramatic hold so the bride could grandly enter the church. The local bystanders applauded this charming choreographic vision. The organ music piped up 'Ave Maria' played by their friend Igor and sung by her sister as a dramatic operatic coloratura version that touched the guests' hearts, when the bride and proud father walked with dignity down the aisle in this vast, broad church.

George smiled happily by the altar, about to marry the girl he had known for seven years, while his best man, Amos Bell, shuffled and pulled at his white tailcoat with matching purple neckties. Some guests thought Amos was the groom due to his nervous demeanour.

The ceremony, planned to perfection by the Neil-Gregory sisters, went smoothly without a hitch. While the vicar completed the signing of the official registry for the couple and their witnesses, a musical trio played masterly classical music, again friends of Igor and Alice. They also will entertain the guests at the reception.

Bunty invited her mother's estranged relatives at Alice's insistence, who quietly whispered to her sister as they walked over to the photography area, "You will get some expensive gifts. Look at this crowd of furs, all your posh lawyers—everyone is impressed with your high-class wedding."

***

The well-trained ushers moved one hundred guests past the flowered pews decorated in white and purple flowers by Bunty's suffragist friends and led them to the church lobby for photographs. All went seamlessly except for one small emergency: toddler Madge needed the bathroom. Alice's neighbour, Mabel, moved swiftly to prevent an accident, which made one flower girl late for some photographs. Then the exuberant crowd transferred into the church hall for a lunchtime meal set out like a glorious Busby Berkeley film, with yards of white, draped cloth across the high archways.

The classical music arranged by Alice evoked a soothing mood while the guests mingled. As Matron of Honour, Alice fulfilled her role elegantly, greeting the guests despite being pregnant with her third child. Amos brought her a high stool to perch upon by the door; Alice held the seating chart for the guests. Plus, she understood her mother's relatives must be close to the bride.

As each guest arrived, she asked, "May I have your name? Then I can give you a number for your table."

The gathered guests turned as the bride and groom made their entrance. Bunty had discarded her purple train and added a white fur stole over her white-silk dress—a spontaneous explosion of applause came from the guests as they entered. George smiled and looked around. "We are all hungry. Let's feed the five thousand. Please serve the starters." The noise and smoking built to crescendo mist as servers handed out shrimp cocktails, and the musicians segued way from classical music to 1920s and 1930s popular tunes. The party had begun.

Once they had eaten, Alice's young daughters had to be shown off to their relatives from Newcastle. Amos had a list from Alice with the names of the wealthy relatives who must meet her girls. They would charm the rich Aunts with their copy-cat appearance of

Pear's Soap ad with their curled hair. The guests oohed and ahh'd at Biddy, the brunette, and Madge, the blonde, who reminded them of their grandmother, Elizabeth Sutherland nee Neil-Gregory, "Biddy is the spitting likeness of my Mother."

Amos followed Alice's orders and introduced them, "Hello, Aunt Hannah, this is Aline and Marjorie, named after the bride."

The girls at their young ages would never remember these people—he even carried five-year-old Madge in his arms around most of the tables—but their adorable daughters charmed the relatives in their matching dresses and flowered headbands. The wealthy relatives purred like cats at Alice's cherubs, the assigned nickname for her little girls dressed in lavender-coloured mid-length dresses with white aprons made by the bride for her nieces. They smiled and continued to curtsey beautifully for the guests. Amos hauled his daughters around ten tables before handing the girls off to Mabel, who took them home during his best man speech, which was about to happen.

Amos was always nervous about speaking in front of a big crowd. He had known George for over nine years; he knew to deliver a worthy speech for his good friend. Alice jingled a fork on the glass to begin the toasts and speeches. Percy, her Dad, would speak first.

She announced, "Ladies and gentlemen, please welcome Marjorie's father, Percy Neil-Gregory."

Only a few of Bunty's work and church friends had met her dad due to living and working in Derbyshire for the last eight years. Alice noted the indignant snobbery and mutterings from the Newcastle Sutherland he spoke in his lilting Geordie accent, an inspiring speech to his youngest, talented daughter.

Percy took a deep breath, and then a shy smile came across his face. "Thank you for coming today to my beautiful youngest daughter's wedding. Thank you to those who travelled hundreds of miles. My girls have grown up to be hard-working, intelligent women like their mother, Elizabeth. Bunty, you have been a joy to bring up, and with so many creative strings to your bow, it's hard for me to keep up with all your talents."

He waved his arms in a large sweep across the room. "The wonderful decor you see around this hall was designed by Bunty. My precious granddaughter's flower girl dresses were all made and designed by Bunty."

Loud applause rippled through the hall as Percy concluded his speech. He said finally, "George will have freshly baked treats his entire life. Everyone will taste her masterly baking today as the wedding cake is served."

The guests were impressed—Percy had wooed many of the Newcastle naysayers. Those who did not know him discovered his calm charm with this speech written by Alice, plus he wore the top hat and tails to impress even the most doubting relatives.

Percy added a sweet ending in his tuneful Geordie accent. "As we say in Newcastle, Bunty, you are a reet pet. So please take your glasses and wish long life and happiness to the bride and groom, George and Bunty!"

The crowd vociferously toasted them. Alice was proud of her Dad, who set the tone of the wedding. Bunty stood, almost crying, and kissed her father. Alice moved slowly to the front again five months into pregnancy number three; violent kicks emitted from the baby.

It must be the boy Amos wants; it kicks like a footballer.

Alice stood slowly and pressed down on her unborn baby, introducing her husband, "Our final speaker, George's best man and my husband, who will be followed by more fine music from our stellar musicians. George and Amos are as thick as thieves. They met eight years ago and took Doncaster by storm. I hope I do not offend anyone from this town, but there is not much storm to make a ruckus within Doncaster, but these two renegades managed to find it. The love of George's life, when not with my sister, is listening to hot jazz in sleazy nightclubs. Now he has Bunty and plays jazz day and night, plus to dance with him. Please welcome our best man, Amos Bell."

Alice moved away, in agony, from the speech table. No one saw her slip away to the bathroom. The best man stood, stared at George for a moment per Alice's direction, and took a deep breath to steady his nerves. He looked around and nervously grinned at the guests as if he were the lead actor in a comedy film.

He launched into his speech at a gallop. "My first duty today is to inform the newlyweds of a telegram from one exceptional guest, Nigel Gresley, O.B.E. For any of you non-train people, he designed the Flying Scotsman train. I have his telegram for the couple: "I hope George you choose your beautiful bride with as much accuracy as your electrical drawings for our train."

The audience laughed and clapped, impressed that the groom had studied with the master train designer in the country.

Amos paused to sip a little wine and said, "George Wiles came into my life as a tutor of electrical systems. He tried to educate us train drivers for the L.N.E.R. This poor man had to teach me and other reluctant engineers how the new electrified tracks worked. But George taught me so much more—how to live life. I learned to appreciate music at a jazz club. He taught me how to live it up at the Ritz, gave Bunty a taste for Daimlers, and thanks to Percy for helping us with a luxury transport for today for the beautiful bride. All of you who know George understand—he always knows a chap who can fix, help, or lend you what you need to accomplish any project or problem. He never tells me where he acquired all these contacts, but some of those chaps are here today. I am thankful he is marrying my beautiful sister-in-law, now called Marjorie 'Bunty' Wiles."

Amos was anxious, as he could not see Alice. He paused and whispered to Percy to check if she was in distress. His list of thanks was delivered fast. Appreciative applause came from their guests, who had enjoyed every moment of this spectacle produced by Bunty and Alice.

Amos quickly left the podium as Bunty had the first dance with her Dad Percy to Bunty's favourite song, 'The Very Thought of You.' Then George and his bride danced fast balboa swing to a Benny Goodman song, 'Let's Dance.'

Bunty noted Amos and Alice had disappeared from the hall. But she went into a love trance dancing with her new husband, which distracted her and made her feel like Ginger Rogers.

After the slow number, George counted the musicians into a fast Benny Goodman swing number, 'Room 1411.' George and his new wife showed off their fancy footwork with Charleston moves and slid smoothly into Lindy Hop steps, oblivious that her sister may be in labour, with more applause at their fine dancing.

***

Amos found Alice sitting outside the cloakroom, groaning and hunched over, and asked, "Is he coming?"

Alice snapped, "He or she is not a train, Amos!"

"But it's not due for four more months. Do you need to go to the hospital?" Alice lay flat down on a bench.

"Maybe, arrgh..." she grabbed Amos' arm. "Yes, I think so. The pain is unbearable."

"OK, stay here. I will ask the Daimler driver to take us. So they can return in time to pick up the newlyweds to get to their honeymoon."

With breathless speech, Alice ordered, "Ask one of the Church people to call ahead. Here is the midwife's number. Pain comes stronger if I stand." She handed him a paper in her pocket; she had not felt well that morning and had jotted down the number for emergencies.

※ ※ ※

Meanwhile, while Bunty enjoyed her superlative wedding dance, an unborn drama took Alice away from the celebration. The majority of the guests had no idea the Maid of Honour was being loaded into the luxurious leather Daimler by her husband, sprawled on the opulent leather seats, perhaps about to give premature birth.

The reception continued with a musical swing, and George and Bunty had a wonderful time with their friends. Guests from near and far were wowed by the well-paired couple and predicted, "It will be a long, blissful marriage."

Unfortunately, the walking honeymoon in the Lake District had to be postponed for a few days while they became substitute parents to the two flower girls.

15

Chapter 15 My Baby Just Cares for Me

Her husband of two hours drove Bunty to the Bells' home. "So while we were dancing to 'My Baby Just Cares for Me', poor Alice was with the midwife, trying to help her little one to survive inside."

"Ironic, isn't it? She can help me plan a fabulous wedding but cannot plan any of her pregnancies. I am sorry it happened during the reception, but at least Alice and the baby travelled home in style in our hired Daimler."

George thought aloud in a worried tone. "What date is the baby due? Can it still come out—oh, what's the word?—prematurely?"

Bunty sighed and shared her concerns with George. "The baby is not due for another two months. The midwife will monitor Alice. However, I am concerned about her unstable health and ability to give birth to a healthy child."

"So, this could affect her health?"

"Yes. But you know Alice's opinions about doctors. She thinks they are vampires, sucking her blood whenever she meets one. My sister sometimes acts like a clueless cartoon flapper. She overtaxed herself by taking charge of the music for our wedding, and too many other tasks depleted her energies. I will live with regret if anything happens to this child, and for the time being, her clueless husband is with her. I am annoyed that I must go to their house on my wedding night and take over for him."

George attempted to keep up Bunty's spirits in the car. "We gave our guests a hell of a do. Bunty, old girl, it was a great day."

"You are the tops."

She reached over and kissed his ear while he drove. "I will be strict with my sister and tell her this must be her last child. No way could Amos manage as a widower. He would probably find a handy train passenger and marry her to care for his girls."

George laughed, then said, "I hope it's a boy. Amos so wants a boy!"

Bunty frowned. "He does? He never told Alice or me."

"Man to man talk—he wants a son."

Bunty replied sarcastically. "Sadly, he does not get to choose."

It was getting dark as they arrived at the Bells' home. Bunty ran upstairs to her sister. Alice lay surrounded by pillows to help relieve her pain.

Bunty hugged her sister. "Hello you. Pleased you are awake."

Alice wrinkled her brow, dazed by the new sulfa medicine they'd given her to ease the pain. "I did not say goodbye to Daddy after the wedding. The midwife put me straight to bed, and he had to return to Derby to get the last train."

Bunty looked concerned and asked, "So, where is the midwife?"

Alice, pale as a sheet, answered weakly, "She thinks I am stable and may come back in the morning. I told Amos to make sure the girls were in bed."

Bunty looked at the baby bump and tried to assess the situation.

Alice yawned, reached for her hairbrush, and ran it through her tangled hair.

"Is the new baby okay?"

With slurred speech as if still in dreamland, Alice replied, "She told me she heard a heartbeat. We talked about inducing me, which means going to that smelly hospital. And I missed saying bye-bye to Daddy."

Despite her sister's meanderings, the baby seemed to be alive. Bunty tucked in some of her bed covers. "Papa will be fine; he also had to return to work. What would he have done here? Family comes first, as Dad always says. So Alice Bell, you've got me."

Bunty poured some water into the bedside glass, handing it to Alice. "Here, keep drinking. It helps you clear out the awful medication from your system."

Alice sounded mournful. "Get back to Derby to his parlour man job."

"You are stuck with me as your next of kin. Of course, you have Amos too."

Alice settled a couple of pillows behind her back and sighed. "I am sorry you had to postpone your trip to the Lake District for a few days."

Bunty looked at her sister, who had nodded off, and after hanging Alice's wedding outfit in her wardrobe, she sat sadly and nibbled the wedding cake left on Alice's bedside table. She contemplated why she and George spent their lives helping the Bells clean up their life disasters.

***

The following day, at six in the morning, Alice's medication had worn off, and the baby was once again hitting her like a boxing champ. Bunty awoke on the couch, as Amos had left early for work, and heard a noise upstairs. Her sister yelled, "Bunty, anyone, help me out of bed; I need the bathroom."

Bunty ran upstairs to help. Alice was half out of bed, barefooted. Bunty put her slippers on her feet. "Are you allowed to get up?"

Alice said, "I loathe using bedpans. Help me, please. This baby is kicking me like it wants to play for Hull City Football Club tomorrow!"

Alice chatted on the way to the bathroom. "Except for my pain episode, we pulled off a wonderful day for you, didn't we? I am sure people had a fabulous time."

Bunty nodded with tears welling in her eyes and said, "Mm, even Daddy danced beautifully with me."

Alice accepted the arm of her sister. Moving around gave her the energy to remember the wedding. "George was the most dashing groom. I am glad I seated the Newcastle Aunts next to Margaret Wiles and worked on their nouveau-rich sensibilities and conservative leanings. Her persuasive rally cry almost swayed them to join their local Newcastle suffragist movement. They understood Mummy worked for the movement but labelled it her eccentricity. First-class snobs—they're the only daughters of a publican. I understand now why our mother left the North East to live her wonderful creative life free from their uptight morality and with our dad."

Her baby moved and kicked. "Argh, it must be a boy footballer or a dancer!"

Bunty helped her sister to bed and, with a cheeky sense of glee, said, "I know you were right about their stuck-up ways. My arrival in the posh Daimler grabbed their attention. We also got Daddy in tails for the first and last time in his life. They did not realise it was all a show presented by Neil-Gregory Productions."

Both women giggled like schoolgirls. Bunty helped her sister slide to the edge of the bed. Alice grinned, but pain showed on her face as she attempted to lie back down. Bunty smiled cheekily and said, "They categorically stated George was a better dancer than Fred Astaire."

"He looked like Astaire in that suit." Alice looked down at her bump and pondered aloud, "I think if it's a girl, I'll name her Dorothy—as you know, I think Dorothy Parker is a wonderful writer."

"I thought you might call her Marlene, as you loved Ms. Dietrich's acting in that last film we saw. So, what about if it's a boy?"

"Oh, the Neil-Gregory women have more girls than boys, but maybe Daniel, after our uncle, or Roy Rodgers is a hoot! If I give birth to a son, he will not be named Amos or George. There is room for only one George in our lives." A sheepish grin spread on her face. She said, "I am delighted to be married." She looked at her hand and ring. "The walk down the long flowered aisle with Papa wearing tails was a cherished life moment. That superlative Ave Maria, sung by a certain pregnant Madame Bell, touched the guests' hearts."

She pulled a bag towards the side of the bed. "Help me open some of these gifts, and I need to make a thank you list. I have not had time to open presents with all these baby distractions. Still, you are correct about the luxurious gifts. I now possess some fine porcelain and Italian glass for my new home."

She opened an envelope, and her eyes popped out like saucers. "Oh my goodness, the Newcastle family all pitched in—I have a check for over one hundred pounds. It's like a year of my wages. How generous of them! It says, *Greetings on your special day—we hope a forever marriage from the Sutherland Family. May you be married for one hundred years.*"

Alice took the check, holding it up and pondering the substantial gift. "Well, our Sutherland relatives were generous with their gifts. Blood money, I call it, or should I say guilt money? Perhaps they forgive our Mum for breaking away from the family and will now bury bygones and scandals. What will you spend it on?"

Bunty added the check to her thank-you list and said, "I am going to buy one extravagant Coco Chanel outfit for myself. The rest of the money will pay some of your medical bills. Money equals freedom to do much more than spend it!"

Alice shook her head. "No, I do not need your wedding money. Amos has some saved—all those extra shifts and not seeing his children need to stand for something."

Bunty agreed, with a nod. "Okay, I must go home and see my husband, who I have now been married to for less than half a day. See you early tomorrow. Love you."

She kissed her sister and went downstairs. She heard George's car drive up to the house as he pipped the horn. She climbed into the car, and she kissed him. They could start their lives as man and wife *away* from the Bell household.

16

Chapter 16 Needs a Little Sugar in His Bowl July 17, 1932

The next day at the Bells' house, when Bunty arrived, she entered the kitchen to find Amos struggling to make breakfast for his daughters and days of dishes stacked high. His demeanour looked like Lon Chaney in the recent horror film she'd seen, 'London After Midnight.'

She stared at his hollowed-out red eyes and sallow skin and asked, "Have you slept?" She noticed him dragging his body along like a hunchback too. He shook his head and said, "Not much. I had to take Alice to the hospital and came back in the middle of the night to relieve Mabel. How do you make a soft cheese sandwich for Biddy?"

Patiently, she explained how to make a sandwich. "With a knife, spread the soft cheese over the bread. I'll do it while you get ready to clean up and return to the hospital. I guess you have lost your Beatrice for a while, Benedick."

The reference to his favourite play, Much Ado About Nothing, almost found a smile on his hallowed face.

Biddy demanded, "Want soft cheese." Though only aged seven, his daughter sighed at her father's incompetence watching his every move. Her aunt whispered, "Ssh," and her niece smiled and became sweet again, as she wanted to please her aunt.

As he washed his hands at the sink, Amos asked, "How does Alice manage this every day?"

"I'll tell you, dealing with two children under six is not much ado about nothing. But I agree you have an Amazon manager as a wife."

She thought her quote might awaken a response. However, a zero response came from her brother-in-law. Annoyed, she grabbed the teapot and poured some lukewarm liquid into a mug loaded with big spoons of sugar and stood helpless with worry all over his tired, drawn face.

She handed him the mug. "Here, sip some tea. Breakfast will be ready after you get showered. You might be at the hospital for some time."

The girls watched and listened to every interaction. Poor Madge, who sat in her high chair, had not eaten yet. Bunty spread a piece of bread with her favourite soft cheese and slapped it in front of the girls. Biddy chewed thoughtfully, and neither child took their eyes off their daddy.

Amos asked, "Where's George?"

Bunty took charge. "I sent him for some basic groceries to the corner shop. You are low on provisions. Children need food."

She stared at him with the arched eyebrows—the Neil-Gregory look—which made him run upstairs with haste. Bunty sat down at the kitchen table and explained the situation of their missing mother to the girls. "Mummy has to have bed rest for a couple of days while she rests with the new baby. The nurse will be here a lot. So I need you all to help me, OK?" They nodded in unison at their aunt while chewing their food.

"Biddy, once you have eaten your breakfast, run a bath for yourself, alright?"

Again, Biddy agreed, and with a serious look on her face, the five-year-old know-it-all said, "But we take our bath together; Mummy said it saves water."

"Thank you, Biddy. Then we will get you both in the tub. If you are well-behaved and no moaning, you can have bubbles."

They smiled happily. They were pleased their auntie Bunty was here. She understood young girls better than their father and behaved for bubbles in the bath. The girls finished their meal while Bunty searched in the larder, looking for some food to feed Amos.

Eggs, mmm. Maybe I can scrape an omelette together. Good, some cold potatoes in the icebox, and I will run out and grab fresh herbs from the garden. I think I see spinach growing—perfect for an omelette aux Spaniards.

Amos returned looking a little less anxious and more human in fresh clothes. "I feel better now."

She gave an indifferent shrug at his comment and placed a delicious spinach omelette in front of him. "Eat."

He sat and devoured the delicious meal as if he had not eaten for days.

Bunty told him. "We all must muck-in this week and keep the girls' schedules as normal as possible. Did you have a plan for how to cope with them while Alice gave birth?"

Amos wiped his mouth on his serviette, "Oh, I thought it would be like her other pregnancies, straight back in here the next day, taking charge."

"Well, you heard what the midwife said—she is in danger and on bed rest until this baby arrives. She may not have milk to breastfeed this child. It might be a slow road to recovery if she has to have the baby cut out."

Amos winced and stopped eating. "What? They did not tell me."

Bunty became irritated. "The midwife explained—what do you think a caesarean is? She might die if the baby cannot get out unaided. They think the baby is facing the wrong way, causing her much pain. She may need a blood transfusion due to her anemia. The clean blood will give her and the baby strength to fight disease when it arrives."

Amos had nodded but was stunned by Bunty's statement, which he had not understood. His eyes darted around, and reality hit him: "Who will take care of the girls?"

Bunty glowered at him and said, "You and I! Who else will care for them? Have you called work yet? You need to take at least three weeks of compassionate leave. You can have three days of help from me. Remember our honeymoon started two hours ago? I am thinking of calling your mum to come and stay. You and Alice should have made a plan."

Amos hesitated and replied negatively, "My mum cannot help us; that is not the best idea. Alice and my mum do not get on. She is not strong enough to pick up Madge."

Bunty, annoyed with his excuses and lack of concern for her sister's health, replied, "Alice will not be down here to annoy your mother; inform her Alice is gravely ill. You had better get her to help temporarily by tomorrow—call her now. Your lackadaisical attitude does not help you or the girls. You have not planned anything over the last six months of her pregnancy."

She showed disgust at their situation. "Planning a pregnancy is a good idea. We no longer live in the Middle Ages, where you need a son and heir to carry on a dynasty. But if your wife needs a little sugar in her bowl, you must take precautions."

George came into the house after parking his car, heard her

passionate comment, and thought they were discussing the song by Bessie Smith. He began to whistle the tune as he unpacked the shopping. Bunty shushed him, which gave Amos time to come out with more excuses: "I haven't spoken to Alice for the last week or so. She was asleep when I came home. I've been working long shifts, saving all we can for the baby."

Bunty cleaned the table of food. "Good, you have money to tide you over while you take some leave. Amos, you cannot make more children. My sister's body cannot take any more births. You wanted a son more than her, and it might be a boy, but it could be another girl. You must say **no** to another baby, whatever comes out this time!"

Amos looked at her confused.

Bunty emphatically stated, "Use protection if you must have sex!"

At this outspoken comment from his wife, George swiftly exited to the bathroom.

Amos responded, "Ah, yes, we know three children are plenty."

He flushed red, embarrassed about having to talk to his sister-in-law about sex. He swiftly changed the subject. "This was a tasty omelette, merci."

Bunty listened to the noise of feet upstairs. "I hear noises. I will go and sort out the girls. You should get back up to Alice and call for time off." With a vehement tone, she said, "You'd better get your act together, Amos. I will not be the only one picking up the Bells' chaos. Much could change this week."

She called upstairs to Biddy. "Hope you're ready for bubbles!"

She pulled toddler Madge from her seat and bundled her upstairs. The child giggled at the tickles and attention. Upstairs, Biddy had dropped her pyjamas in the hallway and walked around naked, turning on bath taps. Bunty noticed the laundry hamper overflowing with dirty clothes. She undressed Madge and added more clothes to the mountainous pile. She placed her in the bath and poured in the bubble bath while showing Biddy the last clean towel to use as she climbed out.

While they bathed, she tackled the colossal pile of laundry. As she bent down to sort, a tear slowly slid down her cheek and dripped on the top of the pile. A thought of fear washed over Bunty.

My sister was busy giving what little energy she had left to my wedding instead of resting or organizing her life. I was so wrapped up in my plans—I had no idea her life was one massive mess.

She heard a sound of splashing and thudding. Bunty deduced Biddy had climbed out of the bathtub and was spilling water all over the linoleum floor. Bunty grabbed a dirty towel and ordered. "Go straight into your room and brush your hair. Can you manage that?"

Biddy nodded, reacted to her Aunt's strict tone, and moved to the bedroom. Bunty soaped a cloth to wash Madge. Once cleaned, her Aunt handed her the damp towel. "Madge, come out of the bath, please. You are a big girl now; dry off."

Little Madge struggled to dry herself while Bunty wiped the wet floor, corralled the dirty clothes from all their bedrooms, and moved the hamper ready to go downstairs. Madge's hair dripped with water, and her Aunt tackled the wild mop hair with an almost clean hand towel. Her niece screamed ear-splitting sounds, so her Aunt handed her the towel and a brush. "Here, do it yourself, big girl!"

Madge sulked and went to her bedroom, tangling the brush in her hair as she trundled along. Bunty found the girl's night clothes strewn all over the room, with a few clothes left in the drawer. *Priority number one: start on the mass of laundry.*

Bunty plodded slowly downstairs, arms bursting with dirty laundry. She passed the hall mirror and laughed at the state of herself, hair falling from the pearl clip she still wore from her wedding and holding a mammoth pile of dirty laundry. She went into the kitchen.

"My dearest husband, please go home and sleep. I have to sort out the chaos here. Take the gifts home, and I will see you in the morning."

For the next few hours, their neighbour Mabel (the Saviour of the Bells, Bunty called her) cleaned all the dishes in the kitchen while the girls played happily together in their room before they dropped asleep.

Mabel, hands deep in soap suds, said, "I saw you were here and thought you might need some help."

Bunty dumped the laundry hampers by the back door. "Thank you. I wanted to get the girls settled. I must update you on Alice."

"I'll dry the crockery and put them away. Have you eaten?"

"No, but I can have the half sandwich one of the girls left."

Mabel nodded. "Yes, I know. With all the wedding planning, Alice was getting incredibly tired. I have been helping her with the girls. I can take on their big wash Monday wash tomorrow and get through the loads you just brought down. On the wireless, they reported sunny and windy for Monday, so hopefully, the laundry should be dry and folded by lunch."

"Can you start on the towels today? We have no clean ones. I am so grateful you came over."

Mabel smiled, ready to help. "I'll go out and put the water onto boil, back in a tick, and it will be hot by the time I finish here."

Bunty sat exhausted at the table to finish the half-eaten sandwich. She updated Mabel on her concerns about Alice's health. This kind, hard-working neighbour immediately told her, "I will do anything to help. Alice's friends will bring food and help with the Biddy's walk to school; leave it to me."

"Mabel, thank you. Alice is so lucky to have you as a neighbour, and the girls adore you." Mabel, the ever-positive neighbour, said, "Bless them!"

***

Later, once towels were hung on the pulley dryer to air dry, the phone rang. Bunty picked up and heard her new husband say, "Hello, my beautiful bride? When do you need me to pick you up?"

"I am sorry, sadly not tonight."

"I think you married me for the ring."

Laughing, she looked at how her diamond ring sparkled in the dark hallway. "It's making my whole hand glow with pride. Stay home, my darling; I love you. Sorry for the delayed honeymoon. Once again, the Bells are messing up our lives—but what's new?"

George laughed. "I still need to unload the gifts."

"Thank you. We are giving up some of our honeymoon, so Amos Bell should be eternally grateful. Thanks, honey; you are the best husband I could have married. You never act asinine like my brother-in-law. I love you more than words will ever say."

She kissed him passionately down the phone, then quietly went upstairs to check on the girls, both fast asleep—both looked like angels. Bunty did not rest until she removed the wheels of chaos within the house. She sorted piles of laundry ready for the wash, put food away in the pantry, and set herself up a bed on the settee in the Bells' living room, using the last sheets and blankets in the laundry cupboard. Then she made some hot tea and prayed for Alice and the baby.

***

For the next two months, Amos' life was not simple. Alice returned home but spent her days in bed with neighbours who helped or offered to prepare casseroles for the family. Amos worked a thirty-hour week over three days and came home to the girls four days a week. He never told Alice he paid Mabel for the weekly laundry duty, planned meals, and some cleaning while his mother took care of the girls. Then he took care of them at bath and bedtime. This action changed his outlook on how much energy a parent needed to have two active children at home.

Amos came to their room the next night with a rare compliment for his wife. "I realize what a great cook you are."

"No, my sister is the cook. I have perfected your favourite dishes. What have the neighbours brought for you that you did not like?"

Amos mournfully explained, as if he had not eaten for days. "Mrs. Engracia sent a chicken casserole, but has red and green veggies in the dish."

"Ah, peppers. Miranda was born in Spain; they use peppers. Did you eat them?"

"The girls loved them, I ate around them, but the chicken was delicious. Would you like some? We left some for you."

"I might come down. I know the orders are for total bed rest, but I need a stretch to help my aching back."

Amos suddenly stood and said, "Take it steady; I will tidy up before you come down." He rushed for the kitchen, which looked like a bomb had hit it recently.

Alice slowly got up, splashed warm water on her face, and then brushed her hair. She moved cautiously downstairs and said to the baby inside her, "I hope you will be worth all this bed rest; you must become a musical genius or something to placate Amos, your Daddy."

Toys were strewn all over the hallway, accidents waiting to happen. She slowly picked up a few and threw them in the front room toy box. Amos cleaned dishes like a man on fire, while she enjoyed the warmth of the kitchen and cuddled her girls.

"Mummy, cuddle."

Her girls took turns in stroking her baby curve. She hugged and kissed the tops of their heads, then spotted the tomato sauce that had liberally painted their faces from the spicy casserole.

"Amos, throw me a face cloth, please." He looked confused, arms flapping like a signalman. "They're kept in the bowl under the sink. The facecloths are blue ones."

He looked under the kitchen sink.

"Please rinse in warm water." He handed the wet cloth to her and touched her hand for a long moment. Alice felt warmth from his empathy. The girls pulled at her, impatient for some attention from their Mum.

"Here, Madge: let me wipe your cheeky face." Madge held her chin in the air, elated to get her Mum's full attention. Biddy pushed her sister out of the way.

"No, you wait for two ticks, my chickie." Biddy smiled at her as she clung to her arm. They had not seen their Mum for a week. This had never happened before in their short lives.

"Now let's wash your face, Miss Biddy Boo. Please pass me the hairbrush, Amos, in the basket on that shelf." She pointed out that even in her weak state, Alice cared for his daughters while he could barely keep up with the mountain of dishes piling up hourly.

Alice asked, "I thought Mabel helped you with household chores?"

"Only on my workdays; I was naïve to think I could do all you do on my days off."

"You should think of the tasks like learning a new job. You would get into the swing of things if I were not here."

She suggested to him, "Take a break and sit in the garden; go rest with a cuppa. Can you bring some books upstairs, and the girls can come up and have story time with me?"

The girl's eyes sparkled excitedly. They loved story time with their Mum. Amos reflected on how the family would survive for the next two months with a new 'son' and a weaker wife.

The girls behaved like angels as their Mummy read 'Wind in the

Willows' to them and executed all the animal voices. The girls lay down on their parents' bed, and by Chapter Two, they were asleep with Alice.

***

Six weeks later, on October 20, 1932, Alice called the midwife—the pain inside her was intense. The baby was ready to see the world, and naturally, Amos was on a train shift. Instead, Bunty and Mabel took over full-time duty with the girls. Alice made it through a slightly premature delivery the next day. The small but perfectly formed baby girl who could breathe unaided. Dorothy was petite and fair-haired, with a strong facial resemblance to Amos. His worries about the difficult birth melted away, and he counted all the fingers and toes. He inwardly responded with joy, but thought, I still do not have a son!

17

Chapter 17 Making Whoopee

After much rest with her new baby, plus her sister and neighbour's help, Alice slowly built her strength to cope with three active girls. She trained her older girls to help her around the house and take more responsibility while she dealt with the new baby. The house seemed to have shrunk; it no longer had enough room for all of them. The baby seat was brought back into action, and nappies constantly dried in the kitchen.

In March 1933, an invitation arrived from her Aunt Alice Curry for a swanky 60th birthday party in Newcastle. Alice and Amos had not had a holiday since they were married. They decided to take a trip north and to stay overnight.

Alice explained to him about her Aunt Alice Curry Joel. "I was named after her, and she is about to turn sixty but pretends that she is ten years younger. It will be good for my Mum's family to meet you. Alice Joel never shunned my Mum. Do you remember I stayed at her house the night before the New Year concert you attended?" He nodded and grinned and remembered their happy courtship.

"We both need a break after Dorothy's difficult birth. I have asked Bunty to take care of our girls for one night, and Mabel will be on hand to help her. We could go up early on Saturday morning and come back Sunday night. Will you come with me?"

Amos happily agreed and said, "We can use my train pass if your Aunt will let us stay for free at her house. It will be a rest. Then I can pick up a driving job to take a train to Edinburgh on Sunday, with extra pay for driving a late shift.

Worried about leaving Alice to travel home alone, he asked her, "Can you catch a train home if I take a Sunday night shift to Edinburgh? It pays double time."

Alice reminded him of her independent life as a singer. "Amos, I sang all over the place before I met you. I came back on trains from the back of beyond after my concerts."

"Oh, I thought Bunty was always with you. Yes, let's attend the party."

They arrived at the well-to-do end of Gateshead—the Jewish part of town—and entered a six-bedroom Victorian house where they met Charles Joel, an auctioneer and her Aunt's husband. Charles auctioned paintings and required the goodwill of those who moved in wealthy political circles to move his business along. Many of the men attending with their wives ran the city of Newcastle. The younger couple slept in a room of this grand home where she developed her love of four-poster beds, where Alice had stayed when performing at her big shows in Newcastle.

They entered the large reception room. A haze of smoke floated to the ceiling as the men smoked cigars. A sumptuous buffet offered seafood, caviar, and more. A classical ensemble provided the guests with live music, and Amos learned why her Aunt invited them.

Alice's vocal talents were to impress the gathered guests as she had performed for George V. Alice sang some of her opera repertoire. A top-notch pianist accompanied Alice. She shared songs by Schumann, followed by the Happy Birthday song. Her Aunt blew out a plethora of candles on a three-tier cake. Amos counted them, amused—only fifty!

Amos' eyes popped out of his head, "This cake is bigger than our wedding cake."

In her bubbly voice, Alice replied, "This swanky crowd gathered here is bigger than our wedding party."

Wondering why Bunty had not come up with them, Amos asked, "Did Bunty not want to come and see your Aunt?"

"No, many of these women are slaves to their husband's political careers. She loathes the crowds in which my Aunt mixes. She constantly holds soirees to help my Uncle's business. Also, if Bunty had come with us, we would not have had a babysitter for the weekend."

Alice mixed with people she had not seen for ten years while Amos ate the sumptuous food, had two pieces of cake and brandy, and sat smoking her Uncle's fine cigars while taking in the crowd. Despite the delicious buffet and free drinks, Amos preferred a simpler life. This party had taken much planning. The hosts constantly greeted people and chatted about politics with their dignified guests. As the guests consumed vast amounts of food and drink at their expense, neither Alice Joel nor her husband sat down all evening. They did not appear to be having any fun, which Amos thought was the purpose of a birthday party.

Alice and Amos retired shortly after midnight, and the party continued. While he cleaned his teeth of the cigar smoke, Alice hummed one of her songs, which aroused him deeply, and remembered what attracted him to her ten years back. Newcastle was their city, the place they came together. He returned to the bedroom, and Alice stood naked—not wearing her nightgown yet. Her lovely alabaster body was not as supple after three children, but it seductively aroused him. He gently grabbed her from behind; she turned and smiled, falling onto the sumptuous bed. Both enjoyed paramount pleasure.

Afterwards, she noted, "That was the best climax since we were last in Newcastle on New Year's Eve, 1923. Do we only get one climatic event every ten years?"

Her throaty laugh rolled out as she curled up to sleep while he remembered their courtship. The night she sang for two thousand people. Only then did the lack of protection hit him. Worry filled his face; he'd promised Alice, after Dorothy's complicated birth, to use protection if they made love. But this moment just happened so fast, he didn't even think. His drunken brain did not process; his need for sex took over.

Their fourth baby was created in February 1933, only four months after Dorothy was born.

***

Alice did not even know until May of that year that she might be pregnant again when she ate some of Bunty's delicious birthday cake. She had never vomited one of her sister's superlative cakes. Bunty entered the kitchen while she was wiping her mouth and stared at her sister in an accusatory tone: "Are you pregnant again? Have you had your monthly?"

"No, we... I miss many periods due to my anemia, so hard to keep track. I sometimes miss a few weeks, but usually, my period starts." She paused, grinned, "Oh yes, February at Aunt Alice's party... the four-poster bed..."

Bunty stopped her midstream. "I do not need the details. Amos did not take my advice for protection."

Alice pursed her lips. "Yes, he has been careful, but he was drunk on this night."

Bunty folded her arms and tutted, "Your acceptance of his behaviour makes me faint! Have you ever thought you might die giving birth to another child? How will your other children cope?"

Alice stared at her sister with wide, insolent eyes. "Except for this sickness, I feel well. My anemia's in check."

"Tomorrow, you must go straight to the doctor. Find out."

She stood with hands on her hips and bit back angrily. "Bossy Bunty, do not be so puritanical about my love life. You have not a clue about giving birth, as you have not got pregnant yet."

The shock of Alice's cruel statement stole Bunty's breath away, and with tears in her eyes, she left the kitchen and cried quietly upstairs so the children would not hear her. Alice had overstepped their sisterly bond. Then Bunty went home early, hurt by Alice's insinuations.

As she rode home on her bicycle, tears dripped down her cheeks. She stopped at the Boothferry Road junction and walked the last half mile to her home. Her thoughts dwelled on where she was in her life. She thought, *George and I are as bad as Alice and Amos, as we have not discussed having children yet. Maybe we work too much? And at weekends, we spend time dancing or helping the Bells, such hectic lives.*

She thought to herself, *I will not be like the Bells. I must talk to George.*

By September, Alice needed bed rest again due to her pregnancy. Amos became the carer for three young girls and worked shorter shifts on the trains; his tiredness made him ill-tempered. Each time he brought Alice her food, she reminded him of how drunk the brandy made him, "This is the result."

She pointed to her belly, which grew daily and she made her weaker. She celebrated her thirty-second birthday on the couch and received visitors who all brought her lovely flowers, plus some long-playing records to listen to while in situ. Biddy, now eight years old, played the music mistress who changed the long-playing records for her Mum.

During the imposed bed rest, Bunty bought her a 'husband' pillow, a padded support with arms, allowing her to sit comfortably in bed or on the couch, to help with her constant backache. She stared owl-eyed at Amos, as she placed the large-armed pillow in place for her sister.

Bunty pointed out, sans subtlety about their reckless lovemaking. "This back support is far more useful than the average pillow. Did you know it's called a husband's pillow? A silly name for a pillow; most husbands do not have the sense to support their wives in pregnancy, like this pillow."

She vehemently told him as she found out about Alice's pregnancy, "You are 'two fools on a folly.' It is ridiculous to have a fourth child as Alice suffered so much with Dorothy's birth."

***

In November, the midwife visited Alice daily for monitoring. On November 23, Roy Gregory Bell entered the world via a Caesarian operation. Unfortunately, the baby was upside down, so it was a difficult birth for Alice, and she had to be taken to the infirmary.

Amos drove into Hull Paragon Station from an early morning train shift. A message left there informing him to go directly to the hospital.

The surgeon in charge told him, "We had to make a small incision to get the baby out. Please visit the incubator baby unit along the corridor and see your new baby while we care for Alice, who is still sleeping from the medication."

He looked for the name BELL on the side of the cradle; it was a boy! Relief surged through his body. Tears trickled down his face, and he stared in complete wonder—a son at last! In his eyes, it has taken seven years for Alice and him to build the perfect family. But his son started to fuss, so the nurse wrapped him up and placed him in the cot. Amos noticed his oversized head, more prominent than his body—*will he always have a big head?*

Around five, the nurse came to tell him Alice had fallen asleep, but he may stay with her. He entered the room and looked at his wife. She appeared so small laying on the vast metal bed, pale, no colour; her hair stuck to her head. He sat beside the bed and held and stroked her hand. She opened her eyes and drowsily asked for water, which he helped her drink through a straw. She quickly fell back asleep with a large sigh. A nurse checked her vitals hourly.

After one of the nursing checks, Alice opened her eyes and said, "You have your boy, Benedick."

This comment awoke Amos, who had nodded off, now disorientated, unsure if he was dreaming. Alice fell into her sedated world again and looked like a breathing corpse, her skin the colour of slate. The medicine administered to get her through the birth had taken her to a dreamy world. She stared at him, scratched her head, and declared, "I need my hair washed!"

Her usual silky hair stuck to her face with sweat. Amos took a cloth to the bedside, dipped it in water, wiped her down, and then attempted to style her hair with a brush. Amos gently brushed her messy hair for the first time, though he created four children with her, including his newborn son. He kissed her forehead and whispered, "Thank you—our son is perfect."

A typical Alice statement shot back at him. "He has a bloody big head. His birth caused me more pain than all the others. I never want pain of this magnitude ever again."

Amos was speechless.

18

Chapter 18 Thanks for the Memory

The next day Bunty explored the legal library at work, a dusty room in the basement with hundreds of law books. The Librarian, Miss Westmore, was an odd woman. Bunty thought she was probably a few years older than her but dressed as if fifty or older, with an Edwardian high-necked lace collar and pleated skirt below her knees. Bunty asked the librarian, "Hello, can you point me to where I might find the divorce volumes?"

This librarian sniffed then glared at Bunty over the pince-nez spectacles perched on her nose; her hair was pulled back in an overly tight bun, pulling the skin back on her face. She asked, "Which year?"

Bunty requested, "1918 to now, please."

"Aisle H, shelves 300-350," she replied, using her pointed chin as a directional guide—she briefly turned her head towards the correct aisle, then looked back to her desk.

Bunty followed her directions. She searched and dragged a finger over the dust; she wanted to give the room a spring clean but needed to find books on the divorce laws. Behind this search was her hope to understand women's official position so that if her sister headed towards divorce with Amos, she would understand the legal side. Bunty remembered one of the court barristers divorcing his wife, and a scandal spread around the law offices as people thought divorce was a societal disgrace.

Bunty found the H aisle, pulled a book out, and a cloud of dust followed. She took her handkerchief from her pocket and cleaned the book spine so she could read it. As she began to read, one of the firm's solicitors entered the library, "Good morning, Miss Westmore. Is this not your lunchtime?"

"Yes, sorry, Mr. Greenbaum, just about to close up—I will return at one o'clock."

He took charge and demanded, "I need to look up several cases now; I will be more than an hour."

Miss Westmore hesitated as she had been instructed to keep the library locked when she left. From her belt hung a chain of keys, and she was intimidated by this man who was her superior. "But..."

"As a senior partner, do not worry—toodle along." He brushed her along as if she were a fly in his way. She reluctantly picked up her handbag, coat, and hat, leaving the library unlocked and unattended.

Bunty heard the altercation with Mr. Greenbaum, the youngest of the senior partners who recently had gained promotion. Bunty ignored him and continued her search. He moved into the K aisle beside hers and sneezed as he blew his nose. She looked through the gap in the shelf as he pulled out an encyclopedic volume from the shelf. His head appeared level with hers.

"Ah, Miss Neil-Gregory, I did not know someone else was here.

Forgive my sneezing—these damn volumes." He took out a hankie from his pocket.

Bunty blushed as he exclaimed, "This library needs a bloody good dusting."

"I agree," she said but thought his swearing was rude.

He continued with a leer, "I suppose Miss Westmore has many other tasks to keep her occupied."

Bunty said nothing, not wishing to gossip about another female staff member.

He asked her, "Are you searching for anything in particular?"

"The Divorce Laws…"

The barrister was full of bravado, interrupted her, and bragged, "Ah! One of my specialities—may I ask, are you married?"

"Yes, recently," was Bunty's guarded reply.

"Well, the best succinct writing you would find in…"

He moved from Aisle K and approached her on aisle H, pulling down a newly bound book from the top shelf. "This is Divorce by Charles Williams, up-to-date on the 1923 changes, including the new laws."

He handed her the book, licked his lips, and slowly folded his handkerchief, which was still in his hand, and stuffed it in his pocket. "Can I help? I am an expert in this field."

Bright-eyed Bunty told him, "I am the organizer of the Hull Women's Suffragist movement, and I thought with the new legal changes, our members should know about the updated laws. So I wish to find someone to speak at our meeting."

He loudly blew his trumpet again. "Intriguing, one of my arguments in my university thesis covered this exact topic. Women's equal rights, but it was pooh-poohed by my ancient Cambridge tutor. But I knew changes were afoot."

Bunty was encouraged by his statement and politely answered, "I think up-to-date information would help those women in unforgiving relationships."

"How elegantly put, Miss Neil-Gregory. Do you have a first name?"

"Marjorie—Marjorie Wiles, I am now married." Bunty started to say her nickname, but promptly decided not to share, as she felt insecure with this man.

"Well, *Miss* Marjorie, I would be delighted to speak on the legalities that women need to know and how to bring grounds for divorce." She noted he stressed the word Miss.

Cautiously, Marjorie replied, "Oh, that would be kind of you."

"But only if you will have dinner with me." He walked like a cougar stalking his prey and came round and past her.

Bunty stared at him and stood stock still. *Did he not hear I am married?*

He moved too close for comfort, "What about Friday evening?"

Bunty shook her head, "I am sorry, I already have something planned."

He continued moving closer to her, "How about Saturday night then?"

She could tell he presumed she would say yes. "I am babysitting my nieces as my sister—a vocalist—is performing at a concert. And as I said, I am married."

He was much closer than socially acceptable. He raised an eyebrow, "Come now, are you playing hard to get, Marjorie?"

Bunty stepped away from the shelving and the odour of his onion breath. He grabbed her breast and attempted to kiss her. Still, she swiftly moved to the side, pushed him against the bookshelf, and thrust the heavy book back into his stomach, and with a dark voice, she said, "I am sorry, Mr. Greenblum, I must return to my office; my lunchtime is over."

She had never been propositioned before and still was dazed

when she returned to her office. Flora, her good friend, who was a few years older than Bunty, and one of the fastest typists for long legal cases, saw something was amiss and asked, "Bunty, are you OK?"

Still breathing deep from the incident, Bunty explained, "I was in the library, and Mr. Greenblum came on strong to me."

"Oh no, not again; sadly, it happens frequently with that man— and he's married too! Make sure you tell your boss."

Taken aback, Bunty thought, *He's known for these actions? How awful for our female staff.* But she did not tell her boss, as she needed the job, but she did tell Alice.

"Arrgh, those powerful men believe as they argue court cases— they can have their cake and eat it too. You should not have to put up with it; tell your boss and your friend in the office was correct. You need more experience on how to handle difficult situations with men."

Stunned at her sister's reaction, she asked, "Have you ever been propositioned?"

Alice sighed, and said, "Sadly, show business is full of powerful men with little minds and small parts ..." She made the shape of a penis with her little finger.

Bunty thought for a long time, still processing a new experience. "So Amos was not the first man you slept with?"

"He was, but I had lots of fumbles and errors of judgement. Just as cars need oil, some men need regular servicing, not only by their wives."

Later that week, Bunty revisited the library and took another office friend as cover in case Mr. Greenbaum returned. During her research, she discovered there were reforms of the divorce laws after the Great War, putting men and women on a more equal footing. She updated herself on some interesting facts. Before 1914, divorce was rare, deemed scandalous, and confined to those who had wealth, plus required proof of adultery or violence from desperate women. So her Mum could not have divorced.

Thank goodness Mum led a jubilant life with our Dad. I know the shame would kill Amos if he had the disgrace of divorce. But he does possess per-war sensibilities.

She continued to read more of the updated law: 'The Matrimonial Causes Act 1923, introduced as the Private Member's Bill. The new ruling enables either partner to petition for divorce based on their spouse's adultery. Before this date, only the men were able to start proceedings.'

Bunty paused and processed her thoughts about marriage earlier in the century.

If I had wed twenty years ago and perhaps was in a bad or worse, abusive marriage with a man like Mr. Greenbaum, who seemed to want other men's wives, I could not have divorced him.

Disgusted, she kept reading with a bad taste in her mouth. The new act offered grounds for divorce: cruelty, desertion, or incurable sanity. But, of course, if Alice wanted to divorce, the grounds could only be cruelty.

Bunty began to understand marriage was almost impossible for women to annul. The aggressive incident in the library had made Bunty appreciate what a good man she had married.

After her altercation with this married man, Bunty was more determined to find a speaker on divorce matters for the Suffragist Meeting. Unfortunately, only a few women worked as barristers in the legal profession in Yorkshire. Still, she found a young female barrister who had studied law. Flora had helped her find a knowledgeable divorce barrister; part of her friend's job was to type up the court documents, and she read of the case of marital abuse. But the case was won by a woman, Constance Zimmerman.

Bunty called Constance, who worked at her father's law offices. She agreed to speak at their monthly Suffragist meeting and be part of the vibrant Movement in Hull. Bunty and Constance created an intriguing title to attract members: "**Why Suffragists Need to Know the Law! (Not Just the Divorce Law).**"

The meeting was attended by a large crowd of members. Constance started with what Alice called a 'sit up and take notice photo.' The blown-up photograph showed a suffragette in London, chained to a railing, who had her rights disproved by the men who'd arrested her.

Constance spoke eloquently, "In 1909, we changed the law so you all can volunteer to serve on juries. How many have you been on a jury?" One woman raised her hand.

She had made her first point and continued, "However, the judges are still all men and believe some women are too frail and should not sit on certain kinds of cases. But this photograph could be you."

Bunty carried a large picture of the chained suffragette around the room. At the same time, Miss Constance Zimmerman continued, "This woman in the photograph was arrested for involvement in suffragette activities. Her husband informed the police about her involvement. She was force-fed by a male doctor and judged by male jurors for simply believing we should get the vote. This could be you unless you all agree and put your name down to serve on local cases to use your rights in the decision-making process from a female point of view."

There was silence in the room as each woman thought about the realities of having the vote and the past treatments of jailed women. The older members had been involved in similar altercations or had suffered abuse from their husbands for belonging to the Suffragists.

Constance finished with a dramatic plea. "I challenge every one of you to sign up to be a juror in your borough and help change the decision-making in the male-dominated courts."

Loud applause filled the room, and the members once again had a goal to achieve.

※ ※ ※

Bunty read many months later in the 'Hull Daily Mail' that due to the Suffragist female members volunteering for the juror lists, the national average of 3% of female jurors was surpassed in Hull and East Riding to over 7%. It made her feel the Suffragist meeting had played a small part in increasing the odds for having a female on a jury.

However, the purpose of her research was to help Alice to have information about the divorce laws if she needed to follow that route, and the local ladies became educated in giving their time to help other women and men.

Walking back to her office, she thought: *It would be better for the Bells and other couples to follow the path of Bob Hope in my new fave film with Sharon Ross—their ill-starred love story reminded me of my sister and Amos. If they could only sing their incompatibility with a clever song like 'Thanks for the Memory.' It would be so much cheaper than a divorce, and Alice would win this case if only life were like a musical!*

19

Chapter 19 The Glory of Love December 1936

On a cold afternoon in December, Alice listened to the radio and sang along to the 'Glory of Love', a chance to enjoy the latest music, while she managed four children and a household. Suddenly she stopped preparing the food for supper when the news came on and screamed out loud, rushed to the telephone, dialled her sister, and yelled, "Bunty, have you got the radio on?"

"No, I am at work, silly. Why, what's happened?"

Alice gabbled her speech, "David has abdicated for the cold prig of a divorcee from America." She used the King's first name as she had met him in London in the 1920s when singing at Wembley Park.

Relieved, Bunty relaxed. "Oh, by your tone, I imagined one of your children, or Amos was hurt."

In her calmer timbre, Alice continued, "No, all fine. The Royal household should make a deal with Mrs. Simpson and allow him to keep ruling. They could lock her up in a crazy attic room like in *Jane Eyre*."

Bunty laughed at her sister's bizarre suggestion, always the actress who responded to the news with such intense reactions. Bunty replied in a calm voice, "I know you sense a connection with them as you met George V and Queen Mary, but the narrow Victorian values of his parents brought on this dalliance. A divorced American must seem fabulous to him after his stodgy parents. Please do not write to them and tell them to lock up Wallis Simpson, or they might lock you up like the madwoman in Mr. Rochester's attic."

Alice, still in her drama mode, continued, but in a worried voice, "I am concerned for the country if his brother takes over; he is so shy and has an awful stutter. He told me as we discussed music backstage at Wembley, he loved to sing—did you know? Bertie can sing fine and fluently but cannot always get the words out when speaking. I think his speech affliction perhaps was affected by strict parenting too."

Bunty knew the only way to distract Alice from her turbulent state was to change the subject: "I am going to the shops on the way home before we go to the cinema—need anything?"

***

Bunty arrived at the Bells' house with the grocery requests later that evening. Amos, for once at home, sat at the kitchen table, trying to read the evening paper, while under the table, three-year-old Roy ran his toy car up and down his father's leg. Disruption became his middle name with his siblings and parents. For only one day the baby was fawned over by his sisters until he bawled louder than any living being; they quickly lost interest.

The older girls played outside as often as possible to prevent

Alice from giving them more tasks around the house. Dorothy, as a four-year-old toddler, tried making friends with this volatile baby boy for a short time but quickly gave up the plight. She spent her time at the piano tinkering until her mother taught her to play some easy tunes. Playing the piano became her secret haven away from her little brother and her family. Dorothy became the quiet child left out or forgotten by the overstretched and exhausted Alice.

Alice looked at her daughter and said, "You are growing. Let's go to your sister's shop (their wardrobe) and get you a new blouse." Dorothy clung to her mother's hand as she went upstairs, and they found two well-worn little girl blouses, her sister's hand-me-downs. She hugged her mother as she fussed over her. This stopped when Alice heard a noise and yelled, "Roy - are you climbing up that bannister again?"

Her son was about to fall off the stairway when Alice grabbed him and smacked his bottom. Roy had been the burden since she gave birth to him, but his son could do no wrong in Amos' eyes.

Bunty heard this calamity as she entered the kitchen and plonked the shopping on the table. Alice carried Roy under her arm in a bundle, placing him by his father. She then dug into her purse with a dramatic gesture to pay her sister for the groceries.

"But…" Alice put a finger to her lips and turned away from Amos so he could not see her. "Thanks for helping by picking up the sausage and liver. I can't wait to see Jean Harlow in the film tonight."

She spoke with tightened lips as she noted her husband's reaction to being the babysitter tonight. Her sister picked up her tone and Amos' reluctance to babysit, played along with Alice with an air of nonchalance, and said, "I prefer Myrna Loy. She delivers comedy lines tartly, just like you do."

Amos snorted at this comment. Alice reacted and posed like Myrna Loy, speaking in an American accent, "Myrna came into this world the same year as me, Bunty? What time do we need to catch the omnibus?"

Bunty played along with the scene sans an American accent. "George said he will drop us off and come back to stay with Amos and the children."

Amos piped up, slightly happier, "Inform George I bought the beer he likes."

Bunty acknowledged Amos for the first time since she arrived with a smile but continued acting the scene with Alice. "Thank you, so kind of you." But she had to hold in her laughter as Alice continued as the actress, "Darlin', (again Alice moved like Myrna Loy and kept up the American accent) - I am leaving soon. Why not take Roy to the park? Here's his hat and scarf, run around with him until exhaustion hits. Then I can fix our supper." (All the 'r's well blurred to copy Myrna's accent.)

Amos gave her another icy look. "Roy drives me round the bend. Put him to bed."

She dropped the accent and pleaded with her husband, "He is the son you wanted, Amos. Please take him outside. His behaviour will be better for you while I am gone. He needs to expend some of his restless energy."

Roy needed constant child-minding. He was a three-year-old stick of dynamite with supercharged energy. Amos now understood that boys behave much differently than girls.

The sisters left to see their film and discussed David's possible abdication again on the way to the cinema. They did not call him King Edward or his brother George, for confusion could happen with Bunty's George.

They entered the newly opened ABC cinema right next to the train station on Paragon Street, with the attractive Streamline Moderne designs on the front door. They always paid for the posh seats upstairs at the new cinema, which housed over two thousand patrons. The Dress Circle view gave opulent seats with arms, plus the best view of the widescreen from upstairs.

They settled in their seats as the organist disappeared into the opening of the stage, but the sisters were disgusted again by the press' viewpoint on the cinema newsreel. The British Press reported the King should not marry an American divorcee and became vitriolic towards him. The sisters disagreed and were disappointed with the Pathé News report. But they enjoyed their toffee-chewing nuts and 'A Tale of Two Cities', starring Bunty's favourite leading man of the moment, Ronald Coleman.

20

Chapter 20 It's A Sin to Tell a Lie January

Alice's youngest child Roy started school today, which was an enormous relief to her. Freedom from her children gave her more time at home alone without distractions. The teachers knew Alice as they had taught all her girls, and now they would teach Roy. So she took him to school but did not stay around.

He wore new shorts and a blazer as the only boy in the family, but she made sure Amos dug deep into his pockets to pay for his son's clothing Alice called upstairs on his first day of attendance, "Girls, make sure your brother gets into his school shorts. I'm busy packing your lunches."

Roy ran amok upstairs away from his sisters, while she sliced off the cheese for their sandwiches, then she added an apple to each lunch bag and swiftly wiped the chopping board down. She grabbed her coat and handbag, stomped up the stairs, and searched for her blood-red lipstick, which she applied in the grand Victorian family mirror hanging on the landing of the stairs.

"Children—10, 9, 8, 7,..." she counted down as she perched her blue felt slouch hat with a large pin on her head, slowly pulling on her matching blue gloves. Dorothy, who would turn seven years old next month, appeared first. She would attend first grade one year ahead of her brother.

"Ready, Mummy!" Dorothy's blonde curls crept out from her grey school hat, a pass-me-down from Madge, and she placed her satchel over her shoulder, ready for action. Dorothy loved school.

Alice patted her head, ensconced in a blue school hat, a little big as it was one of her sister's hats. "Good girl, go down and grab your packed lunch and Roy's too. You have to help him today, as you know the ropes."

Biddy and Madge appeared next—thirteen and eleven years old. "Please pick up lunches and wait for me outside—6, 5, 4,..."

The older girls understand their mother was on the warpath with their disobedient brother. The girls dashed downstairs as Roy yelled; they had learned never to argue with their mother. Roy, who was only five years old, had yet to comprehend this!

Next, they saw Roy under Alice's arms, kicking violently, "Daddy will hear about your behaviour tonight. You will go to school to learn like a big boy and enjoy your day with your sisters."

"Naahhhhhhhhh," yelled Roy.

The day threw a crisp chill in the air, but the sun fought to shine through the clouds. Alice plonked Roy's new school cap on his head. They as they marched along singing, which they did each school day. Each day Alice led them in a new song on their daily mile walk to school and home again. Today, they sang 'It's a Sin to Tell a Lie'—a topical one for Roy. He had begun lying and trying to get his sisters into trouble. His formidable sisters were consistently mean to their little brother.

Plus, Alice threatened him. "If you do not tell lies, you will go to heaven, a better place than hell."

He asked his mother, "But you went there with Dorothy, Mum."

Alice, puzzled, asked, "Where did I go?"

This five-year-old listened to gossip but ignored his parents. "You told Auntie Mabel Dorothy's birth was hell."

Madge again, under her breath, "Plus, it's awful for Dorothy to have to keep hearing about this." She glared down at her little brother, "But due to your big head, Mummy needed a blood transfision." Roy did not understand this word.

Alice stopped and thought about how her children remembered his birth. After the breech birth, she needed a transfusion due to anemia. "I had a transfusion, Madge. Hell's just a saying, Roy. Both of your births were tough for me."

Roy asked, "So going to hell is tough?"

Alice grabbed his hand to walk the mile to school. "Let's sing!"

Despite his initial fears, Roy ended up liking Kindergarten. He liked his teacher Miff Greedday (Miss Greenway—Roy recently lost teeth, so he could not pronounce his teacher's name) and sang for her. Her comment to his mother at the end of the day was, 'He had a good, loud voice.'

Under her breath at the table, Madge muttered, "We live with him, we know."

21

Chapter 21 Oh! We Do Like to be Beside the Seaside! July 17, 1937

The Bell family took their first family holiday together. A big holiday destination during the 1930s was to visit one of the new holiday camps. They chose the camp in Skegness, Lincolnshire. The Butlin's Holiday camp was seventy miles from Hull, but their excitement built like a musical crescendo as if travelling to the moon.

Roy asked incessantly, "Are we going yet?" He asked about three hundred times a day until the girls grabbed him and locked him in their wardrobe, where he screamed to bloody high hell.

Alice herded the girls into their bedroom. "You cannot lock your brother up if he is a pain. Your brother is only little and does not know any better. Please, no more of these high spirits, or I will leave any one of you at home with Grandma Rachel."

This threat, plus a reprimand from their mother, had the desired effect of quieting them down. They loved their Grandma but did not find her fun these days. She was well into retirement and lived in a small cottage with an outside toilet, which stank.

The girls returned to packing quietly and threatened Roy under their breath so their Mum did not hear him. The girls completed their list of chores so they could leave on time.

Alice checked Dorothy's case to see if she'd packed enough underwear for the week but found only her Teddy and piano music in her suitcase and no underwear. "Why are you taking your music, darling?"

Dorothy said with her chin in the air, "You say we must practice every day. Teddy and I are going to play the piano for the other campers. Roy will sing while I play."

Alice could not argue with her six-year-old, as she was her piano teacher, and emphasized to all her students that daily practice made them improve. She left the music in her suitcase and added underwear and clothes. She reminisced about how she treasured her sheet music as a child.

What happened to my love of music? - Amos and babies. No! Today is not a time to let myself wallow in the past; holiday time is here, our first family holiday.

The British government recently had passed a law for all full-time employees to have a week of paid holiday. Holiday camps blossomed all over the coasts of England. The Bells could afford this holiday due to the free train travel. The Butlin's Holiday Camp had a promotion at their new camps—two family members for the price of one, so the Bell family only paid for three people. Amos also needed a break from the long shifts he was driving on the Flying Scotsman. Alice sweet-talked Amos for months to agree to this seaside holiday and hoped a break would save their faltering marriage.

The camp would keep their children occupied while they rested. The children looked forward to sandy beaches, learning to swim, and a plethora of organized games. Once packed, Alice rang the bell used mainly to alert her children for supper. They looked over the bannister from the top of the stairs.

Alice stood at the bottom as chief of staff and gave her orders. "Right, Daddy will be home from his overnight shift soon. I want all your suitcases by the front door ready to go. He will need the bathroom to allow him to get washed and changed, so go now if you need it. If you all carry out these tasks, we will be on the bus to take us to the train station sooner. No arguments or silliness. Madge and Biddy, come and help me finish packing the food and necessities."

The children jumped into action, like a well-trained army with their cases. As Amos walked through the back door, he heard Dorothy playing the piano, Roy chugged along with his toy trains, and the older girls packed the sandwiches and helped their mother for once.

Impressed, he kissed his wife on the cheek, "This is wonderful, Alice. You and the children are all ready to go. How did you do it?"

"Ah! I threatened them with staying with your Mum and not going on holiday."

He chuckled. "Ok! Let me have a quick wash down and change."

"Need something to eat?"

"Nah, I will eat on the way. A cuppa tea would do just the trick."

***

The Bell Family arrived at Hull station on a bright sunny Saturday and caught the morning train to Doncaster. They made the East Coast connection at Louth, Lincolnshire, for their last station to pick up the direct train to Skegness Railway.

Roy sat on the train with his dad, who said, "Roy, on this journey, I want you to write down every train number you see in this notebook." Amos gave him a new notebook to keep him occupied. "And I will give you a penny for every train."

"Well done, parent bribery," Alice muttered. "Splendid way to teach your son about numbers and money."

Despite their differences, the family arrived at Skegness train station, and Biddy pointed out, "Mummy, Daddy—look, a red bus with Butlin's on the side."

Much noise and chaos happened as many holiday families disembarked from the train with all their belongings. Biddy and Madge were all agog and looked for possible friends to smile at—for the girls, this trip was like a story from Enid Blyton's Sunny Stories, which they avidly read.

Amos took charge. "I'll go and find out which coach we are on. Stay here, Alice, with the children."

So Alice stacked their luggage in a pile and waited on the platform. Amos reappeared and announced, "We are on coach five—the one for families."

A young man appeared in a red blazer and white flannels to give directions to the holidaymakers. He carried a large number five on a stick and, in a loud South of England accent, shouted above the crowd noise. "I am Mike, every wun wiv children on coach five. Please follow me."

Amos carried their cases and packed them into the voluminous trunk of the charabanc coach. The family sat together on the long back bench of the coach. The journey to the camp, situated by the sea, took about fifteen minutes.

Biddy, always curious, asked, "Mummy, why does the train not take us to the camp?"

Alice explained, "The camp is outside town. It will be peaceful and near the beach. Better not to have those noisy puffing trains rushing by if you are on holiday."

As they pulled up, the white chalets sparkled in the sun; they walked a short distance to the huts near the beach, with large numbers on the outside: their wooden chalet accommodation for the week. As they entered the chalet, Roy acted out his tiredness and whined, "Mummy, I am hungry."

"You can have one biscuit and then rest while we sort out the beds."

The chalet had two bedrooms plus a pull-me-down bed for Roy in the sitting room. However, he spotted the chalet doors leading almost directly to the beach, opened them, forgot his hunger, and ran and rolled in the sand. The Bells had arrived.

Mike said, "Your young son is quite a ball of energy. Get him signed up for all the active events. Your well-dressed daughters are a delight, Mrs. Bell."

Biddy and Madge, at thirteen and eleven years old, giggled and blushed as he winked at them. A stony-faced Amos saw the wink.

"Mr. Bell, here are your keys. Anything you need, you can find me at reception." He pointed to the wall and tapped his fingers on a typed sign, "The timetable for all activities is right here. Hope to see your lovely girls in the talent show. Lock up as you leave. Lights are here. Enjoy your holiday."

Amos followed him outside to ask how the pull-me down bed worked. Alice had the girls unpack their belongings.

"OK, girls, take your dresses off. Hang them up, please. Then put your shorts on, or if you are getting in the sea, get your swimming costumes on. Biddy, please put the food in the icebox. Madge, please help Dorothy unpack."

She entered their bedroom, surveyed the furniture, and gave her orders. "Leave the bottom drawer for Roy, one drawer each."

They all obeyed their mother and instantly unpacked their clothes. Alice headed to the back chalet door and saw Roy rolling around in the sand. Amos returned to the chalet; Alice gave him his orders. "Amos, please get your son out of his Sunday best and into his play shorts."

Amos ran to the beach to fetch Roy but kicked his shoes off, too. The next time Alice looked outside, they were building sandcastles. Roy was in his underwear, and Amos had no jacket, but he looked relaxed for the first time in many months. Alice smiled at peace with the view. She'd fought with Amos for this holiday to bring them together as a family, and this chalet by the sea made all the scrimping and saving worthwhile.

The next day, their activities began at nine. The older girls attended a class to improve their ballroom dancing, followed by sewing lessons, while Dorothy took the arts and crafts class. They signed Roy up for beach activities, which exhausted him by lunch. With their children occupied, the couple sauntered around the campus. Amos began to unwind, and the pale golden beach at Skegness reminded them of their first date.

Amos dryly said, "The golden beach here reminds me of our first date in Hornsea on September 21st in the nineteen-twenties; you couldn't come earlier that month on your birthday, as you were singing." Alice smiled. "But the same sea here, but a flatter beach here." Alice had beautiful memories, and Amos had facts.

The holiday camp was still in its infancy, with new cabins—the beach shone golden with bracken and wildflowers growing around it. They walked a mile or so south, towards the beach, and took a lined path where they smelt sea lavender. Alice noted, "Your favourite perfume, Amos!"

But a fresh breeze flashed the meadowsweet's bitter odour, which grew out of control on the hedges as they returned to the grounds of the holiday camp.

"Oh, I loathe their bitter aroma," Alice said. "It's not sweet at all —this plant grew by the riverside in Gateshead. Mum used to take us to Uncle Daniel's, when Bunty still warbled in her pram."

Amos began to relax and wind down. They saw the notices for the dance tonight. Alice said, "Can we leave the children and go for a dance?"

"Probably not possible without a babysitter for the little ones," said Amos.

"Oh, look, a talent show—maybe Dorothy would like to play the piano? She packed her music."

Amos looked scared at this suggestion for his youngest daughter. "Remember, she is shy if I listen to her play. A full audience might bring on tears. So be gentle with her; only enter her in the talent show if she wants to play."

Alice instinctively understood why music was essential to Dorothy. It controlled her moods. He would take her to the auditions tomorrow and see if she could handle the performance.

By Monday, the changeable British weather was on the move. Early in the day, dark clouds hung ominously over the sea. Then, within an hour, the rain bucketed down. As a result, some outside activities got cancelled for the morning. In July, intermittent hailstones were a big surprise, but Amos took Roy to the lido pool, though Alice worried and said, "You might catch a chill."

"Alice, we will get wet anyway. The erratic rain can only make us wetter. I want to try and teach him how to swim."

The tryouts for the talent show were at the same time. Dorothy said she wanted to audition. She told Roy, "This is what Mummy used to do. It's called an audition. You can try. If I am not chosen to play in the show, we still can have ice cream."

Dorothy asked her mother, "Can Teddy sit on the piano?"

Alice joked, "He might even be able to have ice cream." Dorothy clapped her hands with joy.

"What do you want to play? How about the Bach Minuet? You know this song by heart, and it's quite an easy tune to play."

"No, I think I will try 'The Teddy Bear's Picnic' for Teddy."

Alice looked at her, confused. She had not taught Dorothy the song. "Do you know this tune?"

"Yes, it was on the wireless, Children's Hour."

Her mother smiled and gave her advice, "Ah, listening to a tune and playing are two different things. So for auditions, you should play something you know well."

"I am good at it," stated Dorothy, looking at her mother with the same look Amos had if she challenged his opinions. With time to assess her youngest daughter, Alice remembered what her kindergarten teacher told her mother. 'Dorothy is superfast at picking up mathematics, plus she reads well beyond her reading age.'

Alice looked at her blonde, curly-haired daughter, who had become an enigma to her. "Well, let's walk over and see how many people are at the audition."

Around the back of the hall, stage mothers fussed around dressing the children's hair, pulled rags out of ringlets, and tied up tap shoe laces. Alice glanced over the room and counted at least a dozen Shirley Temples, one boy with a violin and plastered-down bad hairdo, and a young juggler who kept dropping his ball! Alice looked at Dorothy; she had a pretty pudding bowl haircut, the only way Alice could keep her natural blonde curls tamed. She looked sweet in her favourite summer frock made by Auntie Bunty, a white dress with a printed pattern of oranges and lemons. Unlike some of the girls at the audition, she looked like an average six-year-old, with no fancy hair or make-up, thank goodness.

"If you want to leave at any point, we can go back to find Roy and Daddy."

Alice was reminded of Amos' comment, 'Do not push her.'

Dorothy and Alice sat near the back of the concert hall, a large building with a raised concert stage. Alice scrutinized the staff: a couple of young Redcoats organized the acts. A man in a blue suit was at the main desk. Alice thought she might know him. He may have been a northern-based musical director who played the piano in one of the touring British Empire orchestras. She mused, *"Good, at least he knows his music. But what is he doing working here at a camp talent show?"*

She read a poster advertising the dance tonight: 'Presenting Billy Cotton's Dance Band.'

Ah yes! I remember this man; what is his name? Brian, from somewhere in the Manchester area—Lancashire, Preston, I think, played the theatre in Blackpool every summer. Still, I hope Dorothy is prepared and controls her stage fright.

The young female Redcoat with the list of signups began calling names for each child to go up on stage. Alice was pleased Dorothy would see others perform before she took her turn. Dorothy sat enthralled with the acts, wide-eyed. Her legs swung in time to the music. An older girl sang with her mother accompanying her on the piano, passable but nothing spectacular. Next on stage was a funny-looking boy who told two unfunny jokes.

"Dorothy Bell," called the Redcoat girl with a list of acts.

Alice held her daughter's hand to guide her up the steep stairs to the stage; the piano was on a riser. Dorothy placed her Teddy Bear on top of the instrument and then sat down on the piano stool, her short legs dangled beneath her—then she remembered to announce the song and struggled off the piano stool. The Redcoats and the audience smiled.

She grabbed Teddy and faced the crowd gathered in the auditorium. "I am Dorothy Bell and this is Teddy. We will be performing The Teddy Bears Picnic."

Alice stood at the side and groaned. *There is no way a six-year-old can play this popular hit song with a tricky bass line, but maybe Dorothy will only play the right hand of the tune and sing.*

Dorothy returned to the piano and moved the stool standing to play. Alice held her breath and sighed at her daughter's choice to play standing. Dorothy placed Teddy facing the audience. This action brought an 'Aw' from families at the audition. She played the low-hand bass notes slowly but spookily. Alice looked stunned as her daughter started playing and singing: 'If you go down to the wood today, you better go in disguise...' Dorothy sang to Teddy in a sweet, melodic voice.

Alice had overheard her daughter singing songs from the wireless—she picked up lyrics quickly, and Alice taught her to play simple songs, but Dorothy had never sang and played at the piano together.

After one verse and chorus, she completed the song, "That's the Day the Teddy Bears have their picnic." She finished her playing and added, "Take me with you, Teddy!"

The audience laughed and applauded. Immensely proud of Dorothy, Alice moved over to aid her down the steep steps. A blue-suited man came over to speak to them, "Well done, Dorothy. Of course, I would expect no less from Madame Neil-Gregory's daughter—how are you, Alice? It's lovely to see you again after so long."

He air kissed her on both cheeks and said, "Over ten years since I saw you last. Do you remember me?"

"You have a good memory, Brian."

"Are you going to sing for us too?"

"No! It's a children's talent show."

"No, you misunderstood me. We need a singer for tonight. I hope you will come and sing with Mr. Cotton's Big Band. We have a show every night. I am here covering daytime duty if a child needs an accompanist. Mr. Cotton would love to have a star of your calibre come and sit in for a song or two."

Alice stared at him, and apprehension trickled into her voice but recovered with an excuse. "Ah! I do not have my music with me. I am on holiday with my husband, but maybe we can catch up after you finish today?"

"Wonderful. I am on duty here until four o'clock."

Brian cheerfully patted her on the arm. "Hope to see you later."

Brian bent to Dorothy's height and said, "You are lucky to have such a good teacher."

Dorothy eyed him, unimpressed, and told him, "I know—she is famous." Alice laughed uneasily.

I never told her children directly about singing for the King. Where did Dorothy hear this?

Waving to Brian, she hurried Dorothy out of the concert building to the pavilion area with concrete seats and shaded shelters. "Let's get the ice cream I promised you. Oh! Look, Daddy and Roy are back from swimming."

The children sat with their parents in the red wind shelter, eating ice creams, and looked over the sea, with an erratic wind and occasional rain blowing around. Alice updated Amos on what happened at the audition. "Amos, Dorothy has an impeccable musical ear. After hearing a song once on the wireless, she picked out the tune. She must have taught herself to play 'The Teddy Bears Picnic' from hearing the song on the radio."

"Are you sure Bunty did not teach her the music? She often sits at the piano and practices with her when you are out."

"Maybe she did. They bake every Saturday morning or knit and sew together. Our girls will be self-sufficient if my sister has any say in their upbringing."

"Will she be in the talent show then?"

"We will know tonight. The chosen performers' names will be posted outside the ballroom at six o'clock. I also saw an accompanist friend from the old days—Brian—I cannot remember his last name."

"Whatever happens, I am proud of her, just like our Roy. He learned to swim the full width of the lido today. I was doubtful about this holiday. It took some time to persuade me, but this brings us together as a family." He kissed Alice on the cheek, "I love you, Alice Bell."

Her eyebrows rose. "You have not told me that in quite some time," she stared with sadness while Roy and Dorothy clapped.

Alice looked at her children, puzzled. "What are you clapping for?"

"You tell us to clap if people do good or lovely things." Amos smiled at his youngest daughter, then picked her up and kissed her too.

"Dorothy honey-bee, you listen to everything. You are a funny girl."

Dorothy gabbled away to her father, "Daddy, they clapped for me, so I must have been good. Plus, the judge man kissed Mummy."

Alice now had to explain the performer's air kiss to her husband as they walked over to pick up their older girls.

***

Later in the evening, Alice strolled with Dorothy to the concert hall. They were delighted her name appeared on the list for the Friday Talent Final. Dorothy, with a typical little girl nonchalance, said, "I hope Teddy will behave well." Alice now had to find Brian to book some piano rehearsal time so that Dorothy would be ready for her stage debut.

22

Chapter 22 The Teddy Bear's Picnic

By Monday night, they know the time when Dorothy and her Teddy would perform in the talent show. So Alice went to the telephone box to call her sister, with tons of coins for the long-distance call. "Hi Bunt, do you have any holiday time left?"

"Why?"

"Your youngest niece has been placed in the Butlin's Skegness Talent Show. We wonder if you could come over on Friday night? Billy Cotton's Dance Band is also playing later."

"Yes maybe. I could leave work early on Friday; what time?"

"The show starts at seven. They say it will last an hour. You can stay the night on the pull-me-down bed, then drive back Saturday when we leave."

"I'll work on it. How do I let you know?"

"Just show up at the ballroom or in chalet 55—our hut. By the way, did you teach her the music to 'Teddy's Bears Picnic?'"

"No. I thought you had. I just helped with that morose beginning—you know, the boom, boom, bum, bum—on the left hand. She must have worked the rest out herself. She loves the song."

"Do you think it's pretty good to be able to do that at her age?"

"Alice, she has your genes and an accurate ear. It's bloody amazing for a six-year-old. I will do my best to be there. You have to go. Bye."

So I think Dorothy is my child with the 'natural' or inherited talent, but Roy also sings very well. He sang the lead in the kindergarten pageant. Well, I have passed on my music skills to many students, and two of my children have real promise.

During the build-up to the talent show, Alice asked her friend Brian when the piano might be free for Dorothy to practice. He gave them one time early in the morning and the other during lunch. So Alice had a chance to work on her stage performance, how to use the microphone, and some piano techniques.

At the final rehearsal, Dorothy told Alice, "Teddy is getting fed up with this song; he wants to change to 'Minuet' by Bach."

Alice glared at her. Dorothy had already acquired an artistic temperament. "Your job is to please the audience, Dorothy. Please ask Teddy to be patient for one more day. We can start a new song when we get home. Is that a good idea?"

Dorothy had a thoughtful discussion with Teddy, and Alice breathed a sigh of relief when they both agreed.

✳ ✳ ✳

The night of the talent show came around, and her family became beyond excited to attend. Alice had ironed Dorothy's prettiest dress. At six o'clock, as they smartened up for the show, Auntie Bunty arrived. More excitement was built not only for the show, but

George had driven his new motor car, a 'Triumph called Gloria'—but Bunty named the car—a new woman!

With no time for the family to sit in or drive his new acquisition, they had to go straight to the ballroom to find seats for the show. Dorothy wanted a photograph taken by Uncle George with Teddy in the new car, but her mother said no. She firmly told her, "You must focus on performing for your audience."

Bunty poked Amos and whispered, "Watch out; she already is showing some artistic temperament. Of whom does that remind you?"

He understood this statement; his youngest daughter always wanted her own way, like her mother. Amos sadly nodded. "I predict they may come to blows as she matures."

Flippantly, Bunty stated, "Are you speaking of Alice or Dorothy?"

The ballroom was packed and bustling. Dorothy hid behind her mother and became nervous. Alice asked to borrow Teddy, and in a stage whisper so Dorothy could hear, she asked Teddy,

"Teddy, Auntie Bunty and Uncle George have come a long way to see you both perform. Would you be the best friend you can be to Dorothy and make sure she plays her best?"

She handed the bear back to her daughter. She was fifth in the line-up, and Alice waited by the side of the stage with her. George had his camera ready. Dorothy climbed up the stage steps and placed the bear on the piano as rehearsed. This time, the crew placed a silver metal microphone for her to use so she could be heard. Alice had shown Dorothy how to use it in rehearsal, so everything went without a hitch, and she received loud applause. Dorothy also managed a Madame Neil-Gregory bow, which Amos noticed. He was a proud Dad for once.

At the end of the show, there were awards, with a certificate for each contestant. Dorothy won the 'Most Entertaining Performer' award. The audience seemed to agree it was well deserved, or maybe the Bell brood yelled and clapped louder than most. The 'Best in Show' winner was the 12-year-old violinist, accomplished enough to join a professional orchestra once he had a good haircut.

The performance was a memorable end to a lovely holiday.

Alice hugged her sister and said, "Thanks for coming all this way. You and George stay and dance, while we get the children some snacks and then go to bed."

"We will not stay long, just for a few dances. We are tired after working and then the drive. We thought you and Amos might want to come and dance while we babysit."

"Maybe, I will see if possible. He never likes to pay for drinks or anything extra these days."

After feeding and bedding down her family, Alice spent a few minutes sweet-talking Amos into going back to hear the band. Surprisingly, he was more relaxed than she'd anticipated, and he agreed. Bunty and George came back to the chalet about an hour later, and they changed places with the married couple to allow them to have time off without their children. Alice and Amos danced some foxtrot tunes. The Billy Cotton Band knew how to play for dancers; it had become a popular new hobby with younger people learning to ballroom dance. After a few dances, Amos bought a drink and enjoyed the live music, which had not happened for at least a decade.

Amos dreamed out loud, "When we retire, I will take you out dancing every weekend."

Alice looked at her husband. "Do you think you will make it to retirement? You are working too many hours. If you carry on the way you are, taking extra shifts, I will be a young widow."

"Okay, I will try not to take every weekend shift offered."

She shrugged; he always agreed with her and then would take extra shifts for the money. But she said nothing to spoil their holiday. This was the glum-faced couple that the band leader, Billy Cotton, walked up to. He introduced himself to Alice.

"Madame Neil-Gregory, I am so delighted to meet you. Brian told me you were here with your family. Would you be kind enough to give us a song? I saw you sing in Salford, Manchester, when you were promoting the British Empire event. Your impressive interpretation of the classics stayed in my memory. I would be honoured to have you sing with my band."

Alice looked at Amos and read his face; he seemed quite accepting of this band leader's offer, but she haltingly replied, "Well, sadly, I do not have my music with me."

"Madame, you are a pro. I know opera is your field, but I hope you can find something on our Act 2 playlist that you could share." He handed her a typed song list on their table. "Please look it over and let Brian know. This would be a great help; our vocalist is not well tonight. She has a very sore throat, so we may have to cut some of the vocal numbers. This audience so loves to have beautiful ladies to sing for them."

Alice glanced down at the list and nodded. She was familiar with a couple of popular songs, which she'd taught to students. But doubt crept through her as she had not sung with a dance band or professionally for almost four years.

"I could perhaps present 'Pennies from Heaven' or maybe 'Blue Heaven.'"

She looked at Amos and said, "What do you think, Amos?"

"I think you should help this fine band leader out." He had heard of him from the wireless. "I will pick up Biddy and Madge so they can see their mother perform." As her husband left, Alice said, "I would be honoured."

The bespectacled Billy Cotton smiled, kissed her hand, and returned to the bandstand. She called out to Amos. "Do not wake the little ones; they should be fast asleep. I hope Bunty won't mind staying with them."

She moved towards Brian on the stage to find out the keys to the songs. Amos walked swiftly over to the chalet and told the older girls to change back into their best dresses as they would watch their mama sing. George grabbed his camera tripod. Bunty, who was already in her pajamas, stayed behind with the younger children and said, "I am happy to look at the photos; my sister will be a 'wow'—I am too tired to get dressed and go back in the ballroom."

This night was one of the only times Alice Neil-Gregory sang with a popular dance band with her eldest two children present. She was a huge hit with the audience. Many of the older audience remembered her singing in London over a decade ago. Amos was delighted his older daughters saw their mother on stage as she sang 'Blue Heaven' followed by an encore of 'Pennies from Heaven.' Their daughters were taken to heaven by their Mum's singing. The dance floor was packed with dancers, plus the older audience sitting at dinner tables gave her a standing ovation. This was a night to remember for the Bells.

Back at the chalet, Alice could not sleep.

It was fabulous to be back on stage and sing with the premier dance band. What a night to remember! Amos is smiling in his sleep. Why can't he smile like that when around people? I won't tell him that Billy Cotton asked me if I wished to sing weekends with them during the summer.

If I could get to Skegness and Filey in North Yorkshire, where Butlin's are building another camp, I could work again. Mr. Cotton suggested he could bring me on as a sub, to give his full-time vocalist time off. Oh! It is so tempting to get back on stage. The train goes to both places. Could I get home in the early hours of the morning? However, I think Amos might divorce me; he cannot control two of our brood let alone all four of our children. And I must also prioritise my health. To sing long shows would lay me up all week. I must bring up my funny, opinionated children and see them grow up, not be entertaining holidaymakers, but it was thrilling to be asked!

***

The next day, the family had a morning dip in the water as the weather was sunny again, and Alice and Bunty packed to leave. Alice asked Bunty to keep packing while she slipped out to speak to Mr. Cotton, the bandleader. She sprinted over to the musician's lodge but saw them entering the café. Dressed in her pale blue summer frock with her bright white sun hat, she turned some heads from a crowd of families when she called out, "Mr. Cotton."

"Hello, Alice. May I call you that, now we have worked together?"

"Of course, I wanted to get back to you. I am so touched that you considered me a substitute singer. Sadly, I must put my family first at this point in my life. If I might, I will contact you in a few years when the children can cope without me."

"I understand, and I hope our paths will cross again. Breakfast calls!"

The hungry bandleader shook her hand and smiled. She sighed as she walked slowly back to the family chalet. Her heart was warmed when she saw the children packing sand around George and Teddy until neither could move.

I have made the right choice, but I wish I could be a performer again. Some day!

Their last Saturday in Skegness became a memory of sun, sea, and sand. The two oldest girls thought the holiday was the cat's meow as they travelled back in George's new car. The train trip back was much easier for their parents. They would talk about this holiday for many years.

**

What the Bell family did not know was that Europe would be thrown into chaos by all the "isms'—fascism, communism, and Hitler-ism—and they would not have a holiday together again.

23

Chapter 23 Friendship

By 1939, it looked inevitable that the powers in charge of the country might take Britain to war again. Families were expected to dig up their lawns to plant vegetables, plus people were told to construct air-raid shelters within their gardens, designed and supplied by the county councils. The British public had to muck in and work with their neighbours to build them.

At the Bell household, life continued as Alice's children grew up; they became more bolshie each day as they argued with each other. Their mum often went to bed early, exhausted with their tantrums and discords. One evening, her two older girls finished off a dress at the kitchen table. Biddy had put it together on the sewing machine at her aunt's house. Madge helped her cut off all the final hem threads as they listened to the light programme on the wireless.

The always opinionated, Madge told her sister, "I know we are going to war, but I need music to help me dream life can be better. I adore this song, 'Stairway to the Stars.' Do you know who the band is?"

Biddy, who had a mouthful of pins, answered, "I think it's the Whenn Miller Band."

Suddenly their father stepped through the back door. Biddy took the pins out of her mouth and smiled. "Hello, Dad."

"Still up? A bit late for burning the midnight oil, isn't it?"

"I am trying to finish my new dress for the school dance next weekend."

Madge got up and searched in her coat pocket, where she delved deeply for a coin and took out a shilling. She offered him the coin and said, "Here, Dad, a shilling for the electric bill before you complain about how much it costs to run the lights."

She slammed the shilling down on the table. He grunted but did not take the coin. He put his work boots away, went upstairs to his bedroom, and found Alice snuggled under the blankets, trying to sleep.

"Hello, Alice."

He kissed her on the forehead. "Are you doing alright?"

"I am tired and depressed by the news about the war. I'm trying hard to build my energy for the women's rally this weekend."

If Alice took time for herself, Amos sulked. "Ah, I hoped we might have some time together. When are you going?"

"The meeting starts late Saturday afternoon and finishes by early evening."

Amos calculated the days in his head. "I have territorial training on Sunday."

He looked at her as if she should change her plans. Alice instead changed the subject, too tired to argue, but her tone said everything. "You are serious about being on the fire bomb team, then?"

He undressed and, as an excuse, said, "It brings in extra income for us."

"But you are already in a reserved occupation as a train driver.

You do not have to serve with the auxiliary force as well, as you are over forty."

He snapped suddenly back at her, "I am. Are you insinuating I am too old to serve?"

"No, silly, but I gave up singing to take care of the children. Would it be possible to find something for the war effort that is less dangerous?" Her tone was brittle with sarcasm.

Amos' standard reply to her was, "I'll think about it. Our neighbour Charlie and I will start building the Anderson shelter this Saturday. Have you started getting provisions together?"

"No, I've been too tired." She faded away to sleep.

Amos sighed. "Good night, Gloriana."

Amos climbed into bed and tried to read the shelter instructions. He grew drowsy, so the instructions on how to build the shelter slid off the bed. He fell asleep as images of the shelters he dug when he was sixteen years old in Belgium whirled in his mind.

* * *

During breakfast, Amos started planning how to dig a hole in his garden to keep his family safe from bombing, and memories of digging trenches in Northern France flooded back. He brought out an old spade that folded but also had a trench cutter on it. Charlie pointed out, "They advise digging a four-foot hole."

Amos, who could not find the instructions, replied, "I intend to make it five feet, easier to stand up."

"Mm... I reckon we can put together the sides of the shelter with Roy's help. It will arrive on Monday, so we must get cracking. The top needs to be covered with turf grass. I have already cut up my turf."

Amos' face grew grim. "I will make sure Roy de-turfs our front garden today, as he has not done so yet. My son is bone-idle. See you tomorrow, Charlie. Goodnight."

***

Early Saturday morning, Charlie knocked at the door, wrapped up in a scarf and beanie, and wore his black workman jacket. Biddy handed him a hot mug of tea and said, "Dad will be down in a mo. I hope this cuppa might warm you up."

Charlie smiled. "Thanks, dearie, for a nice cuppa tea. It is a cold morning, but we will warm up once we get digging."

Amos came into the kitchen in his overalls and pulled his boots on.

"Good girl, thanks for making tea. We have five feet to dig today."

The men worked hard on the hole, and with much back-breaking shovelling of earth, it grew deeper and wider. At ten, Alice took out bacon sandwiches and more tea. "So how is it going, chaps? Will eleven of us be able to sleep in that space?"

Amos stated guardedly, "That's the plan."

She saw his Jerry spade. "What the hell is that in your hand?"

Amos held up his old trench cutter. "I never thought I would have to use it again—we were all issued one—as we cut into those filthy Belgium trenches."

Alice shook her head, sarcasm dripping from her lips. "You kept a tool for over 30 years—just waiting for another war? Does the government, in their naive wisdom, believe this shelter will save us?"

To prevent an argument between the couple, their neighbour Charlie pointed to the large white paper he had taped to the side of the shed and said, "Oh, yes, Alice, I have my diagram and have been slicing the turf off my front lawn so we can have a grass roof. I thought of putting a hole in the middle and letting the Jerries think we have a golf course with a little pole and flag. But Mabel said the Jerries might just bomb it for the hell of it—if they think the British like golf."

Amos smirked at Charlie, jesting about outsmarting the Germans. Alice had shown little interest in the air raid shelter and replied to him, "Who knows? She may be correct. Thank you for helping, Amos."

"Nah, this is a joint project. Oh! Alice, the council will drop off the metal sides for the Anderson shelter on Monday. Mabel told me you would be here, as Monday is wash day. I reckon I can put together the sides of the shelter with Roy's help. It will arrive on Monday, so we must get cracking. The top must be covered with turf grass. I have already cut up my turf."

Alice nodded, so Charlie, in his shy manner, continued and added, "Could you move the dolly washer away from the shed so, when they deliver, they place it against the fence? I will do what I can, bolting them together on Monday. Maybe Roy could help after school? On Amos' next day off, we will try and move them into position. Is that okay?" Alice again nodded, processing what her helpful neighbour had told her.

Amos added, "I hope to return Tuesday afternoon if all the trains run to schedule. We should be able to put in all the provisions next week. We also need some wood planks for the bunk beds."

He looked at Alice as if a reprimand might follow, as he did with the children. "Alice, I asked you to have blankets and water ready over a week ago for the shelter."

Luckily, Charlie interrupted with another remembered missive from his missus. "Oh, Mabel told me to ask if she intends to extend them and re-sew, then re-pad them as longer mattresses for your daughters."

Alice nodded, sighed, and left them to their project. She called her sister at work, "Hello, sis. The dreaded shelter is being built."

Bunty replied, "That's good, isn't it?"

"His master's voice is in charge. I have no intention of spending any night in a cold, damp shelter, which would not help my illness. That smell of wet soil makes me nauseous, the earthy odors emulating from the mounds of freshly moved mud. Yuk."

"Look, Alice, impending blackouts will be the norm," replied her sensible sister.

Alice said, "I feel buried already just thinking about it. You know I lived in the spotlight; being hidden underground is not a scene I wish to play. Come over for supper, as George is away—Shepherd's Pie. Bye, Bunty."

Once in the house, Alice sang, which annoyed Amos. She sang the song 'Friendship' from Cole Porter's 'Anything Goes' with his witty lyrics. The men could hear her singing through the open kitchen window. Charlie, with his bright outlook, said, "It must be grand to have a show when Alice sings; you have a free concert. We love her voice and music. She sings with the girls sometimes; it's lovely to hear them together."

Amos grumpily said, "Hmm," as he stopped to rest. Then he asked his neighbour, "Really? I am pleased they do not annoy you."

Amos remembered falling in love with her voice when Alice performed on massive stages. He did not realise why she sang; it helped her not become more depressed.

Alice became more anxious about the safety of her children when she read the papers daily. Journalists during the last year called it the phoney war, but with Luftwaffe bombs killing thousands of people in the London dock area, she surmised Hull docks would be next. The German planes bombed the same area each evening, where Amos patrolled as a member of the Auxiliary Fire Force.

She emphasised lines such as only 'use four-letter words'. Her unsubtle way of intimating that he was wrong!

Amos imagined Alice might be slightly mad and ignored her singing as he dug a deep hole.

24

Chapter 24 Heaven Can Wait

Alice acquired more freedom when her children attended school, but at the beginning of the war in 1939, many lives were affected, and the Bells' home life was not exempt. Early in the year, her father, Percy, suddenly died. The sisters wanted to attend the funeral in Derbyshire, but it was delayed due to an inquest being held, which confused and upset them; apparently, there may have been a suspicious circumstance about his death.

Bunty arrived back from work once she heard the sad news of their father's death. She found Alice talking angrily to the coroner's office on the telephone, her voice strident and high. "What do you mean the funeral will be delayed? Why?"

Bunty listened; the house lay unusually quiet in this mid-afternoon, there were no children, and peace reigned. She put the kettle on the gas and listened to her sister's part of the conversation. Alice demanded, "So, how long is this going to take? I am the eldest daughter. I have to plan a funeral as people will come from far and wide."

Bunty was puzzled by this comment; she thought he only had his new wife, May Brown, and not many friends in Derby. Perhaps maybe Alice had found out more.

Alice, with a firm tone, adamantly said, "I will call back tomorrow, and I hope the coroner can sign off on this 'body' as you call it, but it just happens that this body is my father."

She slammed the phone down and came into the kitchen, where she sat like a deflated balloon with no air left in her. Bunty handed her a mug of tea and asked, "Who were you talking to, the undertakers?"

"No, the coroner's office—I've been on the phone all morning. I got the call from the police, as I am his next of kin, not May. They are not releasing Dad's body for a funeral, as foul play is suspected as his death was so sudden."

"What? Do they know what caused his death?"

"It could have been a heart attack, but according to his wife, he had no symptoms."

Bunty, again the realistic voice of reason, said, "Oh, you know our dad; if ill, he pretends he's not."

Alice sat at the table and poured a cup of tea. "Precisely, but May has verbal diarrhea about everything and thinks the worst always happens. Until the coroner has checked it over, they cannot release the body for the funeral."

Bunty ran her hands through her hair, then dug in her bag for her comb. She'd rushed from work upset with the news, and her brunette locks had become wild as she cycled over to Alice's. Breathing steadier and beginning to think rationally again, she said, "Okay. Well, I suppose that gives us more time to plan how to travel to Derby. Did they inform you when they would release the paperwork?"

"No, but I will call tomorrow. It looks like we'll be going to Derbyshire next week, not tomorrow. Sorry for dragging you away from work."

Bunty stood up. Her tense shoulders relaxed a little. "Ok. I will call work and tell them I will be back tomorrow but need time off next week."

Alice sat, took one of her deep singer breaths to slow down her heart rate, and sipped some tea while tears slowly ran down her face and then dropped into her teacup.

Bunty returned to the kitchen, hugged her sister, and said, "Oh, Alice, don't cry. You'll start me off." Emotions gushed from her lips as fast as the tears. "I feel we are all becoming old with Dad's sudden passing and the pending war. Amos is away all the time, and now we are dealing with a funeral."

Bunty also took deep breaths to stop crying. "I think the fact that his passing was so unexpected. I only spoke to Dad last week; he used to call me at work around lunchtime, but he sounded off. He lacked energy; he had no sparkle in his voice."

Alice assumed the worst and asked, "Weak voice? Did he sound sick?"

Bunty attempted to calm her down. "Oh, don't be melodramatic, Alice. He told me his job tired him a bit too much, being a parlourman."

Angry with the situation, Alice's fists clenched and banged on the table. She said, "Why did he go and take that stupid servant job in Derbyshire?"

Bunty, always the rational sister, replied, "He would have died earlier if he had stayed here as a marine fitter—nasty, gruelling work. Did you know he had a half-brother in Derbyshire?"

Alice's vocal pitch went higher, her eyes wide. "What? No, how do you know this, Bunty?"

Calmly, Bunty explained, "The police got in touch with me after they spoke to you. They found my work number in his pocket after they called you, and this line here was busy. They found his brother's address in his wallet. Sixty-one is not that old, but he never got any retirement. Why did we not know about his relatives over there?"

They both sipped their tea, overwhelmed with grief, thinking about the life their father had endured: married to their mother, working in Harwich during the First World War without the love of his life, and moving her to Hull from Newcastle to have a better life. He took on the daily burden of the household during her ovarian cancer illness, until she passed away. Then, after his marriage to May, he moved to Derbyshire and became a servant in a large home.

Bunty broke the bleak silence. "Have you talked to May?"

Alice sat rigidly and became tense again. "No, will you call her?"

Bunty, as always, completed the difficult tasks. "Of course, let me go and do that."

Alice shivered and suddenly looked up at the kitchen clock. "Oh gosh, it's time for the school pick-up, and I teach two students today. Can you stay and help the children with homework? And have supper with us and explain to the children?"

Bunty nodded, not having any children of her own; her sister's children often seemed like her own. She loved them deeply, and sometimes she played the role of mother more than her sister did. Alice swiftly put on her coat and hat, though she was sad and tired. She picked up her handbag, and, unusually for her, Bunty noted, Alice did not put on lipstick—her sister was off-kilter.

Bunty said, "I'll call May and hear her side of events. I'll start baking a treat for supper; what is their snack today? Have you any apples?"

"Two apples; give them bread and jam. Oh, we do have an abundance of rhubarb in the garden; can you make a pie with that? And we have some of your scones left. I thought I would save them for Amos, but he is not back till Saturday due to taking an extra shift;

they can finish them. Split the scones in half each. Thanks, Bunt, for helping."

She hugged her sister and left to pick up the children from school.

By five o'clock, Alice's voice students arrived for their lessons. Bunty held down the homework front and baked a rhubarb crumble in the kitchen. The Bell children all adored their aunt, who had more patience with them than their mother did. Bunty guided them with homework, all while preparing their supper and baking the crumble.

She told them the sad news of the loss of their grandfather. "Listen to me; after Mummy finishes teaching, you must be on your best behaviour. Today we had the sad news that Grandpa Percy died suddenly. Mummy and I are going to Derbyshire, far from Yorkshire, for one day next week. We have a ninety-mile trip, so you must be well-behaved, and if you are good, I will bring you my special chocolate biscuits every day. Understood?"

They all nodded, for once quietly. Dorothy raised her hand like she was still at school and asked her aunt. "Auntie Bunty, does that mean Grandad Percy is not coming back and going to heaven? Can I put that in my story?"

"What's your story about?"

Dorothy read the title on her page, "My relatives."

Her aunt's smile was encouraging. "I think that would be a fine end to your story that one of your relatives is in heaven." Alice said goodbye to her last voice student. Bunty then heard Alice dialing the telephone and stridently demanding the person on the other end, "Please make sure Amos Bell gets that message today. Thank you. Please confirm this information will be given to him at the next station; it is urgent."

***

The sisters found out the next day their father's body had been released, as no foul play was found, and the funeral could be held the following week. Bunty believed that when May was questioned by the police, she told them Percy was a fine-fit man, and she suspected that someone had it in for him.

Alice agreed, "Of course, she devours all those who-done-its novels! Agatha Christie, the Second. Typical, that woman can never keep her mouth shut. I wish she had gone missing like Agatha did."

Bunty smiled grimly. "Yes, it's a mess, but the police seem to have understood once they spoke to her today. Of course, I am sure she was upset and confused; we should call her tomorrow."

Bunty, of course, made the call.

***

The following week, the Neil-Gregory sisters took the train west to Derbyshire, smack in the middle of the North of England, without their husbands. Amos took two days off to become a father and mother to his four children, while the ladies set off very early for the funeral.

Alice sang Amos' praises. "Thank God for free rail passes from Amos. This would have taken a big chunk from our budget."

Before she left home, Alice had called her doctor friend Patina, who wanted to come and meet them as the funeral was close to her practice. They agreed to meet at the Derby Railway station, close to her medical office, where she ran a rural practice, mainly delivering babies who had complications.

On the train, without distractions such as children, husbands, and work, Alice, with an unusually serious face, asked her sister, "I want to ask you to take care of my family if anything happens to me while they are still young."

Bunty was taken aback. "That's a huge request. You mean you want me to stop working?"

"No, just make sure they do well in life."

"Of course, I will guide them, but you are simply depressed; you are not going to die soon."

Alice continued with a rare serious face. "I am getting weaker each year, as you well know. Some days I only make it through the day as I can sleep while the children are at school. Days off from school are tough. I become weaker and cannot keep up with the children. That's why I asked Patina to meet us; I need her advice."

Bunty did not ask what advice Alice, her mercurial sister, needed; she would find out soon enough. They changed trains at Sheffield to travel to Derby, where they would meet Patina. They exited the large Victorian station and spotted her waiting for them under the white archways in British tweeds, not her usual sari.

She hugged Alice as if she did not want to let her go. In her lovely, lilting Indian accent, sprinkled with Northern cadences, she said, "It's been ten years, Alice. We must get together more often."

She then shook Bunty's hand. With an emotionally filled voice, Bunty said with total sincerity, "Patina, thank you for keeping in touch with my sister. She needs your help."

Trying to lighten the mood, Alice looked at Patina and asked, "Where's your beautiful sari? Why do you dress in tweed and flat brogue shoes?"

Patina smiled elegantly and replied, "It's a costume just like you used to wear on stage. I travel to outlying farms a lot, and the farmers trust me more if I look like their wives. My heart and skin colour hail from Ceylon, but with my white coat, Wellington boots, and tweeds, they trust I can help their ailing wives. Let's have a cuppa in the railway café." Her Bradford accent grew stronger as she spoke.

The sisters only had a layover of one hour, so they visited the small café next to the station. Before their final short journey to Ilkeston, the small town where their father had worked and where the funeral would take place. Bunty ordered the refreshments, while Patina and Alice found a table.

Alice, straight to the point, said to her friend, "Before Bunty returns, I think I have a lump in my tummy. Here is the lump." She pointed to her lower abdomen.

"Ok, let's go to the bathroom and let me examine the bulge."

Bunty returned with the tray of tea and teacakes. Alice and Patina both stood up and said, "We are just going to the toilets."

As they came back to the table, Bunty noted Alice carried an air of deception—as if about to act out a scene—and was not secure with her words.

With an overly sunny statement, Alice, wide-eyed, said, "Some good buttered teacakes that will help tide us over—we left at seven o'clock this morning. Guess what? Patina is heading to a patient in the same direction to near Ilkeston, so we can leave together and not take another train. She will drop us off."

Bunty touched the doctor's arm and said, "That's kind of you; if that will not be a problem?"

"No. I am going to one of the way-out farms, a few miles from the town. Was your father's passing sudden?"

Alice updated her. "The coroner held onto the body; they suspected his death might be irregular. His new wife is not very good at keeping her opinions to herself and reads too many who-done-its."

Patina smirked and recalled how she met May at the British Empire Exhibition. "I remember her in London. What was it, eleven, no, twelve years ago? She is a very loquacious woman."

Alice rolled her eyes and said, "Absolutely! Anyway, she told the police he was in perfect health, and it might have been foul play, as he had no symptoms of illness."

Dr. Patina shook her shiny long hair and answered, "Sometimes, they might call the coroner too if your dad had not been to a doctor in a long time. How old was he?"

Alice replied, "Only sixty-one."

"Not that old, but if he had heart problems and he did not tell anyone, the coroner is called. Anyway, let's talk about you, Alice, so your sister knows the full story of your need to find the right doctor."

Alice appeared shocked by Patina's direct statement. She had not wanted to worry Bunty. Alice said, "I think I have more than anemia to try to control. I may have a cyst growing."

Bunty, shocked, cried out, "What! Where is it?"

Patina, the calming voice of reason, touched Bunty's arm and said, "Do not be alarmed. It's small, and we need her to have an X-ray. This might show the type of mass, or if it is hidden behind other organs, they might not be able to measure the size. Bunty, I want you to research the best Hull doctor in the new field of gynecology so we can find the right one for Alice. I will make sure your GP is on track and gets you a midwife, as newly trained women are often more experienced."

"How do I do that?" Bunty took a notebook and pencil out of her purse.

Patina continued, "Ask around. It's amazing how many women do not tell anyone, let alone their husbands and families, about these personal ovarian matters. First, find out if there are any women at the Hull Infirmary practicing as specialists in this area. Try and ask for a female doctor as your GP; second best would be a young doctor who has recently qualified; they might be more open to new methods and will allow your midwife his fee."

Bunty scribbled Patina's information in her notebook in shorthand and numbered all the requests down. Patina continued, "Your mother died of ovarian cancer, and research recently found it can run in families, so I want you both to have the best care and know how to treat it. If you have the same makeup of cells in your body, you are at risk. You both have great networks of suffragists; someone wealthy in those circles will know a forward-looking doctor. Are you ready, Bunty, to dig deep for information as a female sleuth?"

Bunty nodded. But first, they must attend their daddy's funeral. She wanted to cry but staunchly carried on, writing down notes in shorthand and learning more about cysts and ovarian disease from Dr. Patina.

After they finished their tea, they climbed into Patina's car, a dark green Ford CX saloon. They continued to gather details about ovarian cancer. "Ovarian cancer is a gradual, undetectable disease. Some doctors have been using radiation, but I am not sure that always helps; it depends on where the cyst might be, but it might be used."

Bunty looked scared. "How do you know if it's a cyst? Can you see it?"

"Well, you can feel it. Alice has a hardened mass, and that might be benign, i.e., it might grow but not have cancer. It causes her pain, so it might be connected to the anemia, or maybe not. It happens to women in their twenties and thirties. Sadly, an ovary produces more varieties of tumours than any other organ. Many women have it but have no symptoms; Alice has indicated some symptoms. At the moment, there is not an accepted screening test for ovarian cancer, but as I treat more and more women with cysts, pregnant women, and otherwise, I have lots of notes to compare. I am sorry, on such a sad day, to give you all this information and not exact medical information. But every Sunday night, I will call with any new findings I might discover, and Bunty, can you update me on the search for an understanding doctor, as you are by the phone all day?"

Bunty nodded as Alice said vehemently, "No quacks."

"No ducks or quacks, Alice." Patina's joke lightened the mood.

"I understand Alice's opinion on some of my profession, but some doctors are indeed lazy and do not read the new medical articles in this area, and some are, well, quacks. Having a medical degree cannot help doctors know everything about every part of the body and all ailments."

She pulled up outside the funeral home, and Patina said goodbye, adding, "I will call you on Sunday, Alice."

They pulled themselves together and entered the light-bricked building, with lots of floral wreaths leading the way to the service room. Ten people attended the funeral. May introduced Alice and Bunty to some of the mourners as 'Percy's Daughters from Yorkshire,' as if they were famous.

They entered the large grey room with rows of chairs, where the service would take place. Alice, already in a depressed mood, said to her sister, "The walls are the colour of over-washed underwear."

Bunty, puzzled, asked, "What are you talking about?"

Alice stared around the walls. "You know, if you wash white underwear so many times, it won't come out white anymore."

Her sister inspected the greyness of the walls, gave a wan smile, and nodded. The only brightness in the room was the casket, covered in lovely blue flowers. Bunty endeavoured to stop crying and whispered, "Well, the flowers I ordered in Dad's favourite blue will at least uplift the mood of the room."

The service began; both girls wept and held onto each other. The cremation ended quickly. As they sniffled their way out, following the other mourners, a gentleman approached them and smiled. "Hello ladies, I am your dad's half-brother, Fred Gregory."

They stopped, rooted to the spot in shock, at this man who looked like their father—the same build, slightly more portly, and less hair, but the same cheek colour and stance.

Alice answered wearily, "So, are we your half-nieces?"

Fred continued to smile, hands on his round belly, as he took in the two young women. "I am not sure, but your mother, Elizabeth, was the love of his life. He told me every time we spoke." He paused and looked around to see if May was within hearing, then lowered his voice. "May was a comfort in his last years, and at least she brought him back to where he was born."

Bunty was stunned for the second time today. "What if he was born in Derbyshire, not Newcastle?"

Fred nodded, surprised, and asked, "You do not know about his upbringing?"

Alice, still upset, rudely stated, "But I am sure you could tell us."

Alice's tone stopped the conversation. She did not want any more shocks today; Fred had too much new information to process.

Bunty apologised, "Please excuse my sister; we have had a long day, and a funeral never brings out anyone's best."

He nodded with understanding but continued with family information. "Your granddad George was also my dad, but I grew up with my mom, his first wife. George Neil got Annie Gregory pregnant and may have been with her; nobody told us the situation. Neil was Percy's middle name, but when I went to visit with Dad and his new 'Lady', they put both names together: Neil-Gregory. This gave Percy respect for Jesmond, where they lived, so he was not treated as the family's black sheep. However, your granddad George came back to my mom now and again; she would not divorce him due to being a Catholic. And neither was it spoken about in the Neil-Gregory house, and maybe he never married Annie Gregory, or maybe he was married to both. When I was around nine, the three of them moved from Derby to Heworth near Newcastle. I was left with my mom, who brought me up, but Dad made sure I was always in touch with my half-brother."

The women stared stupefied at the news from this kind older gentleman, who gave them so much information. So Percy, their quite lovable dad, might have been illegitimate, or maybe he was the son of a bigamist? There was too much information to digest; they had no idea how to respond to such news. They understood that in late Victorian England, a family did not advertise an illegitimate relationship. Their mother, Elizabeth, was from a well-known Newcastle Brewery family, but Percy's illegitimacy had to be kept secret.

Bunty graciously said, "I apologise, Mr. Gregory; this is too much for us to take in today. We must leave, and to catch the train home, please take my work phone number. Give me a call; maybe I will have time to understand all the information. It's lovely to meet you."

Alice grabbed her sister's arm as they left the funeral chapel. "Why did Daddy not tell us? Heaven can wait; I am not joining Dad yet. I want to find out why he didn't tell us. Do you think Mom was aware of his background?"

Bunty gulped back her tears and said, "My instincts tell me yes. Mom was so open. But who knows? We may never know. Anyway, who said you would be chosen for entry into heaven?"

They both grinned—their first genuine smile today. "Touché— let's get out of Derbyshire and try to catch the earlier train. Today I do not want to mix with people I do not know."

Bunty apologised to May, who was still sobbing with a group of friends. "We must go home for Alice's children. Sorry not to stay. Talk to you soon."

They left and hurried to catch the bus to the railway station; luckily, one was passing. As they reached the railway station, the whistle blew, so the sisters made a mad dash, leapt onto the train, and sat in the first vacant double seat they found. Out of breath and exhausted with the surprises of the day, both were hung over with melancholy. Bunty, the taller of the two sisters, sat with a protective arm around Alice, who whispered, "We never got to say goodbye to Daddy in person."

Rational Bunty replied, "Dad chose May to give him comfort in his old age. I think he wanted to return to his roots and have peace after living with the love of his life in our fun-loving house."

Alice nodded, and a few more slow tears fell again.

***

George picked them up at the station, as they called him on their train change in Doncaster. Amos was in charge of the children's homework in the living room. He sat in 'Daddy's armchair' as the children called it, as they were not allowed to sit in it. Biddy piped up, "Daddy, can I put on the standard lamp? It's too dark to draw my geometry homework."

"Go ahead."

Alice was surprised. He was in a good mood; usually, he would reply, "No, go in the kitchen and study by the light from the oven to save our bills."

He turned his head and saw Alice. He smiled and asked, "How was the funeral?"

"Very educational," was her succinct answer, and he smiled again.

"All is fine here on the home front. I was about to send the younger ones for bath time."

"I'll do it. Stay here and help with geometry; more your thing than mine."

She put her two youngest to bed after a quick wash-down and told Roy no story time. He loved being alone with his mom in his small room, but she hugged him deeply and promised double story time tomorrow.

After settling her son, Alice went to her room and undressed; tears fell again. She touched the cyst, praying she would live long enough to ensure her children finished school. The crying was also for her father, who might have been illegitimate; her mother's illness, which she may have inherited; but mostly for a future that looked more than grim for her children.

As he came to their newly decorated room and purple-covered bed, Amos found her asleep with her make-up streaking down her face. He thought those tears were only for her father.

Chapter 25 A Lovely Way to Spend an Evening

Alice acquired a rare moment of peace to read the *Hull Daily Mail*. She was thankful her family had not lost anyone in the war. Many of their friends had lost family members. She read about the losses of lives and homes in the western port of Liverpool, which saw the most bombs dropped in the whole of the UK so far in the war, but felt Hull had too—4,000 houses were hit in Hull. Amos reported to her that the docks in the Riverside Quay were the latest casualties last month.

Alice's depression increased with Amos' insistence on carrying out his duty for the war. She felt he had already served his country and gained honours in the Great War.

After a tiring day with inner pain, she snapped at him, "How ridiculous leaving your children and me every night to put out fires. You have done more than most. Are you trying for another medal?

I did not have four children to become a single mother. I need my husband alive."

The couple never sat and talked to each other or came to a conclusion on how to improve their lives.

After reading an article on re-vamping old clothes, she looked through her wardrobe and picked her wedding dress. "I will dye it a pretty spring colour—pink or peach—to update the dress."

A week later, after a trip to the haberdashers for light orange dye and with the help of Bunty's sewing machine, Alice's old wedding dress was altered. The seams of the dress needed taking in as Alice dropped more weight each year from her anemic struggles. The belted flared skirts accentuated her hips in the area of her cyst to appear slimmer in the 'new' dress. She asked Madge, who loved doing hair, to put her hair in curlers.

When Amos came back for supper, he noticed his wife dressed stylishly. The children completed their tasks as Alice put food away in their pantry. Amos asked, "Alice, would you like a walk in Pickering Park once you have put away the leftovers?"

Their daughters all stopped their chores mid-stream and stared open-mouthed.

Alice asked, "What about the kitchen, clean up?" Her husband expected the kitchen ship shape after every meal.

He turned to his oldest daughter, "Biddy, can you be captain of this ship while I and Mum take a walk?"

She nodded; the girls teased her later, "Still Daddy's girl."

Biddy was puzzled why this unusual occurrence had happened tonight. Alice shook her hair and patted it into place. She complimented Madge and said with a wink, "I'll have to have you set my hair every week." Madge glowed with pride.

But the worried twelve-year-old Dorothy piped up, "What if bombs drop while you are out?"

Her dad hugged her. "Honeybee, they drop them after dark as

the Germans fly home over Hull. If they arrive early, the park has a shelter, and Mabel and Charlie will get you into our shelter; you know the drill."

Dorothy still trusted most of what her dad told her, but with monumental dramatic emphasis, stated, "At age twelve, I would prefer no more 'honeybee' – I am not a little girl anymore."

Taken aback, her father paused before replying, "Understood, my Dorothy. I stand corrected. Girls - you all may have an extra treat for letting Mum out for a nice spring evening walk in her lovely new dress."

The girls smiled as they understood the dress was not new. Once their parents had left the house, Madge said, " A typical man, he has no idea he married mum in that dress!"

As Amos and Alice walked towards the park, they saw folks' lives happening in their homes; smells of suppers of cooking emitted from open windows. The predictable Amos had behaved unpredictably. Alice waited to see if he had more bad news to tell her.

She asked guardedly, "So, you do not have territorial duties tonight?"

"I do, but a night off would do us both good; they can do the clean-up without me. Today, I talked to Joe Oliver at the station, and he noted I looked exhausted. I looked in the mirror and saw a tired man. In two years, I will be fifty. I hope this dreadful war is over so we can get back our lives."

She puzzled at his comment and watched him through slanted eyes as they strolled. The last sunshine of the evening flashed across the trees on this late spring evening. The houses bordering the park had large black crisscrosses on their windows, so when bombs landed close by, the glass did not shatter around, making the clean-up easier. The couple walked through areas where the grass had been dug up for growing vegetables, which allowed local people without gardens to grow fresh food.

Alice walked slowly and used her energies wisely. He linked her small hand under his arm and squeezed it. "Our walk reminds me of old times, just being together with no children. Remember walking in Wembley Park in spring?"

"Another life, yes, a good memory, but to what do I owe this honour? We have lived here for eleven years, never taken a walk in the park without the children. However it's a lovely way to spend an evening."

Amos admitted that he had been giving the matter some thought. "Well, I suppose I am slow to change my ways. Joe Oliver told me I should spend more time with you if I want to keep my marriage strong during this vile war, not take you for granted. I realize the war has taken a toll on both your health and the children's anxiety levels. Dorothy even worries about us taking an evening stroll."

Alice sighed and sat on a park bench in the last rays of the sun. "Yes, she is the most anxious, perhaps because of her age or maybe due to reading everything she can get her hands on. She worries the more she reads – newspapers reporting the horrific events of the war and even adult books – the more she seems to understand the bigger implications. Oh! Has Biddy spoken to you about taking the swing shift at the factory? They offered her more money to work the night shift. I told her to talk to you, as bombs are more likely to drop on the night shift in factories."

Amos shook his head. "No, she has not spoken to me. Not happening, I agree with you."

Stretching her face towards the last beams of sunshine, Alice looked up and said, "Thank you. Will you please have a talk with her about the night shift? I could not think why she should not take the job. I understand her wanting to make more money, but we must keep the family together whenever possible. She also wants more income to find a flat with some girlfriends."

"Why?"

"To gain her independence away from the younger ones or maybe she has a boyfriend?" Alice paused… and with care added, "Or more likely the strife we are creating." She stared at him.

He took a long pause, and said, "This is the most civil conversation we have had in several years." He blew out a noisy breath and frowned.

Alice continued, "I am not sure why Biddy wants to move. You have a strong bond with her. If she wants a flat, she would need one of us to sign a rental agreement until she is twenty-one, so please talk to your girl."

Amos felt they were on a safer subject by discussing their daughter rather than their relationship. "She thinks more about money than her safety."

"Like father, like daughter."

He ignored her sarcasm, which cut him deeply as he worked long hours for his family. He changed the subject. "I hope by the time she is twenty-one, the war will be done. One kamikaze fatalist is enough."

She stretched her neck, giving him a smug smile. "Is that how you would describe yourself, Amos Bell?"

"No, but Joe told me in no uncertain terms today he thinks my patriotism is empty. He told me I was being unfair to my family being out most nights at the docks, as I already am in a reserved occupation. My train could be bombed any time."

She clapped her hands in delight. "Good old Joe. Honest home truths, nothing like them! I have always respected him and his wife. Let's invite them over for tea sometime."

Amos bit back, annoyed. "You like him as he agrees with your opinions."

Exasperated, Alice snapped, "Amos, you never listen to *me*. I am pleased a friend will tell you that you are misguided. Maybe you should set an example to your eldest daughter and stop cleaning up the nightly droppings."

"You make it sound like a load of pigeon cages we are cleaning. I am taking a calculated risk to sustain our standard of living."

"Poppycock, Benedick Bell!"

He looked surprised at her use of their courtship pet name for him, as recently their daily interactions had faded into oblivion.

"Hear me out. I never go onto the docks until the bomb wardens call the all-clear. Our unit has our meetings upstairs in the Punch Hotel; we hear and observe the German planes flying past and peek through the eyehole of blackout curtains for clearance. We give the hits twenty minutes to cool down and then head out to clean up. The war needs crews to move the debris as much as soldiers."

"But do you not understand how much your children and I worry about you being away from us for days each week? Even Bunty and George, who cannot drive far due to petrol rationing, are worried for us when you are not at home. Most nights when you are not here, George rides down to our end on his bike during his blackout warden duties to check that we are fine. But they understand I cannot always cope alone."

"But you have trained the girls to clean, cook, and help run the house."

"They need your presence. Roy needs you. My illness causes so much resentment between Biddy and Madge. They want to move out of home as quickly as possible to not deal with so many chores. We are pushing them into early marriages, not the best way to choose a mate. I have no idea where they go dancing on weekends. If they know you are gone, they stay out till one in the morning."

Amos looked at her shocked. "Why did you not tell me?"

"One, you are never at home, existing in your train and bomb squad world. Two, if I did share with you I know you would go off the deep end, which would cause even more resentment with our girls. Why can't you relax and not always be after them? I wonder why it has taken us three or four years to talk about this matter."

He floundered to explain. "I thought the problems were simply your illness - what can I do to help?"

Alice quietly pleaded, "Please take off one to two evenings a week from dock duties and be home and discuss problems with your children, so they do not think I am the Wicked Witch of the West!"

***

Biddy had become a suffragist like her mother, grandmother and aunt. She had joined the union and had become a young leading light at work on Worker's rights at the sweet Factory. One evening, she told her mother, after a discussion about leaders among the Suffragists women, "Well, you and Dad should support brainy Dorothy, and she might make you even prouder than you are of Judge Sybil Campbell."

Alice inwardly felt Biddy was correct; they must find the money to help stay on at school. The most academic of all her daughters, Dorothy could rise high. However with Amos' erratic schedule and her lack of energy it was never discussed.

26

Chapter 26 Trouble In Paradise

 Rationing, blackouts, and food shortages became a way of life for all the British people as England delved deeper into another war. The Bells had problems finding time to communicate with each other, nurture their marriage, and find space for themselves, with four children to feed, clothe, and educate. They had 'quiet fights' as Biddy called their altercations when she'd collect her younger siblings and take them to the park or herd them up the stairs, where they gathered to avoid the discord between their parents.

 Alice's tolerance for pain from the ovarian cyst fluctuated from bearable to needing to lie down all day on the couch in a darkened room. Amos did not know how to support his wife.

 In October 1940, the Royal Family had a wing of Buckingham Palace blown out by a German bomb. The Bells daily treat was listening to the Children's Hour with their mother. That morning, Alice told her children during breakfast, "This evening we will hear the Princess' broadcast; we will listen and not talk. I sang for Princess Lilibet's grandfather, George V, and you must always be aware of the events that are changing your lives. Afterwards, we can discuss any questions you may have."

They listened to the broadcast, which ended with Princess Elizabeth stating in her highly elocuted, crisp voice, "When peace comes, we will be in a better and happier place. Good night from me and my sister, Princess Margaret. Good night."

Alice looked at her children. They all seemed pensive and quiet. Dorothy was the first to pose a question. In a little worried voice, she asked, "If Lilibet's home was bombed, perhaps ours will be too."

Before Alice could think of an appropriate reply, Madge, who had opinions on everything under the sun, informed her younger sister, "Maybe Dot, but we have a shelter. Daddy and Charlie made it pretty solid. And you have two sisters to keep you safe—she has only one."

Roy piped up and managed to insult and care for his youngest sister in the same breath. "And a brother, Swothead, Buckingham Palace is such a whopping big place. You would be as blind as a bat, Jerry, to miss bombing that palace."

They all laughed at his concept of the royal palace and that a German bomb had missed the palace. Alice slapped him on the knees as he called Dorothy swothead, but Roy nevertheless had grown into the joker in the Bell family. Equally, Alice's relationship with Amos troubled her daily and made her feel insecure, as he was rarely home due to his auxiliary fire duties. They chose not to celebrate their wedding anniversary as food shortages affected what they could share with others.

One Saturday evening, when their dad happened to be home, the children prepared a musical concert with scenes written by Dorothy to entertain everyone in this bleak time. Blackout curtains covered the windows. Dorothy played the opening song on the piano, and

Madge took on the role of the compere with her gift of gab. Later, she changed into her costume to dance with Biddy. They both wore their mother's long concert dresses. Roy, the comedian in the family, spent the week, when not on his bike, collecting foul or silly jokes for his family audience.

On their mother's bad days, the siblings learned to keep their heads down, do their chores, and avoid their mum and dad. In November 1940, Alice strove to make something from a small amount of food for their supper, as they had no cheese or sugar left due to rationing. She did not worry too much about sugar, as they had lots of jam bottled from their raspberries and gooseberries last year. Roy lurked near the sink while she headed for the pantry. She saw him move to the treat jar, so she turned back and slapped his wrist. "No snacks before supper!"

Roy whined, "But I am starving now."

"Whining gets you a clip around the ear. People in Africa are starving due to a failed corn harvest. You are hungry." She slapped the back of his head. He yelled.

Alice, at the end of her tether, snapped, "Please go out to the garden and pick a cabbage for me now."

"Yuk, not cabbage again?" Roy's body language looked like she had asked him to fly to the moon.

This flippant comment had Roy sent to his room until his father arrived home. Alice's illness made her less tolerant of her children's behaviour, but Roy's disobedience brought her pain to a new level. By the time Amos arrived home, Alice had calmed down. She informed him of Roy's outburst. "Your son is at it again, answering me back, becoming a rude and belligerent young man. He thinks the world revolves around him."

Amos always trusted his son to tell him the truth and believed his wife might be overextended today. "I understand, Alice, that you do not have the patience for them if you have low energy, but Roy is the youngest."

Her nostrils flared like a bull, ready to attack. "He will not listen to me. His insolence and disrespect will come out with women in the future. You have always been a polite man and courteous to women. Do you want your son to believe he can be rude to women?"

This comment made Amos comprehend that bringing up boys was different from girls. He went upstairs to talk to them. The children were hidden in their rooms to avoid their mother's wrath.

He explained it to all of them. "Your mother blows up like a wind if she gets stressed and sick. Think of her like a tree losing leaves. The pain makes her irritable, and a small comment or being negligent with your tasks can set her off."

Biddy replied, "It's like walking on ice, dad. You never know when she will crack."

"Precisely, and I hope you understand her explosions are due to her illness. The doctors are so busy with war injuries that they do not have time to improve her anemia. Just remember, winds do die down. Hug her, and kiss her to make her moods improve."

Madge piped up, "While you are here sorting out problems, can we discuss Roy, who gets away with murder every day? I do most of his chores so mum won't get upset."

Amos looked at his blonde-haired son, who was sitting off the side, pretending to read his Beano comic. In his father's eyes, Roy could do no wrong. He moved to the doorway and glared at him. "Is this true, Roy Gregory?" Amos used his middle name to acquire the truth from his son.

Roy had all his answers ready, appearing like the prodigal son. "No, I do my chores and more. I dug the garden yesterday. The section you needed is ready for spring planting."

After listening incredulously to his reply, Madge screamed, "Dad, he is lying again! Biddy and I dug that part of the garden! This is exactly what I mean; Roy is a stinker and tells whopping lies." Biddy nodded, and they both glared at their nine-year-old brother.

Amos diffused the situation. "I've got to go and deal with a bomb down at the docks. Will you behave if I take you with me? I will then explain to you the improvements you must make to your behaviour." Roy behaved like the perfect son and nodded.

However, his sisters still believed he got away with too much, and their father did not punish him enough. Alice just shook her head when Amos told her he would take Roy out with him. She retorted, "What about the danger, Amos? I could lose a husband and son in one swoop."

Inwardly, she smiled: *Good, I can have a long bath and an early night.*

The girls came downstairs as their mother went to bathe; they turned on the wireless while they completed their homework; a dance band played a song called 'Trouble in Paradise'—Biddy started to sing along.

Trouble in paradise
Ended our dreams
Trouble in paradise
Strange as it seems
Lonely am I again?
Learning to cry again
Paying the price,
For trouble in paradise.

Her sisters joined in and sang with her. They all had ideas of why their parents did not speak to each other. Biddy believed her mother did not want a boy. "Let's face it, who would want Roy?"

She eavesdropped on the grownup conversation and garnered opinions that Roy's birth caused her mother's health problems. The sisters all had different views of their home situation. Madge voiced her opinion that their dad wanted a woman who was not sick all the time. As the oldest daughter, Biddy summed up all their feelings.

"The trouble is that our parents do not discuss anything with each other or us."

The situation compounded as the bombing of their hometown increased due to being the last port on the East Coast of England. The German pilots daily evacuated their leftover bombs on their way back to Germany.

Meanwhile, at the childless Wiles home, Bunty sat in her high back chair, looking over her garden as the light faded. She placed a log on the fire, read her *Hull Daily Mail*, scoured the paper for discussion subjects to bring to her suffragist meetings, and suddenly burst out with a saddened, "Oh no, another death."

George sat at their dining room table with his T-square in hand, working on a technical drawing, and asked, "Who is it this time?"

"Your mentor, Nigel Gresley, has passed!"

"Oh! I forgot to tell you that a chap at work mentioned that. He has not been well but would not stop working—do not let me work when I am past it."

Bunty went to her husband and hugged him. Mr. Gresley had trained George and taken him as a young man to visit Germany. "It says the memorial is at the Chelsea Old Church; will they give you time off to attend?"

George shrugged and stood up, then replied urgently, "I must tell Amos."

Bunty held onto his hand and said, "Don't bother to call; he's not back until tomorrow."

"What would I do without you?" George asked as he kissed her.

"Starve." Bunty jokingly replied and returned the passion while thinking, *Thank you, God, I chose this man.*

27

Chapter 27 Dream
January 1945

By the beginning of 1945, the noise, dirt, and lack of food brought Yorkshire people into despair as the bombing of the Hull Docks and the surrounding city happened almost every night. The newspapers reported now Hull had been the most bombed city in England, outside of London. Everyone hoped the New Year would bring an end to the war

Most citizens did not want to know the bleak news and simply went down into their shelters, but Alice never slept underground. She always took her children down with hot drinks and said, "I cannot sleep yet, " and left them with her neighbours. She did not want her children or their neighbours to see the pain she suffered from her anemia and cyst. However, by April 1945, people noticed fewer visits from the German warplanes.

On raid nights, as Amos did 'his clean-up duty', Alice would stand near their back door and watch the German planes returning home around five in the morning, just before daylight. She could see them from the orange glow of the fires that Amos might be putting out. As her children and neighbours came out of the shelters, they inhaled the smoke and dust, which often lingered in their throats all day.

Biddy was always the one to ask, "Is Dad back yet?" Alice usually shook her head, but she would serve them breakfast, with the meager rations and mostly fresh vegetables from their garden. Roy joked, "I may turn into a rabbit soon, Mum."

Amos continued his fire duty nights when he was in Hull, helping to clean up debris caused by the German bombs. If tired, he slept on a hard bench at the Punch Bowl pub, which was more comfortable than the places he had slept in the First World War, but he rarely came home to sleep.

***

A highlight of the family's year was when Dorothy's school nominated her as the head girl. Her mother rejoiced that she raised a leader. The school would expand to a high school level in 1946, which had not been a choice for her older sisters, who attended a few years earlier.

Dorothy came home one day bubbling with excitement and said, "Mum, guess what? Students who have excelled this year are being offered a place at the new High School with courses for students aged over 15. This leads to places on college courses."

Alice sat at the kitchen table, holding the pain in her side. "Very good, dear. Can you set the table? I am not full of energy today."

Roy came in and slammed his bag down. "The stupid idiots who run the education department are upping the school leaving age to fifteen, so suddenly I have to take another bloody year of school. I hate the stinking place; I'm not going to show up."

Alice sternly said, "Please do not swear in front of me." He stomped upstairs. Dorothy added, "You know he hates school and rarely completes his homework, Mum. Guess what he said to Mrs. Pilgrim today? She said, "You are not like your sister," to which he replied, "Which one? Pick a card—I got three queens in my house, four if you count my mother."

Alice tutted the best she could do. Dorothy did not tell her Mum that Roy regularly bribed her to complete his homework with his pocket money. She started to move upstairs. "Oh, once I change, I am going to Auntie Bunty's, who will help me organize a school 'D' day party, for the students to celebrate our British War victory."

"How lovely. Which day will it be held?" asked her mother.

"Next week, the second week of the school year when the war officially ends."

Alice was too sick to attend, but Bunty enjoyed the celebration.

* * *

Dorothy received high accolades from the staff for pulling the school celebration together to celebrate 'D' day. She was also offered a place in the newly expanding Francis Askew High School, and her parents would need to sign off on a confirmation letter. Dorothy ran home from school on the first Thursday of the New Year. Today the Principal invited her into her study to inform Dorothy that she wished to speak to her mother or Father, in person or by phone. She had some good news about her educational future.

"Do you have a phone at your home? And will someone be home?" asked Principal Wainwright, shrouded in her black flowing Cambridge robes. Dorothy solemnly nodded.

"You will have to speak to my Mum, as my Dad works all hours driving trains."

Fourteen-year-old Dorothy was floating on clouds when she arrived home but her mother lay on the settee, the usual place she retired when not feeling well. Today at least she was awake. Dorothy explained to her mum needed to be ready for a call from school.

"Mum, I have put the kettle on to make you some tea. Mrs. Wainwright, our Principal will call you at four-thirty."

"Oh no, not Roy again—has he been fighting at playtime?"

Dorothy sighed but ploughed on. "No, it's about me, something good. Can you sit by the phone so you are ready to speak to her?"

Dorothy picked up a high-backed chair with a cushion and placed it by the phone in the hallway while she made a cup of tea for her mother. Alice dragged her aching body to the positioned chair and looked at her third daughter, who had impressively ironed her uniform before school and still appeared immaculate even after a day of running around. She handed Alice a steaming hot cup of tea and a McVities digestive biscuit on the saucer. The phone rang.

Mustering her business voice, Alice answered, "Hello, the Bell household. This is Alice Bell speaking."

Dorothy sat on the stairs and smiled, proud of her mum. Alice had instilled in them in them the importance of speaking well, and she was pleased her mother used her professional elocuted voice with the School Principal. Alice listened and nodded a lot, then replied to the Principal. "Thank you for the fine comments about my daughter. I will discuss it with my husband. Well, we will wait for the offer and then let the school know. Thank you, Mrs. Wainwright."

She placed the phone on the holder and looked at Dorothy. "Well, you are being offered a small scholarship to attend High School, which leads to the college entrance exam in year three." Alice sighed.

Dorothy moved next to her Mum and grinned, saying, "Isn't that perfect? My Dream!" But she saw her mother's worried look and asked, "What is the problem?"

Alice took her face in her hands. "Dorothy Honeybee, Daddy will probably say no."

Dorothy exclaimed, "He cannot say no. This decision affects my future. This is what I dream about."

"What can I *not* say no to?" Amos appeared at the kitchen door to the hallway.

Alice was also startled. "Amos, we did not expect you till later." Alice looked at him in his dirty overalls—*more washing to complete.*

"We had a breakdown on the track. Sorry about the oil; I will get the dolly washer out. What can I not say no for Dorothy?"

Dorothy proudly announced, "I am being offered a scholarship to attend High School, as Head girl."

Alice added precisely, "A small scholarship. We would still have to find the money for books, uniforms, and tests for college applications."

Dorothy stood tall, all five feet of her, and glared at her mother. She thought her Mum was on her side. She perceived maybe her mother would prevent her from advancing her education as she had left school at 14. She had to get her Daddy on her side.

Amos hung up his cap and work jacket. "Well done, Dorothy. Can I get out of these filthy overalls, and then we will discuss the matter at teatime?"

Later on, Dorothy and her parents would eat supper together. Biddy and Madge were both out or working. Alice suddenly remembered Roy was not home and asked her, "Did you notice your brother after school?"

"Yes, he went off with Trevor Needham's lot again."

Amos came downstairs after his bath carrying his dirty overalls. As he dropped them outside the back door, he noted his son's late arrival. Roy put his bike away in the shed and swaggered down the garden path, socks around his ankles, knees scuffed, and mud on his face and hands, like he owned the world. His father commented. "Ah! Talk of the devil, Roy Bell—disguised as a good son."

Roy glared and stuck out his tongue at Dorothy; he believed she had been telling tales about his antics with his friends. Amos looked at his son and then at Alice.

"Please do not set your son a place at the table or prepare him any supper. Due to his lateness, and the fact that he had not completed his chores, he will miss the meal. He will do his homework upstairs, and we will then talk about tardiness."

Amos took off his belt, as he could not abide any tardiness, plus his rudeness to his sister got Roy two belt hidings from his father. But worse for Roy, his father had spotted him earlier riding his bike the wrong way down the main thoroughfare, Pickering Road, showing off to his wild friends.

Dorothy and Alice laid the table to the sounds of Roy's yelling as his father whipped him with his belt. Amos returned, flushed in his face, and they started to eat.

Amos calmed down from his angered state and said, "I am very grateful I have one child who can be a leader within her school. We will wait for the letter and then see what it says about attending high school. I thought you might be like your sisters and want to start work as soon as possible."

Dorothy replied, ready with her fourteen-year-old view of the world. "If the war has been for any reason, Daddy, it's for poorer people to be able to be educated. I want to go to college and take business courses and make you proud."

Amos stopped with his fork in mid-air. "College? Well, maybe you should take a job like your Auntie Bunty and go to night school for your business certificates."

Dorothy had thought deeply about his reactions and had her

speech ready. "That is one choice. However, my dream is to attend a three-year course at a college. I want to go away to Leeds, Manchester, or York and become a full-time student. Then apply for a job in a big business company, or maybe even read law."

Her parents looked at each other. They had never thought one of their children might want to attend college, let alone be in law. They both left school at fourteen and worked hard. They both acknowledged Dorothy already had more education than they had gained at the same age.

Amos mustered up a weak answer. "College costs hundreds of pounds." Dorothy saw her father's lack of understanding of her request to attend a full-time college.

"Uncle George went to a proper three-year college. He's your friend, dad, and I want the same course. I intend to get a local job this summer and help pay for my uniforms and books. If I work during holidays and have a babysitting job, I think I can save enough to attend for three years. I have started a budget and know what I need to save. I already have a babysitting job lined up for the Easter holiday as school is closed."

Again, her parents said nothing—when had their daughter planned all this? They again looked at each other. Alice, who took care of the household budget, knew it would be difficult to find the money, but she had not a clue about Dorothy's plans for college. But their daughter sat and stared at them, determined to hear the answer she needed.

With a forlorn voice, she said softly, "I want you to be proud of me."

Amos came out with a non-committal comment. "In this family, as you know, we celebrate success, and Dorothy, as the head girl, you have trailed a blaze so bright you have given us much to celebrate."

Alice weakly added, "The grandmother you never knew, my mum, used to say it's good to have goals."

Dorothy's anxiety rose as she looked from parent to parent. They were struggling to comprehend this daughter, who had planned a future without their help. Her father finished his meal. "Thank you, Alice, for having that ready for me. We will wait for the letter from your headmistress, then we can discuss it some more."

He moved to the wireless to listen to the news and packed his pipe full of tobacco, before heading to the dolly washer outside to wash his overalls. He had curtailed the discussion for now. The wireless played 'Dream', and Alice sang along. "Sing with me—*Dream when you're feeling lonely*."

Dorothy sang along, enjoying their time together as musicians while tidying the kitchen and trying to get rid of the angst Amos had brought into the house. Dorothy kindly pointed upstairs and showed her mum some of the leftover spam and bread, asking permission to take it to Roy upstairs. Her mum nodded.

Later, Amos came in for a tobacco refill. Alice made an effort to discuss her daughter's request. "Don't start, Alice, I have had a tough day."

She noted his face as he grabbed more tobacco for his pipe, returned outside, and had no more discussion. For some time this had been their way of existing; they were further apart, with a lack of communication.

A week later, the letter arrived. In typical Bell fashion, it was read by Alice and then put on the mantelpiece to wait for Amos to read the contents. When he arrived home after territorial duties around midnight, no one was awake to inform him to read it, so the letter did not get read.

Three weeks after the letter had been sent home, Mrs. Wainwright stopped Dorothy in her tracks at school. She commended her on the excellent school debate she recently delivered, putting forward a concise argument about the need for safer shelters that do not flood and how to help others and share with neighbours their ideas for improvements.

She then asked, "Dorothy, have your parents decided on your high school scholarship yet?"

She politely replied, "My father is still team leader on the bomb team at the docks, so he is rarely home. I don't even know if he sleeps before work." She should not have told the Principal, but she could not hide the frustration of her home life.

The Principal said, "I understand, but if you do not take the scholarship, we will offer it to someone else. Please ask your parents to let me know by the end of this week."

At home, Dorothy asked her mother, "Mum, have you had a chance to speak to Dad about my high school scholarship?"

"You know he is never here."

Dorothy started to emit her thoughts. "You know what makes me mad—you are both so exacting about what time my sisters get home, making sure we all complete our chores and dealing with the rough kids Roy's hanging around with. But with my education, you and Dad cannot, or will not, make a decision."

Her mother faintly replied, "I promise that if he's home tonight, I will bring it up."

She noted her daughter played her angry piano pieces, so she must speak to Amos that night. Alice understood from her own experience, nursing a chronically sick parent, that musicians played harshly to release emotional turmoil and to erase their pain.

Good to her word, Alice asked Amos after his long train shift and then bomb removal—not the best time for asking for anything. "Amos, Dorothy wants to know if you approve her high school scholarship—the letter needs to be returned."

"What? Oh. I don't think we can afford it, Alice. As you no longer teach and the war rationing will go on for a while yet, better she goes out to work."

The reply came through the thin walls, and Dorothy cried herself to sleep. The next morning, with a pressed school uniform, she grabbed a small breakfast until her Dad came down. Her scathing summation spewed out of her. "Father, I am going early to school, and realize this will be my last five months of formal education, where all of the teachers have endeavored to help me get on in my life via a college path. Meanwhile, my parents were too busy doing their duty in the war, making us constantly complete our chores, and monitoring my almost grown-up sister's tardiness. Nothing of real importance gets determined in this house."

Amos sat stunned into silence with this eloquent speech. Even Roy stopped chewing and stared at his Dad, waiting for his explosion. Amos controlled himself and simply replied, "I will not justify a reply to you, as you are upset and angry."

Dorothy stood, grabbed her bag and school hat, and looked from her mother to father, expecting some support from the former. Alice stayed mute.

"It was not enough for you to suppress Mum's singing career, but none of your daughters' education seems important to either of you. If the golden boy there was the one in my position, you would find the money."

Her parents stared and said nothing. Their youngest daughter picked up her school bag and concluded, "I am sorry neither of you had the education you were entitled to, and this made you so blinkered and narrow-minded to understand how important education is for all. I am not going to let your weak, passive decisions stand in my way from this point forward."

She stormed out with a dramatic slam of the door. After a long silence, Roy muttered, "Well, the other students say she is the queen of the debating society!"

Alice's quiet tears rolled down her face, which she dabbed with her hankie, and she looked at her gold wedding ring as a tear dropped on the band. Amos took a swig of tea and stood up, while the others held their breath. "I'm on a late shift today. I will not be back until tomorrow."

Alice believed Dorothy would do well on any course and wanted to help her with the scholarship, but she never found the right time to discuss it with her. To challenge Amos at this weak time in her marriage, plus her illness...it just seemed pointless to argue with him. Arguments made her sicker; consequently, her daughter's ambitions slid into oblivion.

28

Chapter 28 Crying on the Inside

One school night during a bitterly cold February, she arrived at her Aunt's home soon after Dorothy's colossal disappointment of not being able to continue into high school. She entered through the back door and found Bunty in the kitchen baking.

George snoozed by the living room fire. The calm music emitted from the wireless turned to a new hit record, and Dorothy instantly thought, Ha, even the wireless is picking up on my mood. 'Crying on the Inside, Laughing on the Outside'. She smiled at her aunt, who hummed along with the song.

Dorothy loved the warmth of their home, which enveloped her; 'a real home', she told her friends at school, unlike her own home fraught with tension. Bunty smiled at her and noticed her school coat seemed a little too small. Bunty said, "Your coat looks tight; you have blossomed out this year."

Sarcasm dripped off Dorothy's lips. "My mother will not buy

a new school coat for only three more months of the school year. Today we watched the cold rain slam across the window," she mimicked her mother's voice, "but soon there will be warmer weather, and you will not need your big coat."

Bunty wiped her hands on a tea towel and hugged her niece. "Good timing; my apple strudel will be out in a minute. You must have your dad's timing for pastries."

Dorothy reacted with a vile look at any mention of her father, but her aunt continued, "I think I have a gabardine raincoat I can give you. We will have to take it up, but I know you know how to hem now."

Dorothy struggled out of her too-tight coat and hung it on the back door hook, moving towards the oven to warm up. "You are so generous, auntie, but I would like your help with the coat if it needs hemming to make it smooth. Thank you."

"Just finished your babysitting?"

"Yes, the perfect job once the baby is asleep. Their grandma goes home at five and she leaves me to put the baby to bed and sometimes bathe her. Then I can spend the rest of the time on my homework. Both her parents work shifts—their house is well run compared to our ramshackle house; they even leave me a lovely supper."

"Sounds like a grand job."

"Margaret, the mother, has another child coming in September. I had to tell her I could not help much longer. By June, I intend to have a full-time job due to my parents' pathetic decision to not allow me to stay on at school."

Bunty stopped baking and looked at her niece. "Is this the way you are telling people?"

Chin in the air, as if her aunt might challenge her, "Yes, it is the truth."

"But ..."

Dorothy's anger stopped her aunt in mid-sentence, she'd become as outspoken as her mother used to be and continued to vent. "But nothing - my parents may expect me to lie, but I will tell it the way it is." Her eyes displayed inner anger and distrust of her parents.

Saved by her timer, which suddenly pinged, Bunty said nothing but moved toward the oven to check her baking. She opened the oven and pulled out steaming strudel with a mouth-watering aroma and perfectly golden brown. Dorothy calmed down as she took a big sniff of the baking, then smiled—her angst dissipated. However, her aunt saw the tears glistening in her eyes as her niece grabbed her hankie from her pocket and wiped them.

Dorothy, with a stoic tone, said, "If only I could turn my tears into gold, I would have enough money to attend college."

Her aunt stood momentarily speechless by her comment but came back and placed the strudel on a cooling rack. Again, she hugged her niece for some time and rubbed her back like she was a young child. Once revived, she got down to business with a sad smile.

"I came over tonight as your house is closer to my work, where my babysitting family lives. I need help with some more advanced algebra. I wonder if Uncle George would have time to help me with some difficult calculations."

More than content to be brought back to happier tasks, Bunty called to her snoring husband, "Geo...rrge, wake-up!"

He stirred from his armchair by the roaring fire in their parlour. "Yes, my darling. Is the strudel ready?"

"Not yet; needs to cool down. Dorothy just arrived and needs your help."

He stood and stretched like a tall giraffe looking for food in the trees, and stepped into the kitchen. "Hello, Dot, come in here to the dining table. What's your problem?"

"You mean besides having two negligent parents who cannot make decisions regarding my education?"

Suddenly, it dawned on Dorothy that her aunt and uncle were not to blame for her parents' decision, and she weakly smiled at her kindly uncle; regretting the outburst, she said, "Sorry, Dad is your friend. I should not have made that snide remark."

She opened her algebra book and pointed. "This is the page where I am stuck."

George ignored the comment about Amos and focussed on the problems in her algebra book. "Ah! This calculation I understand and can help you with this. Find a pencil."

They sat heads together, working on calculations. Bunty quietly moved to the phone and closed the door to the parlour. She did not want her husband and niece to hear her calling the Bell residence. She said quietly, "Hello, Roy - is your mum awake?"

"She's asleep on the sofa—shall I wake her?"

"Only ask her to come to the phone if she is awake."

Roy stomped to the living room door, with enough noise to wake the dead; she heard a small voice say, "I will call her back."

He stomped back to the phone. "Sorry, not a good time. She will call you back."

"Tell her Dorothy will not return home tonight as George needs to help her with some tough algebra problems. Do you need to write the message down?"

"Writing it down—swothead is doing homework with Uncle George."

Bunty sighed and demanded, "Roy, please inform your mum that Dorothy will stay with us tonight."

"Good! More hot water for me if she's gone," was her brother's delightful reply, "Night, Auntie."

"Good night, Roy."

Bunty quietly replaced the receiver and sighed. The Bell siblings were taking care of themselves. She moved to the stove to make hot cocoa for the brilliant minds working on sums in the parlour. She cut the apple strudel into slices as a treat.

"Do you want to stay the night?" she asked Dorothy as she placed the tray beside the mathematics books on their dining room table.

Pencil in hand, Dorothy stopped and looked worried. "Mum will go spare if I do not do my chores."

Again the voice of reason, Bunty explained, "Look, if their bathroom is not clean for once, the Bells will survive. I know you do the upstairs cleaning. You look so tired; no need to worry about your Mum. I called and told her you are here. I will fill a hot bath here so you can take a long soothing soak."

Dorothy's hands on her hips, indignantly dramatic like her mother's poses, gave her aunt a shopping list of realities. "They will not miss me; the sicker mum gets, the more I feel helpless. Her energies decline a little each day. Dad gets angry if we do not pull our weight with chores. My sisters leave their wet laundry hanging in the bathroom. Roy eats, leaves his plate wherever he takes his last bite, and voracious farting, urgh—disgusting. So I am the unpaid skivvy. Thank you, Auntie, for your understanding; I will stay; I always sleep better here."

With a grim smile, Bunty agreed with her niece; by default, she became the household's maid. Her older sisters were at work, and Roy would not clean if you stood over him with a whip. Tomorrow Bunty will talk to her sister, as she's more responsive in the mornings.

She patted her niece on the arm. "Stay here for a few days if you wish. I will clear it with your mum."

***

Bunty called her sister from work the following day. "I have some time to catch up; the solicitors are mainly in court on Fridays."

Alice seemed responsive and replied, "Just getting ready to go to the fish market."

"Oh yes, fish on Friday! You would think Amos was a Catholic, with his desire for his fish on Fridays."

Alice sadly said, "Going for a walk to take in some fresh air. Did Dorothy stay with you last night?"

"Yes. Did Roy not tell you?"

"Oh yes, he did. I remember I took some pills, which made me fuzzy-headed. Can I ask you if you think dad ever looked at mum's body once she had cancer?"

"Yes, I know he did as he bathed her; he was super meticulous about her care. Why?"

"Oh, nothing; I was just wondering how sick I will get. Going to get off now—love you, Bunty."

Bunty firmly continued, "Well, before you rush off, I want to suggest allowing Dot some time to complete her more advanced homework with George's help. She could stay here for a couple of nights a week. Could one of the others cover her bathroom cleaning?"

"Fine, if she wants to stay. Your place is quieter for her to study."

"I will also loan her my bike until I can find one to buy. This will be my congratulatory gift for doing well at school, so she will be on time for her night classes. She carries so many books. Is there a place to leave their bikes at school?"

A yawn came from Alice. "I suppose there must be. Other students ride to school who live farther away."

"Good. I'll see you tomorrow. Saturday, not too early—anything you need? If any of her chores are not completed, I will complete them. Will Amos be home?"

"Not back until Saturday night, I think."

"Good, we can have some fun together, sis. Bye for now."

Alice sounded listless, as if she were not quite in the world. Bunty believed the medication taken to mask the pain caused this. Having gone through the journey with their mother, Bunty understood the signs.

29

Chapter 29 Varsity Drag

Bunty and George often discussed how the war had an invasive impact on Alice's relationship with her husband and children. By the beginning of 1946, technically, the war had ended. Dorothy stayed often with her aunt and uncle, sleeping in their peach guest room. They rarely saw Biddy and Madge, who were busy with work and friends, except at family gatherings.

Bunty called George to check he did not mind her niece living with them permanently, henceforward. "Hello, sweetheart, Dorothy just came round here and told me she left home to escape from the Bell chaos and wants to stay with us to study in a calm place. Is that all right with you?"

George confirmed, "Of course," but asked, "What has Amos said to upset her now?"

Bunty sighed, "I think he became closed and passive as Dot struggled to reason with him about continuing at high school. I think he may have been an ostrich in a past life, always burying his head in the sand."

George laughed loudly and then asked, "Am I still picking Chinese food then?"

"Let's treat Roy and Dot to tasty Chinese food for dinner."

***

Later, Dorothy talked to her Aunt through the kitchen hatch as she set the dining room table, "I want to try and eat with chopsticks tonight."

Her Aunt passed her the plates and asked, "Set up forks and spoons for eating the Chinese food, in case everyone cannot handle the chopsticks."

"Auntie, using a hatch to pass your dishes through is so dignified. We never eat anything exotic as this, as my father is so stuck in his ways."

Bunty nodded and passed cutlery and condiments through the kitchen hatch. "Well, you may not change your parents' taste buds and push them to explore the culinary world. But Amos once ate Indian food regularly, your mum and auntie Patina changed his conservative eating habits in the 1920s."

Dorothy pondered her statement, with spite in her tone. "Really? Well, I am never going to be small-minded like him—I want to try every type of cuisine."

George arrived home after he picked up Roy and the steaming Chinese food. After serving the food, they delved into the sweet and sour pork, dumplings, and rice.

As if she were a snobby food critic for the local papers, Dorothy said, "I adore the fried rice, and isn't the sweet and sour pork superb, Roy?" With his mouth full of food, he garbled, "Yea," and continued eating. They both loved the meals at their aunt's house, and Roy could always have second and third helpings.

Dorothy continued her tirade about her parents. "Not only are our parents clueless about exotic food, but they are shortsighted about education, and I am going to stay here, aren't I Auntie?"

Roy stopped eating, stunned. "But what will the old man say?" He chewed and ruminated about the problem.

"They may have given birth to me, but I have disowned them. Our parents think, as they did not attend college, we do not need to attend—isn't that small-minded?"

She spoke to all, but no one replied. George began to add something, but Dorothy continued, "Just know, Roy, **your** parents also lie to each other and to us. Mother especially talks about education opening doors, but to open my door for a chance for a college degree—they slammed it shut."

Bunty understood her niece's contempt, so carefully added, "They are not lies, Dorothy—misunderstandings. But I must agree; they are sometimes weak in acting on their supposed beliefs."

George reminded the younger diners, "Remember they grew up in different times. Amos came of age during the war. Plus, Alice was working as a singer at Dorothy's age, correct, Bunty?"

Her aunt nodded, then smiled enigmatically, remembering her talented sister, who sang at concerts up and down the East Coast. Dorothy, trying to get Roy to understand their parents' lack of support, continued ranting, "Your father, Roy, even tries to prevent Auntie from helping me. But he is no longer **my** father."

Roy added his thirteen-year-old perspective as he finished his meal. "It is simply his miserly way. He does not give me any pocket money, even if I complete my chores."

Roy mimicked Amos with uncanny accuracy and lowered his voice. "I never had pocket money at your age; you want money? Go and find a job."

Containing her laughter, Bunty told them, "Please know we are all your family. Families have hiccups. I will talk to Amos alone to make him understand you need to finish high school and attend college."

Roy sarcastically added, "Hiccups, auntie, father chokes all of us daily with his meanness. I doubt the great Amos Bell will change his mind."

Before speaking, Bunty took a measured breath before she answered Dorothy. "I promise I will talk to your father. I will test the waters with your mum first. I will not be indecisive like your parents, and we will get you on the right path. I think her illness is spreading and making decisions more difficult. Try to understand the pain changes her, Dorothy."

The ladies cleared the table and began washing the dishes. Dorothy's face lit up as she remembered something to tell her auntie. "Oh, at my job, the mother is having another baby. So, she will give me more money to take care of two, and each payment goes into my fund for college. I also opened a savings account and have not told my parents. I will leave home for good if my parents do not 'get it,' and I will not return. Will you undersign the account as I am not 21?"

Bunty was impressed with her forward-thinking, a mix of Alice's determined temperament and Amos' saving money streak. "Yes, of course, I'll sign."

The next day, Bunty told her sister of Dorothy's plan. Alice replied, "Dorothy thinks she is in a Mickey Rooney and Judy Garland film—off college and wearing those letterman sweaters. She will be playing the Varsity Drag next time she comes home."

Bunty felt exasperated with her sister, who gave such a shallow comment about her daughter's dreams to educate herself, but again believed the disease invading her sister had squashed her hopes and goals for her children. She did not tell her Dorothy had no plans to return full-time to their home.

Patiently, Bunty continued, "However, Dot does not want to

study music or singing. She wants a career in business or a law degree. Due to her academic ability, the teachers recommended that she should move forward into higher education. George and I want to help. But if she does not attend high school, she will not make the grades for college applications. Our mum always told us to have goals. This is Dorothy's goal—I am impressed by her planning."

Alice sighed, looking weary and tired. "Today, the doctor confirmed I have ovarian cancer, Bunty."

Alice's statement stalled her sister, who fought back the tears. She hugged her sister, fearful of crying and taking deep breaths to prevent tears.

Alice added, "The doctor confirmed with me yesterday. Will you inform Dorothy that attending high school next year is not an option? But we will help her to attend night classes while she works during the day."

Bunty sat mentally calculating the vast sums they paid for their mother's hospital treatments and the medical costs for two years and remembered how it nearly bankrupted the family. So they must follow this path again for Alice, and Dorothy will lose out on her education.

She stoically replied, "I will have to find Amos in a quiet moment and make him understand the pain of his youngest daughter not being able to attend high school and college."

Alice closed her eyes, tears dripping down her face. Bunty inwardly doubted she would be able to change her brother-in-law's mind with a sick wife who needed daily care.

30

Chapter 30 Choo, Choo, Cha Boogie January 5, 1946

Amos was on his way to York to pick up his next Flying Scotsman train when news of a train crash in the northern town of Darlington in County Durham came through the driver's grapevine. Any train crash was devastating to the LNER, but even more emotionally charged for the drivers, who understood the dreaded feeling of all those in charge of trains: 'It could have been me.'

This crash caused havoc on the Northern line; delayed travellers swarmed everywhere at the Railway Station. He fought through the crowds to the administrative offices. He was asked if he had worked with or met the driver—Engineer Burbridge—he said he had not, and the office manager sent him to meet the newly instated Superintendent Edward Thompson.

Mr. Thompson, seated at his desk, looked up from his paperwork and spoke with clarity and speed, "Thanks for coming promptly, Mr. Bell. You may know we have an emergency on our hands.

You cannot continue your shift up to Newcastle tonight. However, we want you to lead the investigation team to run the clean-up operation. First, we must open the line and have the trains running as soon as possible. We ask you to stay up there for three to four days to collect information and to report on the track conditions and the damage to the trains and carriages. Plus interview the people involved. Highly accurate details are required for part of our insurance fact-gathering. A photographer will work with you, he is already in place. We hope you will create a fair, balanced view of the crash. I have read the background of your army service, plus your outstanding territorial record for the recent war clean-up in Hull, and your outstanding honours from both wars. I think you are the best man to head the team. It will include board and lodging, plus extra pay. Is there any reason why you cannot carry out this sensitive role? You have been an employee of over twenty years, I believe?"

Amos understood the team must find out who or what caused the crash.

He replied, "Sir, I am prepared to carry out your requests for the company and will do my best, sir." He also calculated the extra income would pay for Alice's latest medical bills.

Taking a thin folder of details from the Superintendent, he left the L.N.E.R. office.

First, he called home. Biddy his eldest daughter picked up the phone, "Hello, Daddy."

"Can you have your Mum come to the phone?"

"She's asleep, not doing well tonight."

Amos sighed, and the wireless played *Choo, Choo Cha Boogie* - the asinine song his oldest two daughters listened to every night. The girls were probably dancing their crazy jitterbug dance. *Alice must be sick to sleep through that noise.*

"Turn the wireless down please." He heard her shout to Madge to turn down the music.

"OK. Please be sure to give Mum this message. I am on a train crash investigation team and might be away for four days in County Durham. Understand? Please write it down. I will call you once I find out where I am staying; bye love."

"Bye Dad, love you more than you will ever know," Biddy's cheerful sign-off greeting.

Amos headed for the company supply store and signed out two pairs of new overalls, as he was unsure how dirty the job might be or how long he may be away. He crossed the track to the transportation engine, to take him and the three clean-up crew members to the County Durham crash site. He read the basic accident information during his trip up north to the accident site.

L.N.E.R. Report for January 5, 1946: A freight train became divided on the east coastline in County Durham section of the line. It was brought to a standstill, but the rear section crashed into it. The wreckage shows fouled signal cables, giving a false clear signal to a passenger train on the opposite line, which then crashed into the wreckage.

Mm... not much to go on—I have my work cut out with this accident.

***

The team led by Amos arrived at Darlington station via the service line due to the regular line being blocked by the train, which was strewn across the track at jagged angles, the carriages looked like discarded dominoes. They saw the train wreckage as they passed. The police had the area marked off securely. Amos went straight to the Station Master what had been done so far. This small middle-aged man, his uniform distinctly pressed stood awaiting orders.

Former army, great—this means he will do what is expected and help me get the job done.

In a local Darlington accent with a soft twang, the man replied: "Nothing much, except taking the dead bodies out of the carriage. Those living with injuries were taken to the local hospital. I have a list of the passengers; the rest are waiting at a couple of local hotels to be interviewed. This chap here is Bill, our photographer." The man's slight Geordie burr reminded Amos of Alice's Dad, Percy. He shook hands with both employees.

Amos, now in charge, gave his orders, "Photograph the bodies lined up here first, please Bill, and then liaise with the police to move the deceased once you are done. If they have identification written on the tags, please write those up too. My crew, please find out where the clearance bins are kept. We will need two large rubbish carts to pull out the wreckage. Our photos will be proof for insurance people."

The station master said, "I'll show them where they are located. Jack Speck's my name, Mr. Bell. I will be on duty until you give clearance for the wreckage to be moved. There is a phone in my office you can use, and the kettle is on the boil for some tea."

He smiled, a helpful local man. Amos smiled back. He was correct. Jack was army-trained and helpful; his team now had a base to work from to complete the appalling task.

"Thanks, Jack - please call me Amos. May I use your phone now? Then let's all meet back in Jack's office in ten minutes."

They all nodded and went off to begin their first task. Amos entered the welcoming office, where Jack had tea brewing and a blazing fire lit; a Victorian station, cosy in Amos' eyes. It exuded warmth on this cold and icy morning. Amos pondered if the declining temperatures had anything to do with signals freezing. The weather temperatures declined last night and still lingered below zero. The station master should have details of the temperatures hourly - he must ask Jack. He jotted down possible causes while he dialled home.

"Hello, the Bell residence?" This time Alice picked up.

"Hello Alice, so pleased you are up to answer the phone."

Alice abruptly asked: "Were you involved in this accident it's on the news?"

"No, but I am leading the team for clean-up and investigation for the L.N.E.R."

"Oh! Yes, Biddy passed on the message. Amos, what an awful task! Are there dead bodies?"

"Yes, the police and ambulance are moving them. Then my job starts."

"Amos, where will you be staying?"

"Not sure. The office told me to grab a hotel or B&B. But there are many passengers stranded on the way to their destinations. We think the last rooms at the boarding houses within this part of Darlington might have been taken."

"Which station are you at?" He told her which suburb of Darlington and where the station was situated.

"Call me back in five minutes. I have an Aunt Mary-Ann. Remember you met Uncle Daniel, my Mum's brother at Aunt Joel's birthday party? My Mum was close to her and my Aunt stayed in the area after he passed. Just have to find her telephone number."

Amos walked to a railway breakfast café he'd seen as they arrived, situated outside the station and grabbed a sandwich. By the time he arrived back in his makeshift accident office, his team had assembled and completed task one. Jack Speck poured each a mug of tea.

Amos placed his sandwich on the desk. "OK, give me five minutes to eat this. Once you have supped up, start pulling wreckage to the side of the track in a line – east side. Not a pile on top of each other. Bill here must photograph every piece we pull out. I will be along once I have made one more call." The team went out to the track while he called Alice back. She answered immediately.

Full of news, Alice gushed, "I have arranged for you to stay with my Mum's sister-in-law, Mary-Ann, wife of the late Daniel Benjamin Sutherland. Their widowed daughter lives with them: her husband was killed just before the war, and her two boys are in the house too, but one of them will sleep on the settee. You will have a room and bathroom." She gave him the address and telephone number.

"What a great resource you are, Alice. Relatives are everywhere up here. Thank you."

"I hope it is not too gruelling for you. Let me know when you will return."

※ ※ ※

Amos arrived at the Sutherlands' home at about six o'clock that evening, after completing the initial investigation reports. He had completed handwritten notes. Bill, the photographer, had explored every nook and cranny of the tracks and the train and photographed the evidence. The team cleared the blocked track of the debris, and the regular train schedule resumed. Once darkness crept in, freezing fog enveloped the station. Around five o'clock, Amos sent the outdoor work crew to find a boarding house or pub room for the night. Amos sauntered across the town, taking in the unfamiliar area while thinking how he should write up the day-one report of this awful accident.

The Sutherland family resided in a comfortable middle-class neighbourhood on the edge of the River Skerne. Walking up to the house, Amos was impressed with the detached large-windowed Victorian house called 'Willow Villas', with a rambling garden surrounding it. Of course, the well-established willow trees hung, sans leaves. He imagined they must look striking in summer.

He noted the stained glass windows shining through the front door, patterned with art deco diamonds, and highly polished as he rang the doorbell. Mattie Sutherland opened the door, a dark-haired brunette like most of the Sutherland women he had met. She introduced herself and reminded him they met at Bunty's wedding. Amos smiled politely but had no recollection of her. She wore a sombre dress, not like Bunty, Alice, and his daughters, who dressed in the latest bright fashions. She took his coat and hat, while he left his work boots by the door, and then showed him to the room, which held a double bed for him to sleep within.

Mattie told him, "My son John happily has given up his room. He will not be back until later, as this is his last year at school before university and he's out at a debate meeting."

She left Amos to clean up. He saw a white well-pressed shirt on the bed.

How did she know I had no clothes? Maybe Alice told her and was so thoughtful responding to my unexpected need for a place to stay.

Once downstairs, he expected to meet her mother, Alice's Aunt. The house was eerily quiet—he could almost hear the house breathe.

Mattie apologized, "I am sorry, Amos. Tuesday is one of those nights I have the place to myself. My Mother attends bible study and choir on Tuesday nights."

Ah! So, some of Alice's relatives do attend church. She made me believe they were a godless lot.

Feeling like an intruder, he said, "I am so sorry to be a bother." He studied the dowdily dressed middle-aged woman, with a starched white apron over her day dress.

"Oh no, it's a delight for me to have you here—a rest from my Mother! It's good to be alone in the kitchen without interference from Mum. Since Dad passed we both need our own space. I am delighted to be able to feed you and offer you accommodation to help you carry out the important work you have been asked to complete."

"Your home is quality accommodation compared to where the crew will stay tonight in flea-ridden boarding houses. Due to the number of passengers, the better places have been snapped up."

Mattie nervously wrapped the belt of her apron around her fingers. "We are pleased to help. I was worried we would not be up to Alice's exacting standards. Bunty's wedding was so excellently executed, like a society wedding. Captivating; I had a simple wedding in a registry office before my husband went off to sea."

Her eyes carried sadness. He smiled and made an effort to remain positive. "Alice and I did the registry route too, nothing like Bunty's extravaganza. Do you by any chance have a typewriter? I have to make a daily report on my findings."

Mattie came back to life, and said, "I do. I took night classes and helped Daddy with the official letters he used to write. You know he passed away last year?" Amos nodded. "Would you like to borrow it?"

"Yes, please. The L.N.E.R. asked for two carbon copies—what does that mean?"

"You have to place carbon paper between the copies to give you three copies to save typing the information three times."

While Mattie brought out the typewriter, he relished the well-cooked meal on this cold winter's night. The front door opened, and Amos presumed it was one of Mattie's sons.

Mattie called out, "Oh John, this is Amos Bell, the husband of my cousin, Alice. He's the chap on the investigation team of the train wreck."

John stepped into the dining room, a well-dressed, tall young man. "Delighted to meet you, sir," and came forward to shake Amos' hand. He also had a family resemblance to Alice's Mother Elizabeth: strong dark eyebrows, with black wavy hair.

"Mum said you might like to borrow some underwear. I hear you did not have time to go home for a change of clothes."

"I would please, if you have spares?"

"My pleasure, Grandma has no idea what to buy us for birthdays and Christmas, she has no concept of what chaps of our age need or want." Mattie tutted and glared at her son.

"Sorry, Mum but my drawers are overflowing. Please do not return them to me, sir. This will be my gift, for the difficult work you are completing. Also, it will give me extra space in my chest of drawers. I will leave them on the bed. Good luck with the investigation."

This articulate, amusing, young man impressed Amos, who found him engaging. He must work with Roy to learn how to behave around new people.

He again listened to the quietness of the house. This home had no music blaring, no banging doors, or people yelling to use the bathroom; a spotlessly clean, well-run home. Mattie set up the typewriter in the bay window at a small desk, where she moved a large floral arrangement. Scrolling the paper into the machine, she smiled at him: "I'm ready."

"Oh! I didn't expect you to type the notes for me."

"Do you type, Amos?"

Amos looked ashamed, like a little boy, "Only two fingers at a time." He held up his digits. She laughed, again the attractive throaty Sutherland laugh.

"Let me read your notes." He handed them to her. She read them, puzzling over his handwriting and trying to decipher his hieroglyphic written notes.

"I suppose it is difficult to write in the field. How about you read them out loud? I will type. Sit here." She tapped the seat beside her, and he sat and started to read his scrawl. With Mattie's help, Amos completed his first day of typed notes in under an hour.

She pulled the paper out of the typewriter, handing him one copy of the three for proofing. Excellently typed, correctly spaced with no spelling errors, much better than the effort he would have produced.

He added, "Oh, on the last page I should have told you: the one with only six lines upon it should have the time and date. This will be shown to the legal team to read in court."

He leaned slowly over towards Mattie, to show her the page, and as she leaned forward to look at the page, their heads collided.

"Ow!" she looked up, rubbing her head. Amos impulsively kissed her—why, he will never know—it seemed the right thing to do, but then he pulled back worried.

"I'm sorry I overstepped my bounds."

"It was a very nice experience, but unexpected after the head bump."

"You have been so helpful and kind. I have had a long day." Now flustered, unsure how to deal with his faux pas, *why did I kiss her?*

Excuses rolled off his tongue. "I have been up since five this morning Mattie, I am truly sorry."

"I'm not."

This comment stopped him in his tracks. He stared at this helpful woman who had considerable sadness on her face. Unsure what to say next, Amos said, "I will take a shower, or bath if I may?" She nodded, smiling beguilingly.

Disturbed by his sudden actions, in the twenty-three years since he met Alice Neil-Gregory, he had never kissed another woman, except on the cheek. He took a quick bath with wartime allowed four inches of water, as the bath still had a crayon line around it. He drained the water from the bath and picked up his clothes. Wrapping himself around his waist in a large white bath towel, he moved into the bedroom from the bathroom.

"Oh."

Mattie was in the room. She smiled and held the garment in her hand. "I have brought you an old pair of pajamas to use. My Dad was smaller than the boys. My Mum has kept everything."

She moved forward slowly, placing the garments on the end of the bed. She turned and stared seductively, licking her lips at Amos' bare torso, and watched him as he placed his clothes in a nearby chair, folding them very carefully.

She fluttered her eyelashes, with a shy but enticing look. "I thank you for the gentle kiss. It has been ten years since anyone kissed these lips." She gazed not moving, at his freshly clean, half-naked body.

Amos became aroused by her looking over his body, the clean white towel moved with his erection. Mattie stepped forward toward him, and as her soft hands massaged his chest, the towel dropped seamlessly to the floor, and she manually gave him much pleasure. He looked down at her shiny, curly, auburn hair: he did not want this moment to stop until he released his 'Argh' of pleasure, totally fulfilled.

Mattie went into the bathroom while he sank depleted onto the edge of the bed. She returned with a fresh cloth and towel to dry him. He had never been in this position before while married. He simply sat there, relaxed by her caresses.

"I needed this, thank you." Bemused - he simply sat not sure what to do next.

She stood up, took the towels, and then left the room without glancing at him. Stunned but ashamed at what happened, with no histrionics, no drama. Simply pleasure. However, he slept better than he had for months.

***

The next morning he met Mattie's Mother, Mary-Ann Sutherland, a frail, elderly lady with much interest in the investigation. She welcomed Amos with a warm, cooked breakfast. He began day two of the investigation. He walked to the railway station, a couple of miles, allowing him to plan the second day of tasks, including the clearing of the train wreckage damage.

During the morning he worked with Bill, who photographed every part of the damaged carriages for the insurance claims. The afternoon became trickier for Amos. With Malcolm on his team, they interviewed all the L.N.E.R. staff, who worked on the train on the fateful day. They split the twenty people in half, giving each person an interview of fifteen minutes. Some of the crew had worked at the opposite end of the train and did not witness the crash. They only heard the screeching and a jolt from a sudden stop of the train. These interviews moved swiftly with statements easily completed. The more intensive, longest interviews were with those people who worked with the driver personally.

Amos interviewed the staff asking precise questions about signals, weather conditions, opinions about the mood of the driver, and if they thought the driver may have been intoxicated, or simply careless.

Amos completed the interview paperwork by the time darkness fell. He stopped by an off-license to buy some wine and then thought better of taking alcohol back to the house. He would check with Alice if this Sutherland family were tea-total. He knew Mary-Ann attended church but was not sure which religion. He found a telephone box.

Roy answered, and bellowed down the phone, "Yo Dad! When are you coming back?"

"Please say 'Hello the Bell residence,' as you answer our phone."

"Well, only you and Auntie Bunty usually call at this time, Papa Bell." (He said the last word in an upper-crust accent).

My son at only fifteen is getting quite a tongue on him.

"Is your mother up and about?"

"Fighting with Madge, hold on Pater."

Amos listened to his daughter Madge screaming at her mother, like a fish wife at the market, but Alice responded with an equally shrill scream. They sounded like cats yowling in an alleyway.

Alice came to the phone. "Hello, Amos. Welcome to the joys of bringing up too many daughters in one small house."

"If there is a problem, Alice, put Madge on. Screaming at you is not acceptable."

"Nothing I cannot handle. How are things with the Sutherlands?"

"More than good, Mary-Ann, your Mum's sister-in-law is quite elderly but very proper. They are feeding me well..." - he paused, not wanting to give his dalliance away by mistakenly using the wrong words. "They are taking care of me admirably. I want to give them a gift for putting me up - wine or flowers?"

"They are Methodists, no drink, flowers are better."

Thank goodness I called. I care about making a good impression here.

"No, better still Aunt Mary-Ann loves Cadbury's Roses. You know the chocolates in the pretty blue tins. Mummy used to send one to her every birthday. She will love you forever."

"Wonderful idea, Chocolate Roses it will be. How are you today?"

"It's been a good day, except for Madge. She has been smoking and I want it stopped. Some boy she hangs around with bought her American cigarettes and they are untipped - disgusting smell."

Amos was sensitive about smoking near Alice, he always went outside, and he replied, "I will have strong words with Madge as soon as I am home, probably on Friday, or a big maybe, tomorrow night."

"Thanks for letting us know, Amos."

He purchased the Cadbury's Roses chocolates at the local

newsagent, and they were a big hit with Mary-Ann. He then invited Mattie to dinner, as a thank-you for typing his notes.

"Haven't you more work to type tonight?"

"Well yes." He grinned the smile Alice named his boyish grin. "But I thought while I was in the bath, you might be able to finish them?" She laughed, at his cheekiness. Her throaty laugh, a Sutherland family chortle, ironically, reminded him of Alice.

"Of course, pass them to me." She took the notes and gently brushed his hand. The aroma of her perfume tickled his emotions and affected Amos' heart rate. She moved directly to her typewriter, business-like. He went upstairs to shower. After his clean-up, he found another clean shirt on his bed with a tie. He presumed the garments might be from the boys, but also pondered they might have belonged to her dead husband.

On the stairwell, he passed their wedding photograph, probably married around 1928-1930. Mattie looked young, something Alice constantly reminded him she might have become during the war. Then suddenly it hit him that if Alice's illness took her life, he would become a widower.

Suddenly, Mattie came out of the dining room, with the typed papers in her hands, and asked, "Do you want to take the papers with us, so you can check them over? Then I will have time to re-type any errors on our return."

"Yes wonderful idea, thank you." She handed him the folder with his lists of wreckage and his interview names.

Amos in the role of suitor, asked, "Where may I take you for supper?"

Mattie put on her coat and hat and replied, "I wish we could walk down by the river, but it is a black gloss in the dark, the council has not replaced the light bulbs yet. They took them out for blackouts during the war."

"Yes, I saw the lovely River Skerne as I came in on the train."

She picked up her purse and hand-knitted gloves, opened the front door, and told him as they strolled along, "This is a Quaker area with some beautifully built houses—lots of simple meeting houses. South Park is wonderful in spring and summer. We will visit 'The Tawny Owl', one of the oldest pubs in the area. The landlord's wife serves up excellent meals."

Two hours later, they strolled back through the quiet old town of Darlington after a good meal. Mattie did not ask much about Alice or his children. She seemed to know little about Alice or their life with their children. Plus Amos wanted to keep his transgression with her to a one-time liaison, so they did not hold hands. He was also not sure where his crew was staying, and if they saw him with another woman, well, they must appear platonic.

Amos understood this family lived in a different world to the Bells, having high expectations for their sons. It made Amos reflect on his younger children. Roy had begun working on the trains for the L.N.E.R. but disliked the work. Amos must talk to him about joining one of the services to expand his experience of the world and life before settling down. Amos' guilt returned as Mattie told him about her son's education. He should have found the money for Dorothy's schooling; she barely spoke to him now. He wished he could turn back the time and change.

Mattie asked, "What do you think?"

"I am sorry I was thinking about my youngest daughter Dorothy, while we were walking. What was your question?"

"Are the day two report papers correct?"

"Excellent job again, no changes. I am so thankful you are such a proficient secretary. Why do you not work?"

"I suppose I could, but the boys were so tiny and they needed me after their father perished at sea. Now they are young men, and the war is over. I need to look for a place to live, but now Mum needs me around. I prefer to stay home and keep this lovely house clean. I enjoy running a house, cooking, and love doing laundry. This might sound boring and overly domestic?"

Amos shook his head in disagreement and said, "All very important tasks to keep one's life smooth. I hope tonight's meal re-paid you for all you have done for me."

She smiled her enigmatic smile. "I hope we can become better friends, you must spend much time up here driving the Flying Scotsman."

Amos paused, unsure how to reply. "I hope so too."

Was this woman suggesting she wanted more of him or simply friendship? *I cannot start a liaison with her while Alice is alive.*

They arrived back at her home. He pecked her on the cheek and moved swiftly upstairs. He needed to return to his wife tomorrow.

I made a slight transgression ... but this lonely woman seemed hungry for more.

He changed into the loaned pajamas and used the bathroom. As he returned to the dark bedroom, he reached to put on the light, surprised to find Mattie in the bed - naked. This aroused him again but now he had no doubts about this woman's intentions.

"Ssh," she mouthed with her finger to her mouth. She opened the covers so he could delight in her nakedness and lie next to her. Once he lay in the bed, there was no turning back, and he could not resist her beautiful soft body. He had another night of glorious lovemaking with the quietest woman he had ever been in a bed with. He experienced a magical eerie feeling. Mattie left in the middle of the night with a final whispered 'erotically spectacular.' He lay wondering the meaning of this comment until he fell asleep.

31

Chapter 31 I'm a Bad, Bad Man January 1947

Amos arrived back home in Hull from Darlington, after two nights away. The January freeze covered the streets with vengeance, but he wanted to be home to celebrate Madge's 19th birthday. As he left Paragon Railway Station, feeling inspired, he dropped by the local Criterion Picture House, flanked by two large stone lions on the stone steps to the box office. He purchased his daughter a gift card to watch four films. Since she was a little girl, she loved these lions and petted them as 'her lucky lions' every time she visited this cinema.

Back at home, life went on. Tonight Roy had picked up library books for his mother. He had acquired this weekly task from Dorothy, who now only came home if her father was away working. Roy removed his ice-covered boots outside and placed the book bag inside the kitchen door. He hung up his jacket, flat cap, and scarf, then padded to the front room in his socks (one with a hole in the toe). He dragged along the bag of library books. He found his mother snuggled under a blanket on the sofa with the fire roaring, bright red with the hot coals giving the room a cosy hue. Roy shivered and pulled his pants down slightly to warm his backside, and lifted his cold feet towards the fire.

His mother laughed at his carefree need to warm his bottom. "Careful, Roy, I do not want to deal with third-degree burns tonight."

He moved away from the heat and pushed the bag towards the sofa. "Here, Mum! Your library books to keep your brain expanding."

"Thank you, Roy. Oh, please take off that sock with a huge hole in it. Place it in my darning basket. I can still sew and read. Did you pick up my reserved books?"

"Yep, the thick, heavy one is 'Gone with the Wind' and the other 'The King's General.'" She sat up a little and clapped her hands. "Oh, goody, I have been waiting for this book for months."

"Is it a war book?"

"No, it's a love story by my favourite writer, Daphne Du Maurier. Did you have a long wait at the pick-up desk?"

"A little, but the girl on the reservations desk was an alright looker. So I pretended to read a war magazine while peering at her."

His mother smiled at her son, who was beginning to show an interest in the opposite sex and asked him, "Did you read any of the magazines?"

Usually, her son would not be seen dead reading a book, but he had begun to read magazines about war or ammunition. "Yes, I did, Mater. The one I was reading about WWI was about how many soldiers may not have been officially diagnosed with shell shock but might still be suffering from it. Do you think Dad has shell shock? He is so miserable most of the time."

Alice spoke carefully, understanding Roy was often annoyed with his father's strict measures. "Amos finds change difficult, which we have all figured out. This last war threw us more challenges. Your dad deals with the spoils that life throws at him."

Alice noted Roy was growing up and had begun to observe more about people. But she was puzzled about this statement, so she continued: "I do not know if your dad's mindset came from the First War. He has tunnel vision—oops, another train pun—sorry Roy."

Her son grinned, having developed his mother's love of puns.

"I met your dad, and he had little experience of regular life, only army life. He was eager to marry me, ready for a new life, and sharp-looking, always well-turned out. I believe shell shock is more of a brain disease. Your dad's way of life might have been learned behaviour from your Grandad."

Roy thought about this, then asked, "You mean he learned to be mean and penny-pinching from Grandad Bell? Will I become like him if they send me somewhere awful for my National Service?"

"No, Roy. I hope they might send you somewhere exotic like Egypt or India. Countries where you can experience other cultures and peoples, travel broadens your horizons. I want you to understand living in Hull is not the only way of life you can have. You are correct; your dad has not developed a change in his behaviour since I first met him except…"

"Except what…?"

"Recently, he seemed more distant and lonely, almost as if he cannot tell me his feelings. But remember, Dad is an excellent provider and has worked hard to allow us to live comfortably."

Roy shrugged and went no further with the conversation about a parent, who he could never please.

***

Later that evening, Amos arrived home to find a hot and steamy kitchen. He carried the worn underwear and dirty overalls in his bag and was delighted to be home. Biddy kneaded dough while she listened to the wireless singing along with Ethel Merman. Amos removed his boots, scraped the snow outside, and heard the raucous sounds of 'You Can't Get a Man with Gu-uhn'. Her shrillness hit his ears—his daughter's screech mimicked Ethel's but sounded like a banshee.

He opened the door and looked around. "Where's Mum?" She nodded towards the front room while her hands kept kneading the flour.

He asked his eldest daughter, "What the heck are you singing?"

"It's a new song from the musical 'Annie Get Your Gun'. The musical opens soon in London. They are playing all the songs tonight on the wireless."

While his daughter seemed excited by the music, he hated the caterwauling songs. He entered the living room and found Alice had fallen asleep next to the diminishing fire. Her skin had a grey sheen, which made her look ghostly. He nodded to Roy, who sat quietly reading a book. *Wonders never cease!*

Amos returned to the kitchen table and nibbled a biscuit from a plate, saying to Biddy, "Your Mum does not look too good today."

Consequently, it fell to Biddy to tell him Alice had been diagnosed with ovarian cancer. He ran his fingers through his thinning blonde greying hair. "Why did your Mum not call and tell me?"

Biddy licked her lips with worry. "You were not here. Mum found out two days ago and did not want to worry you while you were dealing with the tragic crash. So we have been waiting for you to call. Want me to make you a fry-up for supper?"

Amos nodded then froze mid-bite into his biscuit. His fair face was glowing red from the guilt of not being home for Alice's devastating news; he'd forgotten to call the family yesterday, wrapped up with Mattie's advances.

As his guilt built internally, he escaped to change upstairs as he needed time to contemplate his next move. Biddy meanwhile made him his supper: eggs, black pudding, and bacon, which was easier to buy now that the rationing situation had decreased.

He came down to eat, now more in control of his emotions, and enjoyed the meal. "You're a grand lass, Aline Bell (using her official name). You might become a better cook than your Mum, but don't tell her that."

"Don't tell me what?" Alice appeared in the kitchen, stretching and yawning as he made the statement.

"That our oldest daughter has become a grand cook like you." He winked at Biddy; she was surprised her Dad was in a rare, good mood.

She cheekily asked, "Am I as good as Auntie Bunty?"

"Oh! That's a tough one, Miss Biddy."

Alice sat wearily down opposite Amos and said, "What your father will not tell you, Biddy, on our first date after one of the most painful rehearsals of my life, if I had not agreed to go for a drink with him, your Dad probably would have married Bunty for her pastries."

Their oldest daughter stood open-mouthed. "Is that true?" Biddy loved family gossip and digging into the family folklore of their past.

Covering the rising guilt of his unknown infidelity, Amos adamantly denied the allegation. "Your mother was my *only* choice. I had to ask her three times to marry me. It was love, at first sight, once she sang."

Alice scrutinized his face and narrowed her eyes, while her daughter dreamily said, "Really, I did not know that."

She repeated her daughter's response, adding a more questioning inflection. "Neither did I, Amos. You never shared that snippet of information."

Alice looked at him intently while pouring herself a cup of tea to swallow down a handful of pills. He watched her swig them down with a grimace and reached over to turn the radio down slightly.

Amos aimed for light conversation and, to keep a tight lid on his guilt, asked, "Got some new pills?"

Alice peered at him then raised an eyebrow, but spoke with a matter-of-fact tone, "No, the same ones I've had all year. The doctor may add some new ones soon. Maybe this is a good time to enlighten you about my ongoing illness. You have been so involved with your territorial work during the war and this recent crash that I am not sure you understand how I manage my illness. You must admit the last seven years, we have hardly had time to talk together."

Amos stared at his wife as shame oozed through his body. He looked away again and moved his empty plate to the sink, so she did not perceive his guilty conscience.

The Neil-Gregory women always tell him their truth, but I think she suspects something.

Amos, over brightly, looked at her smiling. "Well, we have time now. I have a few days off for the extra work on the intensive investigation. So now is your time with me, Alice."

The moment he said her name, she saw him blush. Another arched eyebrow, followed by the Alice Neil-Gregory look. Her gaze became distant. After a long pause, she looked out of the kitchen window, and sarcasm slid into her reply. "Well, time for me? That will be interesting. OK, tell me about the crash." She sat down again opposite her husband and gave him her full attention.

Biddy finished drying the dishes but stayed to listen to her Dad's story of the awful crash. "Sadly, ten people were killed, and more were injured. We believe it was the driver's fault and maybe the signalman's mistake too; he did not check the signal as protocol requires. As a result, the train went straight through one signal and did not stop. Your cousin Mattie helped me with my paperwork and typed my notes."

As he stated her name and brought another blush to his fair cheeks. He looked away and took a slice of Swiss roll from the dessert plate to cover his reaction. Alice again saw his agitation, which seemed inconsistent with the details of the crash.

Again to distract, Amos praised the food. "Did you make this Swiss Roll too, Biddy?"

"No silly! You're eating Auntie Bunty's best creamed Swiss Roll. Well, I'm off to netball practice at the Park Recreation Centre. Good to have you home, Dad; we missed you."

She kissed his cheek and grabbed her bag. He looked at her in her trousers, ready for the game. The old-fashioned Amos returned and tutted at the outfit , but she had left before he could say anything. "Remember, Alice, I was shocked when you and your sister began to wear those wide white trousers in the twenties?"

Alice sighed with a cheeky smile. "The world has changed for the better now. Finally, women can wear *the pants*." She grinned and looked at him to see if her pun lifted his spirits.

He focussed on constant chewing to control his emotions. Amos finished the roll. "Indeed it has. I suppose fashions will continue to change?"

Alice rarely experienced small talk from Amos and pondered his statement. "I think so. Fashions and people change too, Amos." Then she hit him with reality, "One day, I will not be here."

He wanted to hug her but was scared that Mattie's fragrance might linger on him. He said, "Let me get cleaned up. Can we sit and talk once showered? I am so sorry, Alice, about the diagnosis. But we are twenty years on medically, from your mother's illness. The doctors can do amazing things now."

He stood and scouted quickly upstairs.

After a soothing, hot shower returned to their bedroom. Alice lay on the bed, reading the newspaper. As his hair was still wet, he placed a dry towel on his pillow and combed his damp hair. He asked, "So, what does the doctor say?"

"Not much; I am to go in for more blood tests. They will monitor my cancer monthly. He told me ovarian cancer is an evil, invincible predator, and he wished to cut it down. I do not want to go to war with my body, but the disease is almost certainly genetic; the same disease killed my Mum. Unfortunately, finding accurate books about cancer seems near impossible, and I cannot find any reliable information on what they call the silent killer. So I am now on my journey to try to drop this disease from my body."

"Alice." He took her in his arms, and her body stiffened. It had been so long since they had such a connection. "Like everything in your life, you read and calculate. I am here to help you."

Bitterly she stared at him and said, "Today, you are here, but what about next week?"

"Alice, I cannot be here daily, or we would have no income. But I love you; I will do my best to help you fight this battle together."

"Argh, you men! Your military metaphors are just like the doctor's comments. I have weekly acupuncture, so you will have more bills to pay for the Chinese doctor I visit. At least five shillings a week. It's lovely to hear you still love me. I also need you to call more and talk to our almost grown-up children. I do not have the energy to corral them through life."

Desperate to please her, he said, "I can do that. I will also try to change to local runs and come home nightly."

"Good. I want to be more part of your world and not feel shut out. Let's change the subject. Please tell me about the inquest. Have they given you a date to report to the court?"

"Not yet, but sadly, it seemed as if the driver was responsible - human error. It was one of the toughest judgments I ever made. I will travel to Newcastle for the court inquest in a month or so."

Alice, in her political mode, said, "But people died? Don't their families deserve to know whose fault it was?"

He took a deep breath and found it hard to explain drivers' responsibilities to keep people safe. "Yes, the drivers, like me, have much responsibility; but in life, errors do happen."

He took her pale hand in his warm, strong hand; she did not pull it away. Alice stretched out catlike on their bed and asked, "So tell me, how was staying with the Sutherlands?"

"Good."

Watching his wife stretch out reminded him of Mattie, when he pulled back the covers as she lay naked on the bed. Guilt again made him move away from Alice to change into his pyjamas. He spoke, unfamiliar with making small talk, while he got changed.

"They treated me like royalty, fed me well. One of her boys, John, gave up his room and gave me clean underwear to keep." He turned back and looked at her with a small smile. "But this crazy, loud house is much more fun. Their house is like a church compared to ours."

"Believe it or not, Auntie Mary-Ann is one of my warmer Mother's relatives. Does Mattie like living with them? How is she faring after losing her husband in the war? How old are her boys now?"

"One about Biddy's age and one younger but well brought up - one at college and the other just started work. They were interested in the case - it was a dreadful local tragedy. But Mattie seemed lonely - no hampered, a better word - still living with her mother."

She watched him intently, trying to read his expression. Scrutinizing his face, she sensed something had changed within Amos.

Kindly he asked, "Do you need anything before you sleep, Alice?"

"No, Biddy made me some tasty chicken soup, but I am losing my appetite for most foods. I think my pills are destroying my taste buds. Amos, I am getting sicker."

"You look radiant."

"Have you been reading women's magazines on how to speak to your sick wife?"

He kissed her cheek like a relative would, not a husband. Then took her hand and kept hold of it. This closeness gave her a chance to speak candidly. "Amos, when I pass, I want you to know you have my permission to marry again. You are a man with too many needs to be alone."

He blushed and turned away at her suggestion.

Something is going on; he's blushing. Has he strayed with another woman due to intercourse being too painful for me now?

Alice snuggled under the eiderdown. "I am tired; good to have you home for once. Will you be here to talk to the children in the morning?"

"Yes, I have two days off for working extra hours. I told you earlier."

"Ah yes, one of the side effects of these pills. They muddle my memory. Try and spend some time with the girls. I suggest the cinema tomorrow night; there is a film they want to watch. Oh, and do not rant at Madge's hair. She has dyed it platinum blonde – she thinks she is Lana Turner."

"Who the hell is …?" He noted Alice's look.

He held his hands up in a surrender position. "No, I will not ask; just tell her she looks like a movie star."

"Just tell her she looks beautiful. While you have helped the country and the L.N.E.R. survive, you have acquired grown-up daughters. Well, they think they are adults! They need to remember they have a father – for the last six years, you have hardly seen them. Oh! Biddy has a new position at the sweet factory; she will train as a supervisor. I am so glad Mattie took care of you." She closed her eyes slowly, their conversation over.

In total, Amos spent three nights away at the Sutherlands. Amos never thought of being with another woman while still married to

Alice. He thought of the needless deaths of so many people over the last ten years and believed it was time to start living rather than existing.

On the final morning at her home, Mattie again intimated she would not mind being his mistress, as he often travelled in the North East. On his journey back to the Bell family, he had much to think about. He even made twenty pounds on the free room as the L.N.E.R. gave him that payment for three nights of accommodations!

32

Chapter 32 You Always Hurt the One You Love

Amos had gone to the pub and would bring back fresh fish from one of the fishermen's pubs, where trawler men sold their fish share on the black market for extra cash.

Alice had a day to herself. She filled the bath with Epsom salts, which, together with the hot water, helped her internal pain. As Alice soaked, she reflected on her mother, Elizabeth, who embodied stoicism during her illness. Her father, Percy, set a high example of how to take care of an invalid. She and Bunty made life bearable for Elizabeth during the four years of battling the disease until she passed away. Alice now insisted her daughters be tested for this awful disease, and use Dr. Patina as a resource for innovations in the disease.

Later, a little revived, Alice dressed and put on her apron for cooking, and Roy came home from school. He'd been riding side-saddle on one of his friend's bikes, as he was not allowed to take his bike to school, as the Bells lived less than a half-mile away.

He wiped his filthy hands down the front of his trousers. "Hi, Mum. What's for supper?"

"Fish pie... and birthday cake."

"Whose birthday is it?"

"Madge's. Did you not make her a card yet?"

"Nah."

"No, but I will make one now is the correct answer." She took her 'bits and bobs' box out of the pantry and handed it to Roy.

"Here. Put on flowers, or glitter, and cut a movie star picture from one of my old mags, please."

"But my friends..." Roy whined and pointed to the boys riding up and down outside, waiting for him to change.

"Nope, Dad is home. We are having a special supper for Madge's birthday and your Dad's next week. While you are in your creative mood, draw a card for your Dad a birthday card too!"

She saw the grimace at the mention of his father. "No, ifs or buts, art is one of your best subjects at school. The choice is to use your pocket money to go and buy a card or make one with lots of care and love. Go and tell your friends to buzz off."

Roy deliberated. He would prefer to play with his friends but was torn between staying at home for the birthday spread. He also hated to spend money on anything but comics and sweets, following his father's habit of not liking to spend money. "OK, Mum." He went out to tell his friends, as Madge arrived home carrying a huge bouquet of Iris'.

Alice's nostrils quivered before looking towards the bunch of flowers. "Hello, Madge. You are early, and what fragrant flowers!"

"The girls in the shop got me them. The supervisor let me off work early, as I worked my lunch break. I need time to wash my hair before I go out to dance. Can I use the bathroom now?"

"Yes, of course. Will you be here for supper? We are having special tea for you with Auntie Bunty's cake." She moved towards her Mum and gave her a big hug.

"That sounds yummy. How are you doing?"

"It's a good day. Thanks for asking."

"Is Auntie Bunty going to be here too?"

"Yes, and Dad is home too." Madge pulled a sour reaction about her father being home and disappeared upstairs quickly: she did not want any problems with her father, especially on her birthday. Amos arrived home a few minutes later, rather buoyant from a little too much drink, and slapped a huge codfish on the sink.

"That should make a few fish pies."

Grinning, he grabbed Alice and kissed her neck, overly amorous from the drink, making him want her more than usual.

"Do you want supper and cake or nookie upstairs?"

"Both."

At that point, Bunty walked in and said, "Excuse me, am I making an untimely entrance?"

Amos blushed. "No, I am going for a bath."

"Madge beat you to the bath. Go and lie down. I am sure you had a tough week up North. Listen for when she pulls the plug, then you can use the bathroom."

He blushed again, which Alice found unusual; he seemed off-kilter. Bunty began baking the cake, while Alice made the fish pie and vegetables.

She called out to her son in the front room. "Roy, I need you to set the table. Then you need to polish the wine glasses." The reluctant thirteen-year-old dragged himself into the kitchen; she handed him a tray of glasses and a bright white cloth.

His mother ordered, "Please take the glasses into the front room and polish not with spit, use this damp cloth, then polish with this tea towel."

Bunty looked aghast and asked, "He spits on the glasses?"

"Bone idle, don't ask, Bunty. It's an uphill battle trying to mold him into a gentleman. The mysteries of boys his age should remain a mystery."

"What kind of cake shall I make? Have you had some chocolate? You know, that's Amos' favourite."

"Of course, I also have plenty of cocoa powder."

The sisters were fully occupied with cooking and baking; a strong odour of the cooking fish in a cream and parsley sauce secreted through the house. Once the cake was baked in the oven, a delicious smell of chocolate seeped into every room. At five thirty, Dorothy waltzed in from work. She took a deep breath, nose in the air. "Mm, chocolate."

"Madge's and your Dad's birthdays. Oh, and be quiet upstairs; your Dad might be snoozing."

Madge pulled the plug from the bath. "I think your sister is letting the water out. So Daddy is next." Dorothy wanted to hide and avoid interaction with her father, so she sneaked quietly upstairs while he ran the bath, and so avoided interaction with her father.

Alice called: "Supper will be in about half an hour."

Biddy returned from work at the Needler's Sweet Factory. She looked around their productive kitchen and kissed both her Aunt and Mum. "I bought Dad some of our new glace fruit drops for his birthday and Maybelline make-up for Madge. Have we got any nice wrapping paper?"

She stuck her finger in the empty cake bowl and scraped off some chocolate cake mixture. "Mm, lovely Auntie. Shall I put some of the red misfits on top, so everybody can have some?"

Bunty nodded as she strategically iced the chocolate cake. Biddy handed her Aunt the packet of red sweets to place on the cake. "Oh! This is a rare treat. Chocolate cake, and Dad is here."

"Yes, an early birthday treat; he probably won't be here next week on his birthday. There are seven of us tonight. Can you help Roy set the table? Also, check the glasses. He has a habit of cleaning them with his tongue." Biddy gagged and pulled a face of disgust.

Alice, with a wooden spoon in hand, as if conducting an orchestra, said, "I am just cooking the vegetables. Once they're done, we should be ready to eat. Find the bits and bobs box in the front room; there is some pretty paper in there for wrapping the gifts."

"Oh, guess what! I have been promoted. They placed me on the wrapping chocolate machines. I am now a checker, with a little more money each week. But don't tell Dad."

"Good for you; why can we not tell your father?"

"He'll want to start charging me rent to live here."

Bunty and Alice looked at each other but did not disagree with Biddy—all the women in his life understood Amos, with his cheap, penny-pinching ways.

The family assembled for supper. It was the first time since Christmas Day they had all eaten together. The fish pie and fresh garden vegetables were enjoyed by all. Alice made a tartare cream sauce with the dish. The cake appeared with five gold candles to celebrate their Dad's 49th birthday. Placed around the edge of the cake are nineteen white candles for Madge. They lit the candles twice for each to blow their birthday candles out.

Roy asked for a second helping of cake. Amos stood and kissed Bunty on the cheek. "Thank you, Alice and Bunty, for such a delicious cake, and we should do this more often." He moved outside for a smoke of his pipe after dinner.

Together, Bunty and Alice's eyebrows lifted.

"We cook every day," Bunty said. "He's the one who misses all the great meals."

Alice said, "Madge, go and change for your dancing. I will dry the dishes, while your sisters clean and wash the dishes."

Amos popped his head around the kitchen door. "Whose is that pale blue bike outside?"

Bunty looked at him with a steady, low voice and said, "It's mine and I only use it occasionally. So Dorothy now has use of it to help her ride to work faster, so she can make her night classes on time. She has many books to carry around."

"We do not need your charity, Bunty. If she wants a bike, she could have bought one with her own money."

The girls slowly washed and dried dishes, almost in slow motion, and handed them to each other—a suspenseful moment as they waited for their Aunt's response. She simply smiled with a dangerous glare at Amos. He understood the Neil-Gregory stare and said, "The money she earns is for paying for her college books. Plus, she needs professional working clothes for the office. You would be the last person to not want her dressed appropriately. I know well, each time you pass a higher course at night class, the books are very expensive in accounting, and they must be ordered from the most expensive Brown's Book store in town."

"Please take the bike home with you tonight."

"Brother-in-law, I will not. I do not take back a loan or a gift once given."

Dorothy had been holding her breath, a tear dripped down her face. Biddy slid a hankie into her hand. She blew her nose, then turned towards her father.

Eyes full of hatred, exploded with drama, Dorothy said, "Please do not abuse Auntie Bunty's generosity to make my life easier, as a weapon against my education. We understand that you think you can be the only provider. I will not ask for anything else from you, Father—ever."

She spat the last word vehemently. "I will help Mummy while she is unwell. I would happily give her all my earnings if it would make her better." Alice shushed her.

Fists tightened, she turned to her mother, and said, "Mum, he will not make me kowtow to his tight-fisted ways. When I am here, I will continue to do chores and help you. But from now on, I am going to live at Auntie Bunty's full-time. I am going to pack now. I will not sleep in Amos Bell's house ever again."

Amos noted she exited dramatically and haughtily, the way her mother did on stage. He also heard how eloquently she spoke, like Mattie's son. Amos comprehended fully, that they had made a huge mistake not allowing Dorothy to enter High School and prepare for a three-year college. He also understood the damage and heartache he had caused, but, like a trained soldier, he did not retreat.

As their children left the room, the adults behaved differently. Alice sighed and held her abdominal area. Her pain came back when she was stressed, and she weakly muttered, "I should have taken more care and found time to discuss with her desire to stay on at school."

Amos looked at his wife, followed by a long silence. "No Alice, I made the mistake. She should have been allowed to stay on. We should have found a way to pay for it."

Alice opened her mouth and stood gobsmacked while rubbing the pain within her. In the time she had known him, Amos never admitted he was wrong about a decision—he either walked away or stood his ground. Alice reflected, "Those people's deaths at the investigation must have had a strong impact on you. I have never seen you change your mind, in all the years we have been married. But we both must share the blame."

Amos looked away. He did not want to discuss anything about his mistake or his infidelities in Darlington. But as a final knife throw, and to cover his guilt of being unfaithful, he stared from sister to sister. With some venom, he replied, "I am taken aback that the Neil-Gregory sisters still want to make decisions in my house without asking me."

Alice under her breath said, "Our house."

Bunty, annoyed, said, "The gift of my bike to Dorothy was my decision at my house to help my niece, and not yours, Amos."

He stared at Bunty and, unsure of how to reply, walked away, grabbed his cap, followed by a slamming of the kitchen door. The ladies moved into the front room and watched him walk down the street, heading west. Alice sank onto the sofa to get warm by the fire. "Off to the pub again. I think he has another woman."

Bunty, who stoked the fire with coal, stopped stunned. "What? How? When?"

She poked the fire with much anger and vigour as if poking Amos' heart.

"Not sure; something within him has changed. We are not intimate any more; lovemaking hurts me so much. But I do not think that is the problem, though."

Bunty spoke defensively to her sick sister, "He should have no expectations, a woman with your condition…"

"I am not fair to him. I lose my temper too easily." Despondency racked Alice's face.

"You worked hard today to have a wonderful meal for all. He needs to wake up and understand your condition. Look how our Daddy cared for Mum. Please do not be depressed. What happened to his carrying out his vows in sickness and in health?"

"Remember we got married in a registry office; we did not say the official church jargon. I understand he has desires to fulfill his urges. I do not think he will be with a prostitute after what happened in the first war."

Alice told her sister of her husband's past with syphilis treatments during the Great War. Bunty again reacted with an open mouth, shocked to learn of his background of VD, a staggering night of truths, exposure, and past actions.

She stood trying to process the evening, and said, "I am going to walk home with Dorothy. Please tell George if he comes to pick me up, I have returned home." She slammed the poker back in its stand.

Alice reached out to her sister. "Please stay with me awhile longer." Tears slowly fell down her face. Bunty moved next to her sister and hugged her.

Alice, in her tiny soft voice, said, "I seem to spend more time with you than I do with my husband. Thanks for being my rock!"

Dorothy came down with two bags brimming with clothes and personal items to find the sisters just sitting together in stillness, both looking dreadfully sad.

Dorothy had washed her face and, with her chin in the air, said, "I am sorry Mum, but I cannot take his bigotry any longer. Are you fine with me leaving tonight?"

Alice nodded. "Yes, of course. I will let Bunty know which days to visit as your Dad gives me next week's work schedule. Come and have supper with me on his away days? You are a very important support for me."

The new living arrangement settled, and the Bells continued their life sans one daughter in their home. Amos came home, and the older girls lived their own lives, going out as much as possible to avoid him or simply to have fun lives. Biddy acquired a serious boyfriend, Bert Bateman, who Alice had met and approved of him. Alice understood Bert as an easy-going man, who paid for all their nights out and was very down-to-earth, the opposite of her father. Bert asked Biddy to marry him, but she told him, "Not yet, maybe at twenty-one."

But she explained to her mother, "I am not going to ask Father's permission to marry anyone." Slowly all his children rejected Amos' tough-as-boots ways.

Madge never sought to please her father in any shape, way, or form. She ignored all his snide remarks about the way she dressed, the friends she chose, and where she went dancing. Taller than him, even without her high-heeled shoes, she towered over him. She always gave him as good an argument as he gave her.

If he said anything to her about hard-earned money, Madge commented, "Just living my life with the money I earn," or "Get real, Dad—you are so old-fashioned," often used as her exit line as she left the house.

Her mother pointed out to Bunty, "Madge reminds me of a sexy actress in a bad play, but do not tell her that."

Alice became the boulder between her husband and Madge. Madge's manner seemed rough around the edges, frequently impertinent. Equally, her mother thought she wore a little too much makeup, tight provocative clothing, and had a laissez-faire attitude to life. She also told her mother was saving to move out of their home, too.

"Dorothy bagged the best room at Auntie Bunty's—there is no way I am going to share with her—so I will get a bed-sit."

Alice brought up independent-thinking girls who would not be subservient to men. Amos' forty-ninth birthday year found him living with four women, well, three, as Dorothy never lived at home again. She visited her Mum, and came to play the piano but chose not to speak to Amos unless spoken to first by him. His daughters grew up, and his world changed again. Amos Bell still hated change.

33

Chapter 33 Sweethearts on Parade

Britons turned their backs on the hardships of the rationed war years. Some changes came with Clement Attlee as the first Labour Party leader since the Bells' favourite Ramsey MacDonald had left office. Amos liked the new politician; Alice disliked his agenda, another subject they chose not to discuss.

But early in 1947, Bunty planned her oldest niece's 21st birthday.

She chattered away to George. "There are three reasons why the Bells need this party for Biddy's coming of age. One: Alice must keep busy to stop her depression from getting worse. Two: I believe their marriage needs some help. Three: After this austere war, a party will help us all be with friends and celebrate together."

George tactfully agreed and asked, "Where are you going to hold it?"

Bunty grinned. "I've already booked for our church hall in June."

The party would be held at the Church of the Transformation, where Bunty married George fifteen years previously.

Biddy jumped for joy as her Aunt told her about the venue for the birthday party. Her voice exuded happiness. "Auntie, Bert just asked me to marry him. Can we have a joint celebration—engagement and 21st birthday? I think it would be fabulous fun to have all our friends and family at a combined summer party."

Her aunt nodded and agreed, "June makes a fine time for an indoor-outdoor party. Could you find a dance band you like? They will play indoors in the hall, after a delicious buffet spread. Those who wish to talk or do not like the music can gather outside in the tree-lined space."

Alice had entered the kitchen, and Bunty, the ultimate party planner, exuded excitement as she told her doubting sister, "Don't worry. It will be easy-peasy to plan, Alice. I thought I would put your number on the invitations. You can talk to guests once we receive RSVPs."

Bunty understood a party would help Alice to stay focussed by getting to know her oldest daughter's friends on the phone. However, Alice sank onto a kitchen chair and broke nibbles of crust off a pie, which lay cooling. "But what if I am tired when they call?"

Alice often made excuses for not getting out of bed. Bunty, who had dealt with Amos' excuses for years and thought her sister was becoming more like her truculent husband, always had an answer ready.

Bunty continued, "Let the phone ring, or one of the children will take a message, and you can call them back. Mostly you will be a great help to inform them of the kind of gifts Biddy would enjoy."

Bunty arranged a list of the guest names to prevent her sister from becoming a passive invalid with few outside interests. Biddy informed Amos of the double engagement birthday party, and her mouth dropped open when he agreed to pay for the rental of the

Church Hall for 'his girl'. Bert found a band and offered to pay for the musicians as all their friends loved to jitterbug.

Bunty took care of the food with Bert's Mum, who happened to work in catering, but of course, the cake was Bunty's domain. Nothing would stop her from making a marvellous cake for her niece's 21st birthday.

Later that week, Bunty arrived one night at the Bell home to discuss the menu for the party and heard Biddy and Alice going hammer and tongs as she walked up the garden path. The argument seemed about the dress Biddy would wear for the party.

With an ear-splitting screech, Biddy yelled, "Mum, I need to be able to dance in it. This is not a formal ball or one of your fancy singing concerts. I will not wear one of your dresses."

"But remember, there will be photos taken that you will look at for the rest of your life. You do not want to be in some flimsy, cheap dress. Polka dots are in fashion. I think twill fabric will be too heavy for a summer party."

Bunty waved her white hankie around the kitchen door. "Hello, have you got time to call a truce? I heard the screaming as I came down the street."

Sarcasm overflowed from Biddy's mouth. "I want to wear a red polka dot dress for my party. My mother thinks I will look common."

Alice threw her hands dramatically in the air, sighed, and sank into a chair. She appeared exhausted, and with her last ounce of energy, she said, "The fabric will be made from cheap and nasty material if you buy from that store."

Bunty quietly asked to tone down the angst, "Where are you getting the fabric from?"

"W. H. Boyes store."

"Ah!" Bunty threw Alice 'a leave this to me look'. "Do you want me to make a dress?"

Biddy, now calmer, smiled at her adored Aunt. "I thought you might be too busy?"

"Well I might be, but I want you to appear stylish and fabulous when you look back at the photos of your engagement, and not be horrified. I have to agree with your Mum, Boyes sells cheap swag."

Alice stood slowly with a hand holding her right side and exhaled. "That's exactly what I said." But she made a stage exit to rid herself of the high tension with her daughter.

Biddy finished cleaning the dishes, turned to her aunt while her mother was out of earshot, and said, "She is such a perfectionist. My mother wants everything her way. You would think it was *her* twenty-first birthday party!"

Bunty, again the voice of reason, said, "We will go shopping on Saturday; you can show me the dress, so I will understand the style you would like. Maybe we can find a pattern and fabric to suit you *and* your mother."

"Yes – but..."

"Look, your mum has not much to look forward to these days. You as her oldest daughter getting engaged and becoming twenty-one will be a day to help her stay focussed thinking about your future happiness and take away from her pain."

"But..."

She stopped her niece mid-sentence and held up her hand. "Biddy, please stop and think of whom you are modelling. Why do you think you are the youngest confectionery section leader in your company?"

Biddy paused then smiled, "I will not allow any chocolate to go into the special golden boxes unless perfect."

"Right, you know those gold and red boxes go to the mums and girlfriends, and people want to give them a luxurious gift, or to say thank you. Let your mother give you the perfect party. It's her way of saying she loves you. You had better get a gold box of chocolates for her too." They both grinned.

***

Back at home on Monday evening, Alice returned telephone calls to those who had RSVP'd to attend Biddy's June birthday. As she began to dial the phone rang.

"The Bell residence - can I help you?"

"Hello, Mum. It's Dorothy."

"Of course darling, I know your voice."

"Biddy told me last night about Grandma and her connections with Doncaster. I did not know Grandma Elizabeth lived here. Can you get me the address of where she lived? I will ask around to see if anyone remembers her. Some of my work friends' parents have lived here all their lives."

"Yes, I cannot remember where I put the page with her address upon it. But will call you back once I have it."

"Yes, I am also calling to reply to the invite. I am attending. Is it OK to bring someone? I'd like to bring a good friend with me."

"Oh? Friend...or a boyfriend?"

Alice understood her daughter was bringing a young man but waited for details. Biddy always kept Alice up-to-date with Dorothy's life, but her youngest daughter seldom told her anything. Madge and Biddy called her 'the secretive sister'.

"His name is Alex, our accounts manager. He seems keen on me and as he has a car, it will be easier to get home and back. We will drive directly to the party."

"Good, that's convenient. How long have you been walking out with him, Dorothy? You do not sound head-over-heels."

Dorothy, whom Alice could tell was at her desk in the office, as she was slamming drawers of a filing cabinet, sighed. "Well, I have been seeing him maybe four months or so. I am taking it slowly; I am too young to get married. He needed someone who could organize dinners and events to move forward in his career, but I suspect he might be using me to get ahead, and doesn't think of me as a serious girlfriend. Thanks to you and Bunty, I am a good organizer. But I want to get on with my career before settling down. It is so much harder for women to get on in the business workplace. You know what I mean?"

Proud to know her daughter was not taking the first man she meets, so she could be married, said, "Indeed I do, that's exactly why we took Biddy to the rally in Nottingham. Sorry, you could not be with us due to work. Do not rush into any marriage; say no to him plenty of times and find out if he will stick around."

Dorothy cheekily answered, "Like you did with Dad, you mean?"

Alice paused, intrigued that her daughter remembered how Amos asked her three times to marry him. Her tone of voice also sounded like she believed Alice had made the wrong choice in marrying her father.

Alice aimed to give her youngest daughter good advice. "Darling, be sure whoever you choose has staying power, and commitment for a lifetime of marriage. Is this man educated and good-looking?"

"In a tall, commanding way, yes. But he always wants his way and is ruthless about getting on in life. That is one of my reasons for not saying 'yes' every time he asks me out."

Alice agreed with her daughter, and said, "I am pleased you understand something about men already and do play hard to get. I look forward to meeting him at the party. Bunty and I will give him the once over."

Dorothy giggled, and said, "Well, he may run a mile after he meets my sisters, and then the Neil-Gregory wolf pack. And then, if he has to meet Dad, he will drive back faster to Doncaster than the trains run. Plus, Roy will probably want to beat him up. If he survives all this Bell scrutiny - he might be worth considering!"

Alice guffawed at Dorothy's comic description of their family. Her youngest daughter always cheered her up. "Indeed. You are a card, Dorothy Bell. I will call you when I find Grandma's former address in Doncaster."

"I find it easier to be funny than dwell on my tears of gold, as Auntie Bunty called them. Love you, Mum. Just so you know I am out every night this week with work parties. You can call me at work in the daytime. I have my desk phone now. Just ask the receptionist for the accounts department. Bye for now."

Bubbly Dorothy, her youngest daughter, rang off.

I know Bunty told me about the anger and tears, despite our poor decision to not let continue her studies at school. Nevertheless, she's moving up in the company and getting dates with managers. I pray she makes the right decision on the right man to marry. Marriage is a testing roulette game if you do not make the right choice. Bunty got it right. I made a mistake - well not a mistake with Amos - but chose the tough path to follow. A strong, secure man would have let me be artistic and...

The phone rang again and stopped her thoughts. Alice spent most of the night calling back Biddy's friends and explaining which gifts Biddy might like for her 21st birthday.

34

Chapter 34 Don't Sit Under the Apple Tree with Anyone Else

Over seventy people attended Biddy's 21st birthday-engagement party. Caroline, her fiancé's mother, catered an outstanding buffet for the event. Bunty baked with the flour acquired by George, which had 'fallen off a lorry.' She never inquired which one, as she needed the flour for the birthday cake and other tasty pastries.

Biddy's guests were delighted with the black and white decor on the tables and the old, black, shellac long-playing records (donated by George) used as plate stands. During the six years of war, most of Bunty's friends had never attended a well-thought-out, creatively designed birthday party. Bunty's distinctive cake table housed the white and black cake, which was decorated with small black records made of black liquorice wound in circles. It was not only remarkable to look at but also incredible to eat.

The sisters came dressed to the nines with their outfits. They had bought them from Flora Brown's shop, a high-class dress shop, which sold the best ladies' outfits and hats. Bunty wore a gold lace top with a classy scalloped neckline and a blue circle dance skirt, which would circle out when she danced with George. Alice went for some glamour in an 'Ava Gardner style' tight blue pencil skirt and a gold lace halter top with a navy short jacket to keep her warm. It was her first new outfit in years.

The swing band set up their instruments, while people ate and mingled. Alice climbed slowly on stage in her pencil-lined skirt and newly dyed red high-heeled shoes, which she used to wear at her professional concerts. Alice first spoke over the square silver microphone. "Ladies and gentlemen, I would like to bring up my husband, Amos Bell, to present the toast."

The younger guests lined up their box brownie cameras, ready to save a memory of the occasion. In contrast, George placed his old Furet camera (with which he had taken Amos and Alice's wedding photos) on a stand for family pictures. Though reluctant to give the toast, Amos agreed, as Alice had written his speech for their daughter. He coughed, "Aline 'Biddy' Bell, our firstborn, came into the world with not much fuss."

Alice loudly interjected, "How do you know? You were at work." Much laughter from the crowd threw Amos off his stride.

Madge whispered to her sister Biddy, "Well delivered, Mum. She could have been a comedienne if she had carried on performing."

Amos, flustered by Alice's interruption, took a deeper breath and continued, "...without fuss. This is how she has lived her life so far. She gets on with the job."

Many nods of agreement came from her work colleagues and close friends.

"Let's celebrate her twenty-one years on this earth, and later, after the band has played their first set, we will tell you about the next step of her life. Biddy, please come up on stage so we can sing to you."

The birthday girl, dressed in her black-and-white polka-dot dress with lace around the edge and socks to match, walked up on stage as a picture of style and happiness. Alice took over the microphone to lead the 'Happy Birthday' song. As a former classical singer, she'd given the pianist her key and directed them. "Let's jazz it up, boys. I sang with the Billy Cotton Band." While her daughter blew out the twenty-one white candles, Alice led the audience in a sing-along jazz style, "Happy birthday to you, yeah." The party had begun.

Alice's moment of being back in her natural habitat came to an end as she introduced the name of the band. "Please welcome, for your dancing pleasure, 'Toasted Tom and the Buttered Bread Quartet.'

She looked through a sea of smoke; since the war, everyone seemed to be smoking, and she could not see Amos. The younger crowd began to jitterbug as the band played lively, up-tempo songs. Alice nodded to guests as she searched for Amos. Finally, she found him sitting with his good friend, Joseph Oliver, and his wife, enjoying his pipe. Their older guests and relatives sat outside, on a tree-lined patio at the back of the church, away from the music. Here, guests could chat without shouting. Bunty came out carrying a tray of cake slices, followed by her niece Madge, whom she had commandeered to help hand the napkins to the guests.

Her niece inquired, "Once you are done with this tray, Auntie, are you and Uncle George going to cut a rug? My friends want a display of your smooth moves."

Bunty smiled. "Okay, once the cake is served."

Madge asked her mother, "Want some, Mum?"

Alice shook her head and collapsed with exhausted air beside Mabel, her neighbour, who asked, "Can you explain what Madge is talking about when she is talking about 'cutting a rug?'"

"Dancing, it's a hip term."

"Oh, Alice, I feel old. Their slang puzzles me."

"I agree, though my three daughters keep me current with the latest jargon. So, Madge, has Dorothy shown up yet?"

Madge, who never wanted to speak to her sister, said, "Yes, just as my Biddy blew out her birthday candles, my midget sister showed up with a tall, handsome catch."

Alice swore under her breath, "Oh, hell, and I wanted some peace and rest. But I promised Dot we would give her new boyfriend the Neil-Gregory inspection, Bunty."

Amos heard their comment and asked, "Dorothy is here?"

Alice nodded. "Of course, she wouldn't miss her sister's engagement party. She drove over from Doncaster with a friend." She informed Amos that Dorothy's friend was male and that he might react negatively. To keep him sweet, Bunty handed over a piece of cake and said, "Here's the last piece of cake on my tray, Amos, just for you."

With a sulky schoolboy look, he said, "Thanks. I thought you'd forgotten me." She noted he looked drained, but remembered he'd driven on a late shift last night and then gotten up early and helped set up the party. "I will never forget you. Your need for my baking is one of the constants in my life, other than George. Ever since you met my sister, Amos Bell appears like a genie whenever I have cake." The gathered guests laughed at her comment.

He smiled, revived by the tasty white-iced lemon cake until he saw Mattie and her son John enter the back patio. Amos chewed angrily at their arrival, then noted that Madge immediately walked towards this tall, dark, handsome boy, offered her hand to shake, and said, "Hello, I think we are cousins. I'm Madge Bell."

Her mother rolled her eyes at the flutter of her daughter's eyelashes—her cheap actress look. Alice noted that John politely smiled back, looked her up and down, and then shook her hand longer than was needed. She heard him say, "John Sutherland, delighted to meet you, cousin."

Alice corrected her daughter. "John is your half-cousin, or that once-removed stuff." She turned towards his mother. "Hello, Mattie. Am I correct about their relationship?"

Dressed in a light beige dress, not the latest fashion like her Hull cousins, Mattie stood behind her son, blinked a few times, and shrugged as if she didn't have a clue.

Madge wanted a handsome man to dance with, so she continued smiling at John. "Well, half-cousin John, I hope you dance well."

"Yes, I believe I do. I attend Durham University. I'm on the ballroom and swing dance team."

Madge grabbed his hand and batted her eyelashes at her cousin. "Well, let's go and cut a rug. I love this Krupa number, 'Sing, Sing, Sing.'"

The young man offered Madge his arm formally and led her to the dance hall to partner dance at a breakneck Jitterbug tempo. Amos eyed them dubiously. Mattie suddenly piped up as if woken from a long sleep and said directly to Amos, "Hello, Amos. I hope we will be able to have a dance too."

Alice commented, without looking at her husband, "Good luck, Mattie. But, unfortunately, Amos would rather have a tooth pulled out than dance."

Mattie suggestively said, "Perhaps to some slower music?"

Amos munched on the last bite of cake, so he would not have to reply. The look on his face hardened; he appeared lost for words. Bunty and Alice looked at him, waiting for an answer. Finally, to diffuse the request to dance, Amos replied, "Maybe a slow one later, but I may disappoint you."

Mattie shook her head and boldly replied, "I am sure that is not true."

The Neil-Gregory sisters looked at each other, both arching their eyebrows. Mattie moved to the hall. They looked at Amos, who blushed.

Alice pondered curiously at what just occurred, then deduced, "She is setting her cap at you."

Amos stood immediately and pulled a face at Alice. "Don't be ridiculous!"

Amos carried the empty plate to the kitchen as if it were a knife in his hand. Quoting the Shakespeare she used to perform as an actress, Alice said to her sister, tartly, "The lady doth protest too much, I think."

Bunty saw their female cousins' inappropriate interaction with Amos. "You're as bad as Amos with your Shakespeare quotes. Well, that was interesting. Mattie is quite bold."

"Oh, I think Mattie has always been off her trolley. Her dad Daniel kept changing religions, so Mum's sisters told me. Our mum was the only one who tolerated him. At first, Daniel was a Quaker, then changed to the Christian Scientist creed, and finally found something in Methodism. As a child, Mattie had no idea what to believe, like a boat without an anchor, but I should not use that tasteless metaphor. Sadly, she lost her sailor husband at sea at age twenty, which left her with two tiny boys. She moved in with her parents. John, though, seems well-educated and groomed. Come with me, Bunty, let's meet Dorothy's new chap."

Arm in arm, Bunty and her sister entered the dance hall, where she saw Mattie speaking to the bandleader. Bunty nudged her sister. "What is Mattie up to?"

Alice turned to Bunty. "Mad Mattie, as we used to call her, do you remember my early performing days in Newcastle? I would stay with them occasionally."

"I do not remember, Alice. I was about eleven or twelve, but look at Madge and John; they are a well-matched dance pair."

They scrutinised Mattie's son, who had a confident, fluent dance style, and were impressed with his elegance and knowledge of fast Balboa steps, the new hip dance on this high-speed number.

Bunty commented, "A smooth mover responds well to the changes in music. His height is perfect for Madge, even in her dance heels. She always complains that most men ogle her breasts as she dances with them. But they are perfectly in sync. I was right to make those matching dance pants underneath; look at her lovely long legs as she twirls."

Bunty was exhilarated by their dancing. Amos, however, looked on in disgust as his daughter danced. Alice saw his indignation as Madge, with total abandon, danced up a storm with her well-matched cousin.

Alice smirked and nudged her sister. "There's going to be Amos trouble; look at his face."

Bunty and Alice watched him while Madge danced wildly, having fun. Amos had disapproval painted on his face; his lips were pursed. Alice admonished his response. "Amos, take that look off your face and do not get a strop on. It's your daughter's twenty-first; have some fun. The kids are just full of high spirits. They are not going to marry or sleep together."

"I am not being stroppy, as you put it. If I can see the tops of Madge's stockings as she twirls, all and sundry will see them. These sensual dance moves can lead to more. John should control his dance leading. Are you not worried by their actions?"

"Oh, I forgot you stayed with them and met John in Darlington, but you sound like a geriatric old man. Most women these days show their white bread thighs at some point if the wind blows up their skirts or if they bend over. Bunty made her matching shorts to cover the important parts."

Amos grunted at her comment but then spotted Dorothy coming his way with a tall man in tow. She was dressed in an elegant, dusty-pink, flared summer frock. Her blonde hair was decorated with a matching pink flower, coupled with a diamante choker around her neck. Alice smiled at her youngest daughter, but Amos instantly disappeared into the nearby toilets.

Bunty hugged Dorothy first and then held her at arm's length. "Love the dress. Only you could wear this style—you look like Dinah Shore."

"Hello," she said, then turned to the man on her niece's arm and held out a hand to shake. "I am Dorothy's Aunt Marjorie, but everyone calls me Bunty."

The well-dressed, tall, bespectacled gentleman took her hand and kissed it. Alice raised an eyebrow, surprised at his assured manner with an older woman. Roy, who had moved over to see his favourite sister, giggled.

Alex gushed with an overdone compliment, "I've been told you helped Dorothy become the creative, organized young woman I find so useful."

Bunty blushed, and she was lost for words at this young man's forwardness. But she recovered. "Well, I taught Dorothy how to sew and bake."

"Mum, Auntie, this is Alex Wright. Alex, my aunt, you have just met, and my mother, Alice Bell." Alice smiled her performer's smile, which gave nothing away, and held out her spare hand firmly to shake, not to be kissed.

"Lovely to meet you, Alex; this is my son, Roy."

Roy looked up at the tall man and asked, "Did she mention me?"

"Yes, Roy, she did." Roy puffed up like a feathered peacock. Alex added, "Apparently, you bribed Dorothy to do your homework so you could finish school."

His mother grabbed his arm and said, "Like father, like son, he will wriggle out of difficult situations like this one." She gave him a clip around the ear. Embarrassed, Roy crept away before his mother asked more questions.

"We are delighted to meet you, Alex," Alice said, waving at him in a regal manner. "You are such an experienced man with women. Sorry, you were too late for my sister's food and cake. However, there may be something left if you check in the kitchen."

Dorothy understood her mother's sarcasm and undertook to change the subject. "No need, Mom—Alex took me out to dinner. Where shall I put Biddy's gift?"

She held a shoe box wrapped in gold paper.

Alice replied, "How delightful! Give it to her yourself. Here she is, coming off the dance floor."

Biddy ran to her youngest sister. "Dot, you are here!" She hugged her sister and gave Alex a look that said, 'Who the heck is this?' while Dorothy handed over the shoe box.

"Here you are; I hope they fit."

Biddy's eyes shone with joy. "You got me some?"

Dorothy nodded and guided her to a chair. "Sit down and try them on." Biddy, excited as a six-year-old, opened the shoebox, revealing black and white peep-toe shoes with heels.

"Oh, I love them." She put on the new shoes and exclaimed, "They fit."

"They are from both of us." She turned to Alex and introduced him. "This is my sister, Biddy Bell, who is twenty-one today!"

Again, Alex took her hand and kissed it. Biddy, like her aunt, blushed like a beetroot, as she was not used to men who were confident enough to kiss the hands of women to whom they had just been introduced.

Alex smarmed, "I am charmed to meet you, Biddy. Happy Birthday, I have heard so much about you. I drove Dorothy to Leeds for the shoes."

Dorothy grinned at her sister. "You will be as tall as Dad in them, so go and dance and try them out! But break them in carefully; they are leather."

Alice watched, eyeing Alex with caution.

Where has my youngest daughter got money for expensive dance shoes? This man has some charm but the gift of gab. I know this leads to the wrong path. Keep your guard up, Dorothy.

"What a delightful gift." Alice looked at the gift label as she tidied up the paper and box. "Such a fine gift from *both* of you—how generous of you, Alex, especially for a young woman whom you never met."

He did not have time to answer before Toasted Tom, the bandleader, loudly announced, "The next song is a tempo change… a slow number, the hit song 'You Always Hurt the One You Love.'"

Alex elegantly led Dorothy to the dance floor. Alice suddenly spotted her husband being dragged towards the dance floor by her cousin Mattie.

Mattie must be needy if she wants to dance with Amos. But, ha! He was not fast enough to get away from her mad iron grasp. I bet he was hiding in the bathroom, hoping she would not find him.

Alice focused her attention on the couple, like a hawk going in for the kill. "Mattie wants something."

Bunty peered at Amos and then Mattie. "Well, she's barking up the wrong tree with Amos; he's a one-woman man. And what about Flash Alex?"

Alice flared her nostrils. "Look at his dance movements. They are like his charm—false and pretentious, a show-off!"

Bunty grabbed her sister's arm and pulled her away.

"Enough, Alice; let them dance. Let Dot make her own mistakes. Come and help me get the champagne ready for the engagement speech."

Alice indignantly said, "I would not trust him as far as I could fling him, but Dorothy has become infatuated with his charm and position, so I will smile and wait him out. She has more in common with her father than she will ever admit, and she blindly trusts people. She finds Alex attractive as he has the gift of the gab, the total opposite of her father—at least she seems to have fallen for a different type. He wants to marry her but will have to wait out an engagement for two years or find another fish to fry. She needs our permission if she marries under the age of 21. Our baby must learn to fly first, where men are concerned."

After the slow number, Toasted Tom announced, "Ladies and gentlemen, please come forward and take a champagne flute to celebrate the engagement of Bert Bateman and Aline 'Biddy' Bell.

"How magical they do not have to get new monogrammed towels, as they have the same initials."

The crowd cackled at his silly joke as the guests' glasses were filled for the toast. Finally, Bunty walked on the stage to present the engagement announcement. "If you do not know me, I am the aunt of this wonderful girl, Biddy Bell."

Bunty waved Bert's Mum to come on stage. "Caroline, this is Bert's mum. She created this wonderful spread tonight."

Much applause and whooping was heard from the gathered guests.

"My husband and I—oh my goodness, I sound like royalty." More laughter. "We want to wish Biddy and Bert a *long* engagement. Her parents told me to make a statement, so they have a chance to save up for the wedding. So my husband George and I will have a jitterbug dance-off with Bert and Biddy and show them how we can still cut a rug at our ancient age. But first, please raise your glasses to Bert and Biddy."

The guests toasted the young couple. Then the band struck up with the song 'Don't Sit Under the Apple Tree.' Biddy danced with her new fiancé to the energetic popular music. The gathered circle of guests clapped along.

Alice and Amos found each other standing side by side, watching their daughters dance. As Alice smiled at him, Amos turned and seriously asked, "Does this song have biblical connotations?"

With a blank look, Alice replied, "What? Oh, Adam and Eve with the apple? I never thought of it with that analogy. Biddy chose it. Maybe it's a warning to Bert not to stray." She stared at her husband. He turned away.

"It fascinates me that you do not like your daughters to show their fine legs while dancing and you often portray a pessimistic attitude towards them having fun. I see how uncomfortable you are with dancing. When Cousin Mattie asked, you looked as if you wanted to run. You could have politely said, 'No, thank you' to her."

Amos turned beetroot red. Alice smirked at him, then turned languidly like a cat and stalked away. Amos saw her deliberate Madame Neil-Gregory exit. She sneaked a glance at him as she stood by the exit and laughed.

After she danced to three songs, Dorothy needed a drink to cool her down; her cheeks were nearly as pink as her dress. Madge appeared at Alex's side and grabbed her sister's boyfriend for an up-tempo number; again, they were well paired, as both were tall.

Dorothy slowed down as she approached the kitchen and saw her father at the door.

Amos asked, "Not going to greet your old dad?"

"Good evening, father. I am going to get some water from the kitchen."

Amos stepped aside and stated, "Your sister's moves with your male friend are very lewd. Are you not worried?"

Dorothy turned to look at their dancing and smiled. "No, I am not. All those dances are called the Jitterbug, which Madge dances very well, not improperly. I am sorry they shock you, but if you compare them to the other dancers on the dance floor, your daughter's steps are exactly like the rest of their friends. It is the new socially accepted way to have fun and keep active."

Amos opened his mouth, but no words came out of his mouth to reply to his well-dressed, eloquent daughter, who'd put him in his place just like her mother. He recovered and counterattacked, "I have not met the young man you arrived with tonight."

Dorothy clicked away from him on her high heels and turned back for the last word. "I will introduce you if you can be polite to him after he finishes dancing with my sister. Excuse me, I need some water."

The crowd clapped loudly at the up-tempo song, so Amos did not hear Mattie slip up behind him and whisper in his ear.

Alice, however, noted that for every move Mattie made, her cousin's body language told Alice that Mattie wanted Amos. Alice, like a snake in the wild, slithered closer to them, unseen. Amos turned to Mattie and showed his annoyance when she appeared right next to him. Mattie stroked his arm to calm him, but his red cheeks and the panic in his eyes told Alice the information she suspected. Mattie and Amos had more than a friendship.

Bunty came up right behind Alice at the right time to break her fall, and she fainted as her knees buckled and she slid to the floor. When Amos heard the commotion, he escaped from Mattie and rushed to where his wife was being pulled up by Bunty and Dorothy. George ran over to the group, looked at Amos, and asked, "To the hospital... or home?"

The gathered group chanted 'hospital.' Alice slowly came around, then, without looking at her husband, and pleaded softly, "Please take me home, George."

"I will get the car and bring it round to the back door."

Bunty and Dorothy helped Alice onto a chair, which she flopped onto like a rag doll. By this time, George had brought his car to the back of the hall. Alice walked carefully, aided by her sister. Amos sat with her in the back seat, relieved, hoping his encounter with

Mattie had not been noticed by his wife, and thought, *Please do not die, Alice.*

Chapter 35 La Vie En Rose

The next day, George dropped Bunty and Roy off at the Bell household while he left to fill his car 'Gloria' with petrol. Entering the house by the back gates, they found Amos in the garden, digging.

"Ah, we thought Roy was with you—thank you for bringing him back."

Amos immediately barked orders at his son. "Get your chores done, Roy. Mum is still in bed and needs rest and quiet."

Roy pulled a face but went inside to change into his work clothes. Amos moved into the kitchen and turned to his oldest daughter, who was cooking for him, and with a rare smile added, "Madge's making me a meal before I return to work."

Bunty picked up a tin and waved it in the air. "Good. I have brought you some Eccles cakes, which I saved for you."

He took the can with another smile and placed it near his work bag. "They will taste even better as my nighttime supper, on my way to Newcastle."

Bunty held onto her anger, which had been simmering since the party, and threw the blame book at him about his promises. "Oh, I thought you were on short runs with Alice's increased health alerts."

She noted that Amos blushed, and as he answered her, emphasized the 'I' in each statement, as if he were the only one running the household. "I can earn more on longer trips and take more time off. This week, I am off Wednesday through Friday night. I can then help Alice on the nights the girls like to go out. I need to be here for her." It sounded as if he was reading a shopping list.

Bunty looked at him with her head on a side, wondering what he was hiding, and replied sarcastically, "Have a safe trip; *I* was not checking up on you. But *I* will take Alice to the doctor's tomorrow, and *I* think we should manage her health needs together, don't you?"

With doubt in his voice, he answered as he hung up his garden jacket and hat. "Yes, I suppose we can." He sulked like a small boy.

Bunty stared incredulously. "Have you given any thought about why your wife fainted yesterday?"

He turned red again and avoided eye contact with his sister-in-law. Bunty persisted and called after him as he stomped upstairs. "She needs to be checked out by a doctor."

Before saying something she might regret, she returned to the kitchen and opened the pantry door. She grabbed Alice's apron so she could help Madge cook the meal. Of course, Madge had picked up on the tension between her father and aunt. With her long blonde hair stuck to her sweating forehead, from the oven heat, she asked, "Auntie, how does Mum make gravy for Dad?"

Bunty re-opened the pantry, grabbed the gravy granules, pulled out a glass jar of Bisto and handed them to her niece.

"Ah, yes! Mum told me – I always forget Dad's favourite. Shall I taint it with some cyanide?"

Bunty almost smiled but was still upset with her niece from the night before. She posed hand on hip and waited for an apology from Madge about her behaviour at the party. However, no apology was offered.

Angry at the rudeness of both Madge and Amos, she quietly went upstairs to her sister's room without a word to her niece. The whole house had taken on a tense atmosphere as if Alice's illness might extinguish them all.

Alice was resting in bed, but awake. "Hello, Bunty; thanks for what you did for Biddy. What a party! Eh?"

Bunty looked around. "Where's Amos?"

"He kissed me and left via the front door, I think." Alice slowly pulled herself up to sitting position and Bunty grabbed her pillow and puffed it up to support her sister's back.

As she fisted the pillow she said, "He's a coward too! He avoids making decisions about your health. Your husband gets more stubborn as you get sicker."

Alice flapped her hand around like she was getting rid of a fly and said, "Ignore him when he's on his high horse. That's how I deal with him."

Bunty, tired from the party and Amos' dire behaviour, sat down and shook her head. She dispersed her boiling anger, as she reflected on the party. "I think most people had a lovely night, but the sudden ending for you was not part of my planning."

Alice grinned at her sister and made a silent movie theatrical faint, hand over her forehead. "Oh! Exhaustion comes on more quickly these days."

"What about having too many stimuli to deal with before you fainted?"

Still acting, with a hand splayed across her chest with wide eyes, she asked, "What do you mean?"

"The high drama bubbled all night. First Amos' simmering anger at Madge's wild dancing with John. Then mad Mattie followed your husband around like a lost dog, stroking his arm, and Dorothy with her overtly charming Alex, who seemed keen to put his hands all over Madge. If it had been a farce, I would have laughed myself silly until my sides ached."

Alice said, "I told you I do trust Alex as far as I could fling him, and in my weakened state, that's not far. Dorothy has become infatuated with his charm and position, so I will smile and wait him out. She has more in common with her father than she will ever admit, and she blindly trusts people. She may find Alex attractive as he has the gift of the gab, which is the opposite of her father—at least she seems to have fallen for a different type. He wants to marry her but will have to wait for a long engagement for three years or find another fish to fry. She needs our permission if she marries under twenty-one. Our baby must learn to fly first, where men are concerned."

Resigned Bunty shrugged and told her sister about the altercation between her nieces. "Sadly, I stopped Madge and Dorothy from having a catfight in the kitchen after you left in front of Caroline."

Alice dismissed her daughters' behaviour. "Oh, they never agree about anything. Sorry, you had to deal with their vileness. Caroline must be wondering what kind of family her son might be marrying into. My daughters had to bring themselves up as I became more tired."

Bunty reached for her sister's hand and with much concern, asked, "But what about your fainting, Alice? Did you feel faint, or was it great acting to diffuse the situation?"

"What do you think, Bunty?" Alice's expressive eyes asked mysteriously.

"Well, the climax certainly got the guests' attention, and Amos only had eyes for you once you fainted."

"Really, how interesting? My relationship with my husband has been complex since I got ill. He has no idea how to help me, but why should he? He was away in the Great War when first his father passed, then his youngest sick brother was brought back to Whitby on a boat, and got gangrene from lack of treatment, and died also. Amos may not have it in him to acknowledge any more deaths. He has not developed emotional growth like George, who has grown into a real man under Margaret's and your care. Also, I am not like you. I am demanding and will not admit this dreadful disease, or behave like an invalid. Amos is my rock. I am clinging to him till Death's door opens."

Bunty looked at her weak, pale sister, sighed and took some time before answering. She wanted to yell, '*He made pathetic excuses thirty years ago; he should grow up*', but she took several breaths, and then she said, "I believe Amos fell in love with the Madame Neil-Gregory at the Lord Mayor's concert where you were playing a part. But you have continued to grow as a great mother and a woman with strong opinions, with which he cannot cope. Sadly, I have not seen much growth in him. You have been together for almost twenty-five years. If he cannot accept your personality, beliefs, and amazing endurance after knowing you this long, he should start doing so, or you should divorce him. That man seems clueless about how to deal with your situation, except to bark orders at people."

"I doubt he will change. I agree the Great War did much to shape his cynicism. He has a shroud over his thoughts. He rarely allows his true thoughts out. He never allowed the children to experience his kind side. I witness it occasionally. I do understand why he is not in love with this thin, insipid, weak Alice, but he will not stop supporting me until I am no longer here. I have told Amos to marry again when I pass."

Bunty was astounded by this comment. She sat straight up in the chair. "What? How magnanimous of you! You are way more selfless than he deserves. Alice, how incredibly forward-thinking! I would not be so generous with George."

Alice pulled a sardonic look. "I am being practical. Amos and

Roy cannot exist without some female help in the house. I hope he will find someone who will give him what I lack. The misery we both create is more painful than my illness and has affected how our children conduct themselves."

"That is true. I was so embarrassed by my nieces' outbursts last night, in front of Caroline."

"You have been a fine example for them, have guided my brood, and have been a wonderful influence on Dorothy. Amos' guilt may stem from having a mistress, he comes home happier - I perceive whoever she is releases some of his angst."

Bunty looked at her sister. "What? Do you know who it is?"

"No, not sure. At first, I suspected it was someone local. I could smell her perfume. But it might be someone on one of his stops up in the North."

"You are so calm. What, in Edinburgh? What perfume?"

"Maybe Newcastle—who knows? L'Air De Temps is an expensive brand of perfume. I prayed the bombs would get me, but sadly, that was not my fate. I am still here, and the party was fabulous, and to find such a reliable man for Biddy…"

Bunty cut her off and said, "Just like when you first knew Amos. You said the same phrase when we were in London, and he kept asking you to marry him, and you replied, 'He's a reliable man, Bunty.'" Bunty mimicked her sister well.

Alice showed more concern for her daughter's alliance. "I feel Bert will stick with strong-minded Biddy unless he strays like her father, but he knows how to have great fun. Caroline has brought up a great young man."

Bunty became deadly serious. "If you want to divorce Amos, I can get a good lawyer from where I used to work and aid you with compensation. We could also have him followed."

Alice laughed. "A private eye, how would that help me? I am happy to read about them in my novels. Soon I will be gone, Bunty;

I do not care about a divorce. Maybe Amos' unhappiness has come from my pain, not the war. But some people with this disease experience more suffering than I do. For example, look at Edith Piaf, the French songstress, displaying her pain as she performs. I adore her 'La Vie En Rose'. Or am I wearing my rose coloured glasses?" She giggled at her silly imagery, and Bunty laughed with her music-loving, madcap comedic sister again.

But she pushed on with her opinions. "Amos should become your total support during your illness, but as usual, he sweeps the problems under the carpet!"

Alice ignored her sister lost in the thoughts of the beautiful French song; suddenly, she turned to look at the rose on her bedside as if coming back to the real world.

"Amos can be thoughtful. He bought me a delicate pink rose to cheer me up. He supports me monetarily, and we are still sleeping in the same bed, which comforts me. From early on, I had to be the strength of our relationship. I no longer have the energy to spar with him, so he is adrift. Not everyone is blessed with the kind of love you and George share."

Bunty folded her arms and said, "He should be here more to give you his strength. Thank you for sharing so much with me. I understand now where you are with Amos. I want to shake him profusely most of the time. But I'm pleased that Bert is a good prospective husband for Biddy."

Alice smiled and nodded, "I think so and hope. But who can tell? People change, war can convert anyone into a demon, and being ill switches your priorities. I am not sure we are a good example of a normal marriage to them. Marriage is like a deck of cards. Some are handed aces like George and Bert; others get a mixed hand."

Bunty wanted to keep Alice positive and suggested a way to support her sick sister. "Hey, we had an idea. George and I want to set you up with wireless in the bedroom. Would you like one?"

"I would love it! However, I am afraid I might not get out of bed; I would listen to music all day."

"Well, are you saying yes or no?" Alice took time answering and smoothed the bed sheets with her piano-playing hands moving to an imaginary song. Her face became taut as a pang of pain travelled through her body.

"No, I am good for now. I need a reason to go and sit with the children if they are around. Can we plan my next visit to see my doctor? Can you call and book an appointment for me one afternoon soon? I can get my energy up by then."

"Do you need another tablet to help with the pain?"

"I rattle around with those pills inside me; I am not sure they are helping me. I am not as magnificent as Mother was in her illness. I feel like an old Harridan. I'm surprised Amos comes home at all. Did he say, 'Alice, don't die' when we got in the car?"

Bunty pulled herself up from the bedroom chair and said simply, "George told me so. Am I to believe you did not completely blackout? In sickness and in health, he should remember those vows. Madge has tried to cook corned beef and potatoes—do you want some?"

"A few potatoes with the Bisto gravy would be good as I have to take some medication. I cannot take it on an empty tummy. Thank you for giving up work to run the house and take care of me, plus guiding my children to be kind as people. But let Amos get on with his job and ignore him."

Bunty said, "It was time to give up work."

She did not add that Amos' ambivalent behaviour worried her more than anything.

"I am not sure your almost adult children listen to me much, and I do not have a cat in hell's chance of guiding him."

Alice rearranged her pillows to get comfortable. "Look my kids never listen to me either, and Amos requires sculpting like an old Roman statue; you have to chip off his rough edges, day by day."

They both giggled and shared a sisterly moment. Bunty hugged her sister but tears fell as she left the room and she wiped them before she called the doctor's office for an appointment. As she finished the call to the Doctor's surgery, Alice's neighbour Mabel knocked on the kitchen door with a pan in her hand. "Here you go, Madge, carrots and peas for your mum."

Both Biddy and Madge together said, "Thank you for cooking them." They both knew but did not tell her, that Alice would hardly eat any of the vegetables.

Mabel, ever positive shared with Bunty, "I have great news! Philip is doing well at his carpentry job with a lovely man who also has a non-verbal child and can sign to him. Philip sweeps their floors and cuts simple jobs for him. Soon he will get to use screwdrivers. Plus he brings home sawdust for our compost – should I put this bag outside straight onto your compost?"

Bunty clapped her hands. It was the best news she had heard for weeks. She said, "Thank you, Mabel, what fabulous news for you about Philip getting a job. Yes, please dump the sawdust in the compost heap, but I'm not sure if Amos will be back to do more gardening."

She turned to her niece and asked Madge, "Can you put a little sausage and gravy on a plate for your mum?"

So Bunty became her emotional support during the last year of Alice's life in place of her husband. The girls managed the daily running of the house and cooking between them. Their parent's relationship changed. Amos came home, ate, paid the bills and slept, but had little interaction with his adult children. Instead, he or the children brought a rose to cheer up Alice every few days to allow her to dream of 'La Vie En Rose' and sing along with Edith Piaf.

36

Chapter 36 Serenade of the Bells 1949

As Alice became sicker, the British people rebuilt their lives in the aftermath of the war. On good days, she would arise and get dressed; on bad days, she lay in bed all day. Alice lost weight and lived on soup and hot drinks. But, just as Bunty had nursed their mother Elizabeth with Alice, she now assisted her sister with care, love, and compassion, so her nieces and nephew could get on with their lives.

Amos still worked shifts and sat with his wife a couple of days a week, his 'wife sitting time' they named it, to give Bunty a rest. However, during this time, she would complete the weekly shopping for two households and bake for the family on those days. Amos gave her the housekeeping money, which had been Alice's domain. His sister-in-law kept the household in food supplies, which came back to the British stores after years of rationing.

Her children took turns to sit with their mother, feed her, help her to the bathroom, take over the chores, and have almost zero communication with their father when he was at home.

The wartime had been a boom time for railroads moving troops around the country. With the nationalisation of the railways in January 1948, Amos worried about his job. As an employee of the L.N.E.R., he had faithfully served them for 26 years; its new name was British Railways. In late December, Amos grumbled to Alice, "They are getting rid of all the steam engines; they might put me out to pasture with them."

Alice understood that he made mountains out of molehills. "Have they officially told you they are not employing you any longer?"

"No, but..."

"You are worried, and you do not like change. Your lovely Flying Scotswomen might end up on the scrap heap. But with the dreadful economy, people cannot afford to travel regularly; families are not taking holidays or trips, and imports to docks are declining too! I believe you will have your job until you wish to retire, as they have a strong regard for your work, plus you still have your pension from your war work, accumulating interest. We would manage."

"I know, but they will ask me to drive diesel trains, and they stink!"

"However, it is much safer than getting burned in steam trains! You sound like Roy; he wants out for the same reason."

Amos reacted to the memory of his wartime experiences, and said, "It's all a mess; I know I voted for the Labour government, but I had no clue the nationalisation of my profession was going to be the outcome." He looked sulky and boyish.

Alice smiled her old, sly smile and expected to win this argument. "You should read the Daily Telegraph rather than the Daily Herald; they only tell the Labour Party side of the story."

He lifted his head and looked at his wife of twenty-five years, astute about the political landscape and the foibles of politicians.

Their conversation was a rare one. He smiled at her as she attempted to complete the newspaper crossword in less than twelve minutes daily, as the wartime Bletchley scientists had; this activity helped keep her mind sharp as a steel trap, even though her body brought more pain daily. He asked, "If I went to pick up fish and chips, could you manage to eat some?"

She lifted her head, eyes alert. "Not really, but I would love a bacon sarnie." Her childhood Geordie accent came back. "Yours will not be burned like the offerings Roy gives me."

Amos grandly said, like a waiter. "Coming up for Madame Neil-Gregory—one bacon sandwich."

She reacted cheerfully to the use of her old stage name. "Roy must marry a girl who can cook, as he manages to burn a boiled egg."

While her husband fixed the food, she picked up her newspaper to read the headlines about the new hospital and a proposed National Health Service, which she believed was a local necessity as much as a national need. Unfortunately, subsidised hospital care was not available for her, and only Amos' well-paid job allowed her to pay for treatments; not all sick people were so lucky. Alice understood she would have died sooner if not for her husband's income.

She switched on the radio, which Bunty had installed by the bedside, and ironically, they played the Jo Stafford song 'Serenade of the Bells'. She laughed out loud. "Must be our song," under her breath as she heard her husband bring up the food.

***

Alice did not live to experience the new decade of the 1950s. She believed this decade would be a renaissance of music and the arts like the nineteen twenties were after the first war. She passed away on a cold autumn day on October 19, 1949. Edith Piaf's La Vie En Rose was played at her funeral by top-class musicians.

FINIS

This book is dedicated to those men and women who worked for the Flying Scotsman as it travelled on the rails for years and maybe even worked with Amos Bell.

Research is paramount to historical fiction writers, and many of my people lived in the North of England, so I wanted to get all aspects of telling their saga correct. Neil-Gregory Bell, the only descendant with the family name and his wife Julie Bell helped me tremendously with family trees, Amos' War records, which still exist, and more to get the detail correct.

I am also indebted to my first see editor, who is an American Rita Catanzarite, but she has a European soul (Italian), and she always tells me when it's enough, "cut it!" Following her was Tracy Neis, an Orange county writer who also made the book edits easy with much insight.

Then my beta-readers Matt Landig – actor and writer, and British editor Lynne Collinson, who encourages me to write for the Society of Speech and Drama Teachers - Word Matters – so is well used to commenting on a manuscript.

Finally to Matt. J. Bartley who puts up all e-books and print jobs to where they should be with love and compassion when I am stressed. So before a book is ready for you to read there is an army of work that happens before libraries and booksellers can get a hold of **The Soundtrack of Their Lives.**

www.DebbieWastlingAuthor.com is my website. Please sign up for my monthly newsletter for more free short stories. If you are a book club and would like me to visit or send Reading Group questions, please do get in touch and I'm happy to supply them.

Here is a list of people who I included in the book who lived in the best of times and the worst of times – I love Dickens and wrote a TV script, so I feel justified in borrowing his phrase.
The people who lived their lives, which I fictionalized:

Opera Singer Alice Bell, nee Neil-Gregory
Train Engineer Amos Bell

Alice's Children:
Marjorie 'Madge' Bell, nee Wilson
Aline 'Biddy' Bateman, nee Bateman
Dorothy Bell, nee Wastling
Roy Bell

Her sister, Marjorie 'Bunty' Neil-Gregory/nee Wiles
Engineer George Wiles
Bert Bateman
Mattie Sutherland (became Mrs. Bell)
Edward Thompson (Regional Manager for the LNER)

Music Credits

Chapter	Title	You Tube
Prologue	I'll Be Seeing You	https://youtu.be/ 5o4xKEm0OFs Vera Lynn
Chapter 1	The Wedding Glide	https://youtu.be/ oJ7H687mY3I Paragon Ragtime Orchestra
Chapter 2	Tea for Two	https://youtu.be/ WJe9aBeNVQA Marion Harris
Chapter 3	I Married the Bootlegger's Daughter	https://youtu.be/ vCw0ZWOyk7k Frank Crumit
Chapter 4	Hold Me	https://youtu.be/ RlkFUyLy8No Hotel Commodore Dance Orchestra
Chapter 5	Best Things in Life are Free	https://youtu.be/ IMX9XIs9V04 George Olsen
Chapter 6	Baby Face	https://youtu.be/ 3z-yV4tkihc Jan Barber

Chapter 7	My Blue Heaven	https://youtu.be/U1Ycn2Lk9Dc Gracie Fields
Chapter 8	March of the Women	https://youtu.be/qTYv4wT8g4E Ethel Smyth
Chapter 9	Old Man River	https://youtu.be/df4VdyGIqJ8 Paul Robeson
Chapter 10	The Love Nest	https://youtu.be/T5jq-85VUs John Steel
Chapter 11	Is Everybody Happy Now?	https://youtu.be/h-3ibSwnanE Ted Lewis
Chapter 12	What'll I Do?	https://youtu.be/4aUSEgi3I2w Walter Pidgeon
Chapter 13	Brother Can you Spare a Dime?	https://youtu.be/FIuSTT277XI Rudy Vallee
Chapter 14	I Wanna Be Loved By You	https://youtu.be/hclK-UKJNgk Helen Kane
Chapter 15	Needs A Little Sugar in His Bowl	https://youtu.be/meuwKhPGItk Bessie Smith

Music Credits - 301

Chapter 16	My Baby Just Cares for Me	https://youtu.be/nvcfgRQ4_Pg Jack Payne and his Orchestra
Chapter 17	Making Whoopee	https://youtu.be/ANRPmTZRqkg Eddie Cantor
Chapter 18	Thanks for the Memory	https://youtu.be/KmE7gVkK14I Bob Hope & Sharon Ross
Chapter 19	That's The Glory of Love	https://youtu.be/hQdsS_VhxMg Billy Cotton Band
Chapter 20	It's a Sin to Tell a Lie!	https://youtu.be/Q9IQb_sKTEg Fats Waller
Chapter 21	Oh! We Do Like to Be Beside the Seaside	https://youtu.be/q3LuhZNGMdI Florrie Forde
Chapter 22	Teddy Bear's Picnic	https://youtu.be/dZANKFxrcKU Henry Hall
Chapter 23	Friendship	https://youtu.be/NZY5b9kC8YE Judy Garland & John Mercer

Chapter 24	Heaven Can Wait	https://youtu.be/uBSlQgwduCo Heaven Can Wait (Vy Van Heusen-De Lange) by Glen Gray and the Casa Loma Orchestra, vocal by Clyde Burke
Chapter 25	Trouble in Paradise	https://youtu.be/qP5kYfnigJM Al Bowlly
Chapter 26	Dream	https://youtu.be/o2HLZnqRC44 Pied Pipers
Chapter 27	A Lovely Way to Spend an Evening	https://youtu.be/Q1nVibkdDVM Frank Sinatra
Chapter 28	Crying on the Inside	https://youtu.be/kL1ehKTnv-o Dinah Shore
Chapter 29	Varsity Drag	https://youtu.be/wiENqi2jfgg Movie Good news
Chapter 30	Choo, Choo Cha Boogie 1946	https://youtu.be/P1EG__jgefA Louis Jordan
Chapter 31	I'm A Bad, Bad Man	https://youtu.be/E1X4Bxd_IGc Bruce Yarnell

Music Credits - 303

Chapter 32	You Always Hurt The One You Love	https://youtu.be/mS9U75YC-jA The Mills Brothers 1944
Chapter 33	Sweethearts on Parade	https://youtu.be/tG4udzyZpeY Lionel Hampton
Chapter 34	Don't Sit Under the Apple Tree with Anyone Else But Me	https://youtu.be/YcyiC79l9l0 The Andrew Sisters
Chapter 35	La Vie En Rose	https://youtu.be/kFzViYkZAz4 Edith Piaf
Chapter 36	Serenade of the Bells	https://youtu.be/rABoq0R8Z4Q Jo Stafford

Dear Reader

The above You Tube URL codes evoke the music from 1925 through 1949 to click and enjoy the music as you read. I hope this will bring knowledge and joy of how the Bell family lived and survived with their music - the good times and bad. Thank you for reading true story about my ancestors which was intrinsically connected to music.

I would love to hear your feedback on my website – www.Debbie-WastlingAuthor.com

Printed in Great Britain
by Amazon

56940358R00175